PHANTOM LIFE

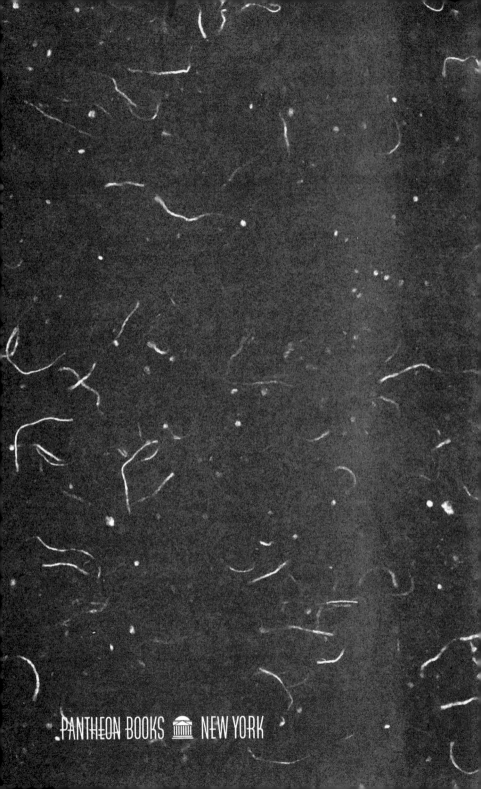

PANTHEON BOOKS 🏛 NEW YORK

PHANTOM
LIFE

DANIÈLE SALLENAVE

TRANSLATED FROM THE FRENCH BY LYDIA DAVIS

Originally published in France as *La Vie Fântome* by
P.O.L. Éditeur. Copyright © 1986 by P.O.L. Éditeur.

Sallenave, Danièle, 1940–
Phantom life.
I. Title.
PQ2679.A52367V5413   1989   843'.914   88-43203
ISBN 0-394-56453-7

Book Design by Fearn Cutler
Manufactured in the United States of America

First American Edition

PART ONE

CHAPTER 1

NIGHT was falling. They sat up in bed, and Laure put her hand out to the bedside lamp.

"Don't turn the light on," said Pierre. "Let's stay this way a little longer."

With his face turned toward her, his eyes still closed, he let his lips wander to her shoulder, her neck, the top of her breast. Noises came in through the half-open window, through the venetian blind partly drawn: the shouts of children, the sound of running water, the rustle of dry leaves. Laure sank back in bed and, laying her head on Pierre's arm, gently stroked his hip. Pierre smiled. He was sitting up, his back straight against the pillows, moving his hand slowly over his bare chest. Delicately he freed his wrist and turned it to look at his watch.

Through the doorway a bright reflection could be seen shining on the bathroom floor. Pierre lifted the sheet and slid one leg out of the bed.

"Where are you going?" asked Laure drowsily.

"Sleep a little longer," he said softly.

"Do you want me to make some tea?"

"No. It's late. Sleep."

Laure opened her eyes again. Pierre had his back to her; the dark tan on his hips ended in a distinct line just above his round buttocks.

"Sleep," he said again.

"What time is it?" asked Laure. "Five o'clock?"

"Six. Even a little after."

"You have time."

He did not answer, and Laure heard water running in the bathroom. Suddenly she was overtaken by a sharp sense of loss; her head felt heavy, her mouth sour. The room was darker now, and the children's shouts mingled with the cheerful splash of water. Outside the beautiful September day was ending, and they had not seen anything of it. In the kitchen a sliced fruitcake on a plate next to two clean cups was drying out.

Pierre, back in the bedroom, stood at the foot of the bed buttoning his shirt.

"How hot it is in here," he said. "Help me roll up my sleeves."

With some effort Laure got to her knees on the bed.

"You were asleep again," he said tenderly.

"No, but I didn't want to get up."

Pierre rested one knee on the mattress, which sank under him; head bowed, he reached out one arm toward her, and while she rolled up his sleeve in neat folds, he brushed the supple underside of her breast with his fingers.

"Stop," she said.

He was already reaching out his other arm toward her, and with his free hand he stroked her belly.

"No, don't touch me."

He withdrew his hand, straightened up, and felt his pockets. There was a muffled clink of keys.

"How do you usually do your sleeves?" Laure asked.

He looked around without answering.

"How do you do them?" Laure asked again.

He shrugged. "I don't know what you're talking about." Then he fastened his watch around his wrist and adjusted his pants.

"I'm going," he said. "Is this the way you say goodbye to me?"

He leaned toward the bed, his eyes tender. Laure's anger had faded. Pierre went on looking at her, his hand resting flat against the wall for balance. Laure grasped him by the neck, pulled him toward her.

"No," said Pierre. "It's too late, I really have to go."

They struggled for a moment, then Laure released him, her anger returning.

"Come here," said Pierre. He was already in the entryway and was holding out his hand toward her without looking at her. She followed him.

"When do you start?" Pierre asked.

"Monday," she said.

"I don't begin until Wednesday," said Pierre, "but I have to go in before that, anyway."

He saw that she was not smiling. He turned back and hugged her.

"You're not wearing anything," he said. "Don't tempt me, it's already hard enough to leave."

Her face was against his neck. "Go now," she said, and kissed him under the chin. "You have a little beard."

"Am I hurting you? You're right, I do." With the back of his hand, he felt the stubble on his cheeks. "You're right, I look like a savage."

With his mouth brushing hers, he said, "I'll see you tomorrow, or sooner if I can. I'll call you in the morning in any case."

She did not watch. He closed the door behind him and, as always, gently scratched the other side to say goodbye before going down the stairs. Almost immediately she heard the door of the building bang shut and, turning away, saw the low sun reddening the tiles of the kitchen floor.

As he walked along the sidewalk between the rows of dusty trees whose leaves, thick from summer, were beginning to turn yellow, Pierre remembered Laure's question and somewhat impatiently rolled down his sleeves, buttoning them though they were a little tight, his keys jingling between his lips. It was six-thirty, so the boulevard would be impossible. Slowly he pulled away from the curb, met the flood of traffic at the corner, managed to cut into it, then came up against a long line of waiting cars. His head felt heavy, his heart was beating too hard. He took two slow, deep breaths. To his left, behind the iron grating of a store window lit for the night, stood parallel rows of motorcycles crowned by glowing red spheres of helmets. He approached the railway bridge, forced himself to take another deep breath, turned the radio dial, and looked out the window at the old silted-up canal. Then he lowered the volume, ran his fingers through his hair twice. He felt damp still, but calmer.

He glanced left, shifted into second, and reached the Boulevard du Château without any trouble.

Laure had gone back into the bedroom. The heat, the close air felt oppressive, but she did not open the window wider. With one finger she parted the slats of the blind. Outside it was quiet again, the concierge's children had gone into the kitchen for their dinner. Laure paced around, walked from one room to another, came back to lie down for a moment on the warm, rumpled sheets, then got up, filled the bathtub, and stayed in the warm water without moving, eyes closed, while the steam rose around her, beading in her hair, dulling the glazed ceramic tiles. She grew drowsy. It was nearly eight o'clock, and night had fallen. In the kitchen a slight breeze rattled the loose window.

Laure drew on her bathrobe and sat at the table without turning on the light. The seat of the chair stuck to her naked thighs, and she raised them slightly and pulled the cloth under her. She ate a little cake and listened. Silence. She heard footsteps on the stairs, and her heart beat faster. Then the footsteps faded, disappeared. Now water was running in the courtyard again, the stream struck the base of the walls, the potted plants, and splashed against the flagstones. With her fingers she raked together a few raisins, put them mechanically in her mouth. This is the last week, she thought. On Monday it will all begin again.

Every day she left the library at four-thirty. It was a convenient time of day to see each other, except on the two days—maybe three this year—when Pierre had his classes. Wednesday couldn't be counted, that day belonged to the children. They usually met here. Pierre had his own keys.

For some time now, however, Laure no longer hurried home on the days when Pierre was waiting for her. She would linger in the office, sometimes tell one of her colleagues to go on and leave, she would stay a little longer; the other woman, surprised, would thank her. Once she did not get home until Pierre had already left: she found a note saying, "What happened? I'm worried to death, I didn't dare call the library . . ." She had gone too far: now she compromised. She made him wait a little so that she would not seem entirely at his disposal. Actually, she enjoyed arriving home after him, ringing her own doorbell, the way people do when they live together and forget their keys. She did all this without really intending to, or only in response to a vague intention, almost independent of her own will. He would open the door for her, impatient, his voice tense, warm. "I'm disappointed!" he would say. "Now I only have an hour, but come on, come on anyway, come quickly." She would follow him docilely into the bedroom. Then she would be alone again, she would think how they had barely had time to say anything to each other.

Laure was back in the bedroom; she lay down, smoothed the rumpled sheets with her hand, looked at a spot on the dark sheet, scratched it with her fingernail, then brought a damp washcloth from the bathroom and rubbed it. She lay down again. The smell of earth and freshly watered plants came in through the window along with a child's soft chattering from the floor below. With her foot Laure reached out to the television set and pressed the button. After a moment, between closing eyelids, she saw a helicopter land against a jungle background in a great roaring of blades and thrashing of broken branches. Armed men jumped out and scattered, bent double, under the bamboo trees. A smiling face appeared in the left-hand corner of the screen and then filled the whole surface of it: "Troops landed throughout the morning. By about five o'clock Greenwich Mean Time it appeared that . . ." She did not hear the end of the sentence. She had closed her eyes and was drifting off, aware of the damp spot on the sheet against her hip. The room was bathed in a yellow light. Words formed in her head, a vague reproach rose from her tired body, she moved her hand over her belly and fell deeply asleep.

Once he passed the station, Pierre was not far from home. As it turned out, there was more time than he had thought: he always forgot that Annie stayed at the bank until six-thirty on Fridays. He parked the car by the curb, got out, and pushed open the wooden gate. His son had already seen him.

"Want me to open the garage for you, Papa?"

"No," said Pierre, "I'm not going to put it away. I'm off early tomorrow morning. How's it going?"

"Fine."

The boy stretched to reach Pierre's face. His hair smelled of sun and chalk.

"I'm fine," he said again. "You look tired, Papa."

"I'm all right," said Pierre. "What did you do this afternoon?"

"Oh, nothing," said the boy. "The new teacher is sick, and they won't have a substitute till Monday. I went to the swimming pool, but Françoise twisted her ankle."

"Where is she?" asked Pierre. "Why didn't you tell me right away? Is Mama here?"

"No," said Bruno, "she brought her home at four o'clock and went back to the office. She said she'd be back late."

Pierre gently opened the bedroom door. At first he didn't see anything. Then he heard the child's voice.

"Papa?"

"Hey, there, bedbug. What happened?" And sitting down on the small bed, he felt his heart swell. "What happened, angel?" he said again.

"Know what?" said the little girl. "I didn't cry at all."

Pierre took the small hand between his. "You're warm, bedbug. Now tell me all about it, tell me what happened."

"I slipped," she said. "I didn't see the little step. The teacher always tells us to watch out, but I didn't see it."

Pierre helped her lie back down and pulled up the sheet. "It doesn't hurt too much, does it?"

"No. Do you want to see my bandage?"

"No, don't move. Go to sleep. Mama will be home soon."

He remained sitting on the bed for a short time. The little girl's face was in shadow, but her forehead glistened with sweat under her sticky hair. She shifted a bit, then fell asleep. Pierre's eyes were used to the dark now, and he could see the familiar disorder—pictures cut out and taped to the wall, a large Indian bird swaying in the breeze. Soon he, too, felt overcome by a strong desire to sleep, and he barely heard the front door open behind him and Annie's low, tired voice ask, "Are you there?"

The little girl woke up. "Come kiss me, Mama. Give me a kiss!"

Annie passed in front of Pierre, brushing him with her hair as she leaned over the small bed. "Yes, sweetie, a big kiss for my brave little girl." The child put her arms around her.

In the dining room Pierre turned the television on.

"How did it happen?" he asked.

"I have no idea," said Annie. "They called me at the office. You weren't home yet, there was no one at the house. The doctor said her ankle wasn't sprained, so they just put a very tight bandage on it. Do you want to eat right away?"

"No, I can wait, but I wouldn't mind something to drink. How about you?"

"Oh, I'd love a drink. You know Combet didn't come back? So of course I'm saddled with everything."

Pierre looked out the window. A black bird had landed among the hydrangeas, and the bush was shaking. Pierre forced himself to answer: "Didn't come back from vacation?"

"No, no, he didn't come back at all, and his replacement hasn't started yet."

On the screen a mottled green-and-brown helicopter appeared, landed among the bamboos in a confusion of broken branches, then the image blurred and was replaced by a row of vibrating green-and-yellow lines.

"I don't know what's going on," said Annie. "This TV doesn't work anymore."

"No," said Pierre, "I think it's the picture."

And in fact a bright, smiling face, in color, soon appeared.

"Is this Cambodia?" asked Annie.

"I was just trying to find out, but you were talking."

She came and sat down next to Pierre, handing him a glass. "All this?" said Pierre. "You gave me too much."

"Drink it, it's very good. You begin Monday?"

"No, Wednesday, but I have to go in before. I have all sorts of stupid meetings."

"Not as many as I do. Sometimes, I . . . ." She broke off in midsentence and slid over toward him almost without moving.

"Come here," she said. "I need your shoulder. I'm completely worn out. I don't even know if there's anything to eat."

"There must be some chicken left," said Pierre. He swallowed a second mouthful, and in the pit of his stomach he felt a bracing warmth that spread up to his shoulders. He took a deep breath. "See?" she said. "It helps."

Bruno's voice reached them, muffled, from the other end of the house: "When are we eating?"

"Don't shout," said Pierre. "You'll wake up your sister."

The announcer's face disappeared from the screen.

"Bruno, honey?" said Annie. "Would you set the table?"

Pierre stood up.

"No," she said. "Let him do it. He has to earn his allowance. You should rest. Stay here next to me a little longer." With authority she lifted Pierre's arm, put it around her shoulders, and planted his wide-open right hand on her breast. "Oh, that's good," she said, her eyes shut, a smile on her face. Pierre did not move, did not close his hand completely. Bruno came in with a stack of plates. As he passed he cast a contented and inquisitive glance at his parents, then quickly turned his eyes away.

CHAPTER 2

LAURE was awoken the next morning around eight by the violent, repeated ringing of her doorbell. Her first thought made her heart contract. The interlude of sleep, too short, was over already, and Laure saw herself being led against her will back into the hard calculation of the days. It was like leaving the kindly shadow of the trees to cross an empty square, fired upon by the sun and by curious gazes through closed shutters. She sighed, sat up. A second volley of rings sounded. Yet there was no way it could be Pierre, anxious, standing behind the door and saying, "I forgot my keys, I couldn't wait any longer." At last she opened the door.

"I was about to take off," said a young man wearing a

windbreaker, a tool-bag slung over his shoulder. "Sorry to wake you so early, but you were the first on my list."

"I'll show you where it is," said Laure. She went over to the window and raised the blind. Bright autumn light entered the room.

The young man dropped his bag on the carpet. "It's heavy," he said. Then he turned the telephone over, unscrewed the base, and took out the cord.

"This will take me a minute," he said. "I'll put in five yards for you. Will that be enough?"

Laure nodded.

"You'd be better off having a second outlet installed, like in the bedroom, in case you have to use the phone at night."

It was barely eight-thirty, and Laure wasn't listening. Had they woken up yet in the other house? What was Pierre doing? Her heart contracted again. Certain times of day, every day, were more difficult than others, and she had to get through them. This hour, for instance, and the hours just before night. These were times when it was better to sleep: when you woke up, the danger was past.

But the young man's voice brought her back to broad daylight. She had to confront the empty square again, and the sun.

"That's a nice couch," he said. "It must be comfortable. I could put in the other outlet right away, if you want. I've got everything I need here with me . . . You really have a nice place," he added.

"The bed isn't made," said Laure. "Sorry."

"That isn't exactly unusual this early . . . But look at this, this whole thing is barely holding."

He was standing in the bedroom doorway, pushing the closet door with his finger. One hinge had come out.

"I know," said Laure. "I'm going to change it."

"Your husband should've done it long ago, because the other one's wearing out, too, it's going to come loose."

"I'm quite capable of doing it myself."

"Oh, I'm sure you are, but if you ever need a hand, I can be here any evening after six."

He finished screwing on the cover, put away the drill, and swept up the dust and bits of wire with his palm. "I'm done. I'm going to call verification. Now you're going to need another telephone, or else you can bring that one into the bedroom at night."

In the entryway he briskly shouldered his bag again and glanced at the small bookcase. "You've read all those? Takes me a year to get through one book."

Laure did not smile. She was too hot and wanted him to leave. "It's my job," she said.

"What are you? A teacher? A professor?"

"No, I work at the library."

He whistled through his teeth. "So you're surrounded by books all day long. And you don't get sick of them?"

He had clear eyes and a short blond mustache that moved when he spoke. He smiled again.

"So what do you do in the evenings? I have a motorcycle, and I like good music. I know a place you can go to hear it."

She shook her head.

"It could happen, you never know. A librarian!" And he whistled through his teeth again, with surprise, admiration, a touch of scorn.

She closed the door behind him. Should I have given him a tip? she wondered. How does one do it? Slip it into his hand, into his pocket?

She put the cube of pine back by her bedside where it belonged, and set the lamp and the alarm clock on it. The sun was higher in the sky, it was still summer, and the heat made her feel groggy. Mechanically she turned on the lamp, turned it off again, went to get the telephone, plugged it in, then set it on the bed. She waited. Just once, she thought. What if I called him just once? Her heart was beating fast, her breath came quickly, she felt her legs tremble, her palms dampen.

She lifted the receiver, dialed the number, listened to the phone ring, and hung up after three rings.

Someone in the house must have said, "Pick up the phone—my hands are wet," or "I didn't hear it," or "Listen, it's stopped ringing, it must have been a wrong number." Like a skittish animal, her mind shied when she forced it to imagine where the telephone was, in rooms she did not know: on a low table next to a couch; on a small stand in the hallway, a shelf; on a bedside table. At that her mind balked altogether. For one moment, however, she had felt the concrete, though immaterial, presence of the house, as though by causing the telephone to ring there she had introduced a sort of promiscuity, a disturbing, vague, almost obscene connection that moved, bothered, upset her. As the vision faded, Laure felt overcome by an immense discouragement. She lay down on the bed, turned onto her back, her hair spread over her face. Its fragrance comforted her, it's always the same, she thought, oddly. The sun reached her feet, rose over her legs, and she fell asleep breathing the smell of the wooden blind.

Years ago her parents used to rent a little house in Charente for the summer, always the same one. She and her brother slept in two corner beds in the back of the large kitchen, under a window where a wooden blind hung. Her father had contrived a bedside light for them, a bulb dangling from the end of a wire and shaded by a paper cone that would soon scorch, then burn through in a hole fringed by crumbling black.

She and her brother would fall asleep listening to the stream murmur under the trees outside. In the dark she would hear her brother calling, "Mama, mama!" Then her mother answering, "Be quiet, go to sleep, you'll wake your sister." Even when he was asleep again, her brother would go on talking. Laure, wide awake, could hear the shuffling of her mother's bare feet on the tiles, the deep creaking of the big bed when she got back into it, then her father's drowsy murmur. The memory faded, and Laure was asleep.

When she told Pierre about this, adding, "I had my own fishing line, and I sometimes went fishing!" he shrugged his shoulders impatiently. "My stepfather always wanted to take us fishing. I hated it. My brother did, too. We would stay home, pretending we had homework to finish, but that was actually when we began smoking. One day we even finished off a bottle of port. My brother filled it with water he'd colored with caramel and red ink."

"What happened?" asked Laure.

"I don't know, I can't remember what happened. We were little idiots, really. I wanted to be like my brother, or like the worst kids in the class, hanging around doing nothing, never opening a book. My mother was in despair. So was my step-father—he knew what it costs not to have any education. Anyway, that didn't last. What do you expect! I was a good student, you can't change what you are."

Then, after a silence, Laure said, "I would have liked to know your parents."

"Me too. I would have liked to know my father." He snorted sarcastically. "The truth was that for a long time I couldn't have been more unhappy, I didn't like anything, especially myself, I couldn't stand myself."

"You still don't like yourself," said Laure.

"You think so? Oh, I don't know!"

Laure woke up steeped in the smell of the little house where they used to go. At first she looked around for the window and was surprised not to find it. Then everything returned to its proper place: in front of her the framed reproduction of Rouault (a figure in orange-and-violet silhouette, kneeling under a deep-green sky), then the hall door, then the window to the left. The image of the little house came back to her again.

One summer night when she couldn't sleep—her brother had awoken her with his crying, then gone back to sleep—she heard her parents' voices in the darkness, her father's low, urgent, and her mother's higher, like a chant. "Oh yes," said her father, "oh yes!" She had glanced over at her brother's bed, but he hadn't moved.

It's the blind, she thought now, the smell of wooden blinds that's making me remember all this. She knew she should get up. If she stayed in bed any longer, her head would begin to ache.

Keeping an eye on the water as it rose and trembled in the kettle, she looked out the window at the concierge's children, who were circling the small courtyard on their bicycles. It was close to noon. Pierre had not called. She drank a cup of tea, smoothed the surface of the table with her hand to remove crumbs of biscuit, and caught sight of her tanned shoulders in the window pane. She was starting toward the bathroom when the telephone rang. She did not sit down, she held the telephone in her hands.

"It's me," said Pierre, "I only have two minutes. How did you sleep?"

Laure said nothing.

Pierre did not wait. "My sweet," he said, "I would so much have liked to stay."

Laure still did not answer. She looked around the calm, orderly room, sheltered from the heat by the pale blinds—the walnut table, the small bookcase, the reproductions on the wall.

"Can you hear me?" came Pierre's voice.

"Yes, I'm here."

"What's the matter? Are you angry?"

"No." No, she was not angry, she was trying to defend herself against that deep, warm, serious voice, only against that voice and nothing else, as though in it there was something not exactly dangerous, not even threatening, but out of keeping with the orderly furniture and the pale walls of the room.

"No," she said in a tender voice that did not quite correspond to what she was feeling, "I just have a slight headache." As she said that, she thought she had no courage whatever.

She was all the more surprised to hear herself say, immediately after, "Are you coming this afternoon?"

"No, I can't, I have to take Bruno to the dentist."

Laure thought of her brother Jacques, of the house in Nantes. She heard a child crying and Nicole's voice saying, "Jacques! You can't forget the dentist!" That confident, impatient, authoritative voice.

There was a silence. "I haven't washed," said Pierre. "Not yet. I kept your smell on me all night."

Her smell? This reminder shocked Laure. She felt cold, distant. She heard Pierre's voice again, more urgent now: "Don't be angry, I beg you." It was obscured by a crackling noise. "I love you so much, if I think you're angry, I don't want anything anymore, I'm paralyzed, dead."

"No," she said firmly—and this time it was true—"I'm not angry. I'm going out."

"So am I." Pierre's voice was suddenly happy, his tone lifted, cleared, lightened. The sensual, nocturnal, dangerous glow disappeared from it. And at the same time something between them broke, their shared attachment to a secret world, the world of the night. "At five o'clock," he said, "I have an appointment with the auditor. On a Saturday, if you can believe it."

"Bertoin?"

"No, the new one, Samson. My sweet, I love you so much."

He hung up. For a moment she listened to the loud hum of the line close to her ear and looked at her tanned feet on the carpet. "I'm sad," she said out loud. The sound of her own voice surprised her. Then, "I'm also hungry."

CHAPTER 3

AS though magically restoring a continuity that everything else tried to fragment, the telephone played an almost organic part in their lives that went beyond the unavoidable function it performed in their separation. It played the part of a vital conduit, essential to the secretion and flow of some humor, even in their imaginations, even in the way they described it to each other: sometimes laughing, more often complaining, they spoke of it as a cord, a membrane, a vibration, distance, heat, cold. "I feel you are so close," the voice of one would say. Or the opposite: "Why are you so distant?" Then they would be comforted with a word, reassured by each other's imaginary presence; if they could not feel the breath of that distant voice, at least the receiver was warm against their ear, providing a soothing substitute.

Yet whatever their exchange, whatever the quality of their closeness, they would always have to hang up: "Look, I'm going to have to hang up," Pierre would say. It was always Pierre who hung up, just as, for other reasons, it was always he who telephoned. For some time now she had accepted this with more or less good grace, as though it were natural that he, being a man, would take the initiative in all areas.

Anyway, it took strength, courage, decisiveness to break off, and Laure had none: such an intense exchange could only be interrupted violently. "Look, I'm hanging up," Pierre would say, or "Let's stop." Sometimes they were angry, or on the verge of anger, and it was better to avoid a quarrel they had no time to get into anyway, even less to resolve, and which would have meant hours of solitary torment for both of them. To hang up was as necessary as it was to wake up, suspend this disturbing, sensuous continuity so marvelously established over distance by an electric connection, the ideal extension of their fleshly connection—their voices low, their dream shared—a daytime sleep lulled by the soft trembling of their breaths, their whistled exhalations, the little noises of their tongues, their coughs.

More prosaically, it would also happen that Pierre had to hang up because of some outside circumstance: a child would enter the room, a neighbor would come by to return a pair of pruning shears, the doorbell would ring, the mailman would knock, Annie would return unexpectedly, having set off on some errands and left her purse or checkbook behind. If there was time, Pierre would warn her, saying, "I must tell you right away, I may be disturbed at any moment," but if there was a greater urgency and the intrusion was unexpected, he would say nothing and Laure would quickly understand. He would continue more quietly, "Yes, I'm going to hang up. I'll call you back." At these times his voice was deep, as though strained by the annoyance, the overexcitement of danger, and a reawakening of thwarted passion. Once or twice he was even forced to cut the connection abruptly, leaving Laure helpless, furious, on the edge of tears. The worst was to imagine Pierre taken by surprise next to the table or the shelf, pretending to move the telephone ("I was afraid it would fall") or look for something in the address book; Pierre running out of excuses ("I answered, it was a wrong number") with a gesture she knew so well, running a hand through his hair twice, then once over his mouth and chin, as though to wipe off the sweat: a gesture that expressed awkwardness, embarrassment, his fear of being discovered, and, even more, his shame at being a coward.

When he lowered his voice to speak to Laure, Pierre was not only yielding to the demands of passion—uncomfortable in the harsh light of day—but also to the requirements of prudence and respect for his family. Laure was never able to make out the exact composition of this mixture of "contained passion" and "adulterous caution," just as she was never able to enter into Pierre's reasoning, imagine it, or understand it. When she discovered his caution, she simply took offense, reading it as a sign of his weakness. For she owed the discovery not to an increase in perceptiveness but to a growing disenchantment, and the appearance in her feelings of a kind of scorn for her lover. Starting then she began to watch him, surprise him, and judge him without indulgence. And she never guessed that if Pierre spoke so quietly on the telephone, it was also because he derived a sort of sensuous pleasure from the muffled sound of his own voice, from the response of his own body as well as that of his mistress.

And what torments the use of that word *mistress* caused them! Pierre pronounced it with an old-fashioned solemnity, as though making a literary allusion, as though quoting a word, and therefore a custom, from another age, referring to a more conventional and cynical kind of affair than theirs was—or perhaps a more chivalrous one. Laure, who would never have dreamed of calling Pierre her "lover" when she thought of him or spoke of him to her friend Ghislaine, had never managed to rid the word *mistress* of the superficial images that linked it in her mind with men's intimate conversations, with salesmen's confessions in back rooms of cafés. But at the same time it had lost for her the secret beauty that Pierre meant to restore to it by applying it to Laure, always enhanced by an adjective—"my beautiful mistress," he would call her—even if, when he spoke it to himself secretly, he took a less noble pride in it, a more commonplace, virile satisfaction: that of being a man unconstrained by the strict observance of the bonds of marriage.

"I'm Laure, just plain Laure," she would say.

"Yes, of course," Pierre would say, and for a few weeks he would not use the word, except in the privacy of his own heart and his marriage bed, feeling his wife's warm hip against him while the delicious, though rarely satisfying, sensation of his duplicity rose in every part of his body.

So when he had to warn Laure on the telephone, telling her at the outset, "I'm going to have to hang up," he actually never hung up abruptly—or only once or twice—because that would have been the most obvious sign of an illicit conversation. Rather, he continued to talk, only he would raise his voice, change his manner—becoming so animated, so artificially jovial that Laure would be stunned—introduce trivial, unexpected subjects, in which a cordial and anonymous formal tone would appear suddenly, wounding Laure more than anything else. (Laure imagined that afterwards he would still have to make some explanation—"It was that bore, X. . . . Couldn't get rid of him.") And he would finish the conversation with a few coldly polite phrases that wrenched Laure from her dream and brought her back to a view of their situation that was more correct in every regard.

The worst of it was that at these times she believed she saw Pierre as he "really" was, as others saw him, without the masks he assumed in their passion and their secret understanding, without that warm, nocturnal, private voice, restored to the appearance of a man who had nothing to hide, who was speaking to a colleague or a relative on the telephone: a simple, jovial, friendly man, someone people at parents' meetings or student conferences or family meals would describe by saying, "He's a good man, Seguin," or "Pierre's a great guy."

Was this really Pierre? For a long time Laure had thought she was the only one who knew his secret, the only one who knew that the image she had of him was the real one. But as she grew both more perceptive and more disenchanted, she came to feel that in fact Pierre showed his true nature to everyone but her. (In both cases she was wrong. In the first case she was wrong to believe the convenient fiction that passion is the secret revealer of human natures; in the second case, moved by a secret meanness and unavowed rancor, she was wrong to believe that the signs of weakness and banality she found in Pierre were part of his "true nature." This second mistake was perhaps more serious and more difficult to correct than the first, for we always see more truth in the unprepossessing or simply displeasing traits of those close to us, just as medicine seems more effective if it tastes bitter. So the discovery of defects in those we love leads us to conclude once more that love is blind, and that we have been blind, and we are crushed by that blindness when we have ceased to be proud of it, when we have forgotten the time when it seemed flattering to be duped by love.) Entire episodes in Pierre's hidden life now appeared before her eyes in this light. Her imagination went to work with complete freedom, unchecked as it was by any kind of inspection or verification. And so she pictured Pierre to herself in an intimacy she did not share: Pierre unshaven, in unbuttoned pajamas; Pierre sitting on the arm of the couch while talking distractedly on the telephone to a pupil's father or his wife's brother, meanwhile thinking, Look at that, my toenails need cutting; Pierre yawning, the receiver nestled against his shoulder, while the smell of coffee and toast came in through the kitchen door, mingling with the stale odor of unaired rooms that everyone had been sleeping in, including the dog.

But anything—anything—was better than the two times Pierre had hung up without a word and she had sat for a few minutes incredulous, thinking the line had failed, keeping the useless receiver against her ear, listening to the rapid beeping that was like an ironic commentary on her abandonment. And both times, when she put the receiver back in its cradle, her rage was as strong as her distress.

But however calm they were (if Pierre, for example, had chosen to call in the afternoon just before school started again), however absorbed in describing, remembering, or anticipating their embraces (which took up most of a conversation whose main purpose was simply to make or change an appointment), they had to end the conversation one way or another. Then each would always pretend to be leaving it up to the other— even if in the end it was Pierre who made the fateful break— or to reproach the other for going on too long. Often, if he was alone and really sure that no one would be coming in to bother him, Pierre would call Laure back immediately. She would laugh, saying, "I knew it would be you." And they would stay on the line without saying anything, their warm mouths pressed against the mouthpieces; and for some time even after breaking the connection they would hold the warm receivers against their cheeks or the vein pulsing in their necks. But the game would have to end, and then they would wander around their rooms, in their separate homes, their heads heavy, their hearts torn.

Once Laure's telephone rang just after she had been talking to Pierre. "It's you," she said right away, "I knew it." But it wasn't him, and they laughed about that for a long time. Sometimes she would pick up the phone on the first ring, because it was the time he usually called, and she would simply say, "Yes," and so would he, and they would be like worshipers in some cult. Sometimes he would call her during the night, once at three in the morning—she did not ask how he had been able to do that—and she would go on saying, "Yes, yes," even after he had hung up.

Though they both made the same loving use of it—Pierre pushing from time to time at the limits of propriety Laure had clearly assigned—the actual location of the telephone expressed distinctly the difference in their respective situations. Before she had the cord lengthened and another outlet put in her bedroom, Laure could only try to bring the receiver close to her bed. But in Pierre's house, where was it? She had happened to learn that there was only one telephone, in the dining room.

"Anyway," he had added somewhat enigmatically, "I always get up early": a remark that, on another level, Laure had of course immediately profited from. In the old apartment on the Rue des Minimes—which occupied the shortest side of a trapezium on the site of a monastery of the same name, destroyed during the Revolution—where Pierre was living when they started seeing each other, the telephone had hung on the entryway wall, above the shelf for the directory. Off the entryway were the kitchen and the baby's room—that was Françoise, who had just been born. Its ringing would wake her, so it was moved, which did not make Pierre's and Laure's conversations any easier: the common room with the new outlet lay in the heart of the apartment, all the other rooms opened onto it, it had to be crossed to get to the bathroom. But Laure never knew anything about all that, as she knew nothing about many other things.

Of course, the telephone was also used—though only by Pierre—for arranging an impromptu meeting or changing the place for a meeting, or for canceling. Because of this, Laure began to dread the ring of the telephone, for that was how the unexpected would enter into their carefully regulated order. That it might announce an additional meeting was scarcely less upsetting, and in the end scarcely less sad, than if it were canceling one, because it always disturbed the patient and precarious equilibrium that Laure had built up for herself, the fragile, complicated system of psychological compensations she had put in place in order to be able to accept the fact that Pierre was not with her. At a time when there was all the justification in the world for his not being free, suddenly, inexplicably, he would be free—and Laure would be hanging over an abyss, over the unknown depths of the life he was leading somewhere else, feeling confusedly what a threatening freedom Pierre would have found if he had wanted to, and how thoroughly he had accepted chains that could be loosed by the smallest thing but that his will alone helped to maintain. At the same time, however great her joy at seeing him again, she knew very well that one is no less chained when one "frees oneself," when one "finds a few minutes," than when one cannot leave the house at all. For by changing the hour or the date of a meeting, Pierre transformed even the image of the time he had created: a vast, glacial, rigid surface with a few free spots, the way an icefield is pitted with wells of open water. Suddenly everything would begin floating. Nothing was inevitable anymore: anything could have happened. But nothing did. Only "a few minutes" had been "found," that was all.

On top of that, the order that Laure had imposed on herself, one congruent with Pierre's order, was shaken, cracked. After all, she had already found a way to occupy the time Pierre would not or could not spend with her. By freeing himself at the last minute—at the expense of an afternoon he would give back to her the next day, and which would therefore be empty, since they had meant, before this last-minute change, to spend it together—Pierre forced her both to postpone what she had planned (a visit to Ghislaine, an appointment with her hairdresser) and to find something to fill a suddenly empty afternoon, something she hated to do. He would arrive at eleven o'clock, at a time when she was supposed to have left for the hairdresser or met Ghislaine for lunch. And she would have to go back to bed, to put it crudely, in the middle of the day, whereas she had risen late, looking forward to a free, solitary afternoon. As for the future half-day he would give back to her, she didn't want it: it was like a gulf, an irreparable hole in the fabric of time. Then at the end of the day, when Laure was worn out by these perilous readjustments, which forced her into an acrobatic reversal of her feelings, hearing from Pierre—who thought he was doing something nice by calling her to congratulate himself on this additional meeting, or to reassure himself of her forgiveness for his change in plans— would plunge her even deeper into pain, because the warm timbre and contained passion of his voice managed to awaken all sorts of desires without satisfying any of them.

What Laure did not know, on the other hand, was a fact that sometimes became an exhausting obsession for Pierre, the cause of burdensome organizations of his time and the occasion for a thousand childish lies: that he had to telephone from outside the house. She did not know this, and would not have understood it, anyway. There were few public telephones in R., and Pierre did not want to risk standing exposed at the street corner in the harsh illumination of a telephone booth, always at the mercy of some chance surveillance, some report, some piece of slander, some suspicion. It was better to call from a café, but most were closed on Sunday, not all had telephone booths, and when there was one, it was usually in the basement next to the toilets, dirty, cluttered, smelly, airless, covered with graffiti. Or else it was a simple hood of laminated plywood or hardboard from which the conversation in the café and the whistling of the percolators were audible, and Pierre, unhappy, his heart tight in his chest, his back curved under the pitiless cover, trying not to see, among the hastily scribbled telephone numbers, the obscene symbols that seemed to allude directly to their relations, answered Laure's questions haphazardly, surrounded by the brutal smell of disinfectant and the moldy reek from the nearby cellar. Did Laure understand that it wasn't always easy to talk about love, or to delve into the exact nature of their feelings, in such squalid proximity to an uncleaned toilet frequented by drunken soldiers and haggard mothers dragging howling children who had already soiled themselves?

Sometimes the waiter behind the bar simply pushed over to Pierre, or nodded toward, a greasy telephone on which a long succession of mouths had left minuscule traces of tobacco and a persistent smell. Pierre's desperate eyes, fleeing the ironic or indifferent glance of the waiter, would move from the row of bottles to the packs of cigarettes lined up behind the tobacconist's glass case and return with mechanical obstinacy to the beer tap, which dripped a dense foam of unpleasant color and smell. With all his strength he would try to keep the dirty receiver away from his ear.

"You're not listening to me," Laure would say.

"Of course I am," Pierre would say, then add "I am," in a burst of irritated tenderness. He would buy telephone tokens beforehand to keep from being caught short, but this telephone would accept only one kind, the kind he did not have. Or he would feel despair mount in him when, having taken the flat tokens and pierced tokens, the tin tokens and white-metal tokens out of his pocket, he would hear the words "The telephone is reserved for customers" drop from the waiter's disdainful mouth. Then, so that he would not have to go look somewhere else, because it was raining or it was All Saints' Day, he would order a glass of Vichy water or Dubonnet, which he would not finish. And then there were the telephones that didn't work, that kept the coins without giving a connection, the booths from which he would see an exasperated woman emerge in the distance, and then at last, relieved, he would descend the cellar steps of a sordid café at the owner's resounding invitation—"Go ahead, it's working!"—as he barely avoided the yellow fangs of a dozing German shepherd. And when he had to return home, miserable, defeated, he knew very well that Laure would not believe his "I couldn't find a booth" or "the telephone was broken," and that she would always read it as a convenient excuse, a mark of his ill-will, and a sign—unfortunately true—of his state of subjugation. To Laure's credit, however, was the fact that in four years she had called Pierre at home only twice.

CHAPTER 4

HANG UP the phone, head aching, return to the kitchen; finish tidying the bedroom; dress, go shopping; leave for the library; feel the pain of a short time before slowly vanish, for no reason; see it followed, for no more reason, by a lighter feeling of cheerful expectation, a new-found confidence; by evening sense the return of the sadness that had been so difficult to get rid of in the morning . . . it seemed to Laure that she had already traveled this road a hundred times. She would have liked to forbid herself this discouraging thought, but she could not. Then she managed to shake herself—that was her word for it—and stop thinking about it.

But there was a new element in it that September, the fourth since the beginning of their affair (though "affair" was a word

Laure did not like, one she found trivial, yet the one, she imagined, feeling some shame, that Pierre's colleagues used, if they knew about it, and her friend Ghislaine, and her cousins, and probably her brother, Jacques; some for lack of delicacy, others for lack of vocabulary, and all of them, more generally, because they lacked her reasons to look for a word more appropriate to the lofty conception she had formed of her relations with Pierre). What was new was this: for a long time—in fact, she said to herself, until that very moment—the difficulties they had encountered had seemed to her temporary; "one day" everything would be different, soon, maybe even tomorrow. Now she felt this was not true: all the time that had gone by looked dreadful to her; and so did the time ahead. What she had taken until now for a passing circumstance of their arrangement was actually its true nature: they would never know anything different.

Thinking this, Laure would be overcome by an unshakable despondency. The worst of it was that the more painful it seemed, the more certain she was that she was right. To plunge into the pain was to plunge into the truth. What hurts is the light, she thought, rather grandly.

Tuesday, September 8, 1976, eight-thirty in the morning; she hung her raincoat on the coatrack and glanced quickly at the mail. A few parcels had arrived yesterday evening after she left. She sat down at the long table, opened a box of index cards, closed it again. A little sunlight came in through the tall windows, the smell of the books soothed her, a silent morning lay ahead. Around ten her colleague Claire arrived. They had agreed that Claire would stay on in the evening after Laure left—she preferred to come in later in the mornings because of her little boy. Laure was sitting in the vertical light. After four years Laure still did not know if she liked her job. What did it mean to like a job, anyway? In her family having a good job meant not having to perform repulsive or unpleasant tasks, working in sheltered surroundings, keeping the job for a long time, and being able to look forward to a decent retirement. If the work itself was monotonous, tedious, or even poorly paid, that didn't matter. In this sense, then, Laure's profession was a good one. But whether she liked it or not was another matter.

She liked the silence, punctuated by the quiet motions of the people in the room. She was less fond of Wednesdays, when the library was noisy, crowded with children whose outbursts of laughter drove away the retired people who came in to read the papers in a warm spot and the old schoolteacher who sat covering index cards with his faultless handwriting. Sometimes she felt a sense of emptiness, but she always loved handling the books. She would not have liked to sell books, it was enough for her to have a surface sort of contact with them, like the contact of a nurse with her patients: to pick them up, classify them, put them away, sometimes give them a touch of glue that would hold well enough until they were sent back to the bindery.

Laure looked at the window to her left and saw her profile reflected against the shelves of books behind her. Claire had taken out a copy of *Elle* magazine and was leafing through it; they smiled at each other. Claire liked her because she was calm and quiet. Yet Laure knew that inside she did not really fit the sober image people had of her—her passion for Pierre, their "arrangement," did not correspond at all to that image. A secret lay hidden in her, shining beneath her smooth surface. And something else in her, she felt, was different, but she did not know what it was.

The previous June it had quickly become apparent to Laure that Pierre would not be quite as "free" as he had thought. When Laure guessed this, she talked about it to Ghislaine on the telephone. Ghislaine immediately proposed that she go with her and her new boyfriend to Sicily, where they would do some camping. Laure declined but talked to Pierre about it.

"Where?" he asked.

"To Sicily," said Laure.

"I would so much have liked to go there with you." Maybe
that remark was too much, yet Laure felt the sadness of his
tone, which expressed his obligation to deny himself certain
things, the strength of the commitments he had undertaken,
a fundamental honesty that, even though in these circumstances she did not benefit from it, was necessarily auspicious for
Laure. Pierre remained silent, so as not to be drawn into a
conversation that would take them nowhere. And yet he allowed a touch of rebellion and bitterness to sound in his voice
as he concluded, "Yes, I'd have liked that very much."

They had just drunk some coffee together, it was June 25,
very hot, and Pierre was trying to pick the price sticker off a
box of crackers. Laure felt a sudden compassion for him and
laid her hand on his hair. "It doesn't matter. Come here."

Pierre did not wait for her to say more. He closed his eyes
and, without standing up, turned his face and lips toward her,
and she ardently pressed her own lips against his. It was three
o'clock. This year the early summer was scorching, stormy.
Even so, in the end they fell asleep. When they woke up, they
were damp with sweat and the blinds cast a grooved shadow
over the floor. The smell in the room was almost the same as
in a hotel room at noon, foreign, anguishing, laden with
perfume.

"I'm thirsty," said Pierre, and that was exactly what he
would have said in Rome or Palermo. And he added, as though
commenting on a decision they had not yet talked about, "I'll
work, I'll really buckle down this summer, I know it."

The sticker from the cracker box was stuck to the back of
his hand. Laure took it off. "Seven and a half francs?" she
said. "You're not very expensive."

"I know. You're right. Sometimes I don't think I am."

Then he rolled over toward her and put his eyes up very
close to hers.

"I can't see you when you're so close. I can't see you."

"I can't see you either, but I can smell you. I love your
smell."

Laure gently ran her hand over his burning-hot back, which was reddish brown and covered with freckles. "You feel as though you have a fever," she said.

"I'm going to go take a shower."

They saw each other one last time at the beginning of July, just before Laure left for a librarian's conference in N.

"And what about the end of July?" she asked abruptly. She had sworn to herself not to say anything, but she could not hold back the words.

"No. Maybe the end of August, though I'll have the children on my hands all day long. They go off to camp in July."

"In July?" Laure felt cold. That meant he and Annie would be alone in July at Guérande. Guérande, or was it Croix-de-Vie? It didn't matter.

"Are you feeling bad?" he asked. He took her in her arms, held her against him, kissed her neck. "Try to leave your session two days early," he murmured. "I'll have some time at the end of next week."

She did not answer.

"Don't cry," said Pierre, "oh, please don't cry."

He stroked her cheeks, and she felt the pain subside. She had no one but him to comfort and soothe her, even for the pain he caused her. He also suffered with her, there was no question of it, he could not bear Laure's tears. So the comfort he gave Laure split him in two, and in the end his own pain became abstract, fictional. He hugged her to him and began kissing and licking her swollen face, her streaming eyes. Suddenly he remembered the nurse, Babeth, reaching out to him (in the wallpapered entryway with the barometer on the wall), her thick lips covered with lipstick, her tongue wet, red. He slipped his hands under Laure's shirt and plunged his lips into hers. Her lips parted, wet, swollen with tears, and she continued to sob quietly. Now Laure grasped him by the neck and kissed him full on the mouth, trying to find in this kiss the strength of will that was failing her. Little by little she ended by convincing herself: wasn't their happiness so great that it hardly mattered whether or not, say, they went to Sicily together that summer? Blindly they made their way to the bedroom without quite knowing how they got there, without letting go of each other.

They left the bed a little later, ashamed, happy, exhausted, and took a shower together, eyes closed in the fragrant foam of soap. Still later, by the time Laure shut the door behind him, the clouds that had hung between them were gone.

The conference began on a Monday. Laure arrived late Saturday afternoon. They had reserved a room for her over-looking the port; a trail of smoky clouds reddened in the west, and drifts of mist ascended from the horizon, while rows of cranes stood out black in the estuary. When she opened her windows, the sea suddenly entered her room, and she was assaulted by a scene of violent, incessant, disorderly activity, something noisy and real, something essential, in whose presence she felt, confusedly, that she lived a life of futility and deception, in an excess of private happiness and melancholy. What she had left behind suddenly seemed ridiculously inconsequential in the face of this world, so entirely occupied with serious things: these sweating men, these cranes, these open, yawning freighters. Despite the late hour, the sun was still dusting yellow light over the metal of the cars, the sides of the ships, the roofs of the dock sheds, and then the gusts of sea wind blew it away, sweeping everything clean. Next to this, to these lives governed by a rhythm of strong, savage work, the love whose secret burden she carried everywhere with her was merely an "adventure" such as a bank teller or a warehouseman might be indulging in at this very moment. Her "secret" was no different, and it was nothing compared to the regular, powerful forward march of the world: nothing but a little twist, a little deviation from the great order that everyone observed and respected.

Everyone was in agreement, that was clear, everyone was in league to preserve the secret; and the very ones who exposed it, by spreading gossip, by letting innuendoes slip out, even by sending anonymous letters—though they took very particular care in doing so, a care they no doubt also found to be in their own interests—were only delegates of the community, determined not to let the truth shine out but to bury it deeper in the shameful obscurity of illicit liaisons.

A general consent, indulgent and cowardly, surrounded this sort of thing, based on a complacent philosophy that tacitly recognized these "weaknesses" up to a point—sure as everyone was that this philosophy would be to his own advantage sooner or later. And the men and women Laure was observing right now as they worked so energetically, rushing here and there, continued to live, it seemed to her, in a kindly half-light, always on the brink of exposing themselves, always protected by the condemnation and the muted resentments of the community.

This was what "life" was, whatever share she had in it: not an ever more stalwart defiance of hypocrisy and bid for freedom but a precarious balance between the demands of a sense of duty that was abstract but, in the end, respected—a duty to continuity, faithfulness, the education of children—and those of the flesh, of desire, which everyone allowed, on condition that they did not exceed certain tolerated limits. For a period that was sometimes longer and sometimes shorter— during one's youth and the early days of marriage—the two demands were compatible; but when, inevitably, they diverged, one had to adjust as best one could, not do anything irreparable, "salvage what one could." Or "give it all up." But that was more dangerous, and rarer, and sooner or later one would have to start all over again, reinvent new forms of a compromise as old as the world, to the benefit—or detriment, depending on how you looked at it—of a new partner, of a new husband or wife.

This was the substance of a revelation that flashed upon Laure and left her feeling discouraged, exhausted, broken; the brilliant light in her eyes jumped and sparkled through her tears. She sat down on the foot of the bed between her open suitcase and her purse. On top of everything else, she was having cramps. What should she do? She had no particular answer to such a general question. She was crushed. She seemed to see around her a crowd of men and women, worn out, yet impelled by a secret force that tangled their limbs on beds in furnished hotels, in rooms rented by the hour or the month, sometimes even in the marriage bed before the children came home from school. Afterwards, painfully, they would separate and return to their respective homes, by common agreement. Weren't these people right? And shouldn't one submit to this way of life, whatever the cost? Her images of the arrangement she and Pierre had—its secrecy, its beauty— now seemed illusory.

The smell of the sea and the sight of the large white birds gliding above the pale waters calmed her, and she turned around without standing up; behind her, in the mirrored door of the wardrobe, the sky and the sea formed two bands of delicate blue, the sea a little greener, the sky a little whiter. And when she opened the wardrobe door to hang up her coat, the reflected light joined the light from the window, isolating the bed in the middle as though it were a boat. She let go of the door, drew back the bedspread, and lay down. Her eyes were just closing when the telephone rang. It was Pierre.

"My darling," he said. "Were you sleeping?"

"How did you find me?" asked Laure. And her voice was full of joy.

"How hot it is!" said Pierre. "Did you have a good trip? I'm a wreck. It's over ninety, and the orals lasted all afternoon. I jumped right into the shower when I came back, I'm completely naked, luckily there's no one here."

The house, the shower, the heat, Pierre sitting on the couch. Where? In his room? In their room? A glimmer of the old pain approached Laure, then receded without having touched her.

"It's hot here, too," she said. "I was going to take a nap."

The picture came back to her: Pierre walking around his house naked. How could she say it to him? How could she say to Pierre, without feeling ashamed, "I don't want any-one"—meaning *her*—"to see you naked"? Yet when men lived apart from the women they loved, they could say it—they could say, fiercely, "I don't want him to see you naked." She closed her eyes.

"You're tired," Pierre said, anxious.

"Yes."

"And . . ." He hesitated. "Has it come yet?"

"Not yet, but now I know it's coming."

"Oh good. I feel better. I was getting a little anxious."

Laure turned her head, and once again she felt the bright light full in her face, the smell of the sea, the cries of the birds.

"I'm surrounded by water," she said.

"Wait," he said. He came back right away. "It was the neighbor, she had a package for us."

Was that "us" inevitable? Laure did not think so. Nothing was ever certain: at any moment the earth could drop out from under her as she walked, the tranquil day could be swept away by darkness, betrayal, falsehood. Yet Pierre's calm voice seemed miles away from this distress, this pointless agitation.

"Try to come back Thursday," he said. "We could have a whole day to ourselves, and maybe the evening, too, I don't know. But I'll call again." Laure felt the old anguish settling into her again, but a fresh gust of sea wind in the curtains drove it away.

"I'll try," she said.

But she did not try. She stayed through the last lecture of the session, even though it did not interest her and almost nobody else had stayed for it. And she arrived in R. Friday evening feeling quite tranquil. She knew Pierre would not be free for at least two months. She would pack her bags—tran-quilly, yes—and leave for her parents' house on the Atlantic coast two days later. And that is what she did.

* * *

Pierre was surprised to get no answer when he telephoned Thursday evening. On Friday he called only once, in the morning. Actually, he admitted to himself, this was a relief: now they would both have a vacation. And for a few days Pierre felt he had avoided something oppressive.

Annie's last day of work ended at noon on Saturday, Pierre had already washed the car, they packed the children's bags and then their own, and Pierre put a last coat of paint on a chest of drawers for his wife's parents. Annie leaned toward him as they were loading it into the back of the car, and kissed him on the hair.

"How good you smell," she said.

"Oh yes," said Pierre. "Sweat, paint, turpentine."

Two days later they were in Guérande, and after the meal Pierre lay down on a chaise longue.

"Where are the children?" he asked sleepily.

"At the Rs' house," said Annie. "They're swimming."

"Good."

"This is nice," said Annie.

He nodded weakly, overcome by drowsiness again, then fell asleep.

On Monday he felt a twinge of uneasiness. Shouldn't he have been more persistent about telephoning, or left a letter? But what would he have said? For lunch Annie's mother cooked a guinea hen and an apricot tart. He was surrounded by a gentle quiet, a comfortable family atmosphere; his uneasiness vanished. After a while it became too hot outside, and he went upstairs to take a nap in their room. On learning that Pierre "would be working," Annie's mother had had a beautiful, polished wooden table taken upstairs and put a bouquet of flowers on it. He lay down with a feeling of sensuous pleasure. Yes, the time would pass quickly, they would be together again when the summer was over. He felt gentle, strong, and patient.

That evening the heat became almost intolerable. Pierre was not sleepy. The air in the floral-wallpapered bedroom was heavy, stagnant. Pierre turned over and sighed noisily.

"Can't you sleep?" asked Annie. He did not answer, and slowed his breathing. Then he felt Annie moving over against him gently, touching him with the whole length of her warm body; at his back the velvety softness of her breasts pressed against his naked shoulder blades. He shut his eyes tighter.

CHAPTER 5

PIERRE knew that Laure would not write. He would not try to get in touch with her, either—it was better that way. Once again the summer stretched before them, a neutral, colorless space. According to a tacit fiction they had created, their vacations "with their families" were only a succession of unimportant, tiresome "chores" to which they submitted dutifully without talking about them. This was empty, dead time, at the end of which they would meet again.

Pierre had sat down at the beautiful polished table. He could hear Annie and her mother chatting in a confiding way on the terrace below. He leaned forward but could not see them. Where was Laure? Had she already left for her parents' house? Or her brother's? He thrust the questions away. His head felt heavy. He should go swimming. He stood up: on his way back he would do some errands, pick up a copy of the paper. And he felt heartily relieved that he would not have to suffer any remorse or uneasiness when he passed the post office, since there would be no letters from Laure waiting for him, or the row of public telephones, since he did not know where to reach her.

In fact, they had never been very clear as to corresponding. At first they had decided not to write each other when they had to be apart for a day or two, a week, that it was too hard to wait for letters, especially in the summer, when there were so many obstacles to receiving them—backed-up mail delivery in the places they were staying, long lines at the general-delivery window—and both of them had cruel memories of scorching afternoons spent waiting for a letter that never came. Sometimes, though, in the pain of separation—one of them would have cheeks wet with tears—they would decide to write, unable to bear the pain of silence on top of the pain of separation.

"Write to me," Pierre would say. "Write to me at my in-laws'—or rather, no. It would be simpler to write me care of general delivery, I pass it every day." Laure would promise with a silent nod of her head, and Pierre would go on, "I'll write to you, too. I can, can't I?" But back together again, they would see how pointless their anxiety had been. This was the last time, they swore; it was definitely better not to write.

In July, the first summer after they met, they parted from each other breathless, desperate, and Pierre set off on his vacation after a sleepless night, eyes red with fatigue. Every time he stopped the car on his way to join Annie and the children, he tossed into the mailbox a brief, hasty, anguished postcard written with an old Bic he had found in the car that left blots on the crossbars of the letters. He chose the cards at random without looking at them, sending off pictures of fountains surrounded by flowerbeds, of ugly provincial monuments, factories, suspension bridges. "I couldn't sleep. I love you. I want to die. I am kissing every inch of your body."

Laure received only the first postcard before she left, two days later, to visit her brother. All the others were waiting in her mailbox when she returned. She read them with an incredulous happiness and a deep feeling of unreality, for in the meantime she and Pierre had already seen each other again and now she found herself transported back, helplessly, to the summer's unhappy beginning, to a paroxysm of passion that had been soothed by their reunion.

The following year there was no question of writing, because Pierre had to join a couple of friends in Italy. But the year after, Laure promised, reluctantly, to write to him—care of general delivery, of course. Reluctantly, and yet she would have felt hurt if she had not been able to write. Pierre had begun smoking again, partly to calm the anxiety of waiting for Laure's letters—an anxiety heightened by the fact that he could not go to the post office every time the mail arrived—and partly just to have an excuse for going out. But the post office did not keep convenient hours. It closed in midafternoon when everyone was resting and he could have gone out alone. So he would let Annie do the food shopping with her mother, begging off because of the traffic jams, his fatigue, the crowds. "Go on," he would say to them indulgently, as though they were children. "See what you can get done, we'll meet later at the little café."

The question was how to enter and leave the post office without being seen and without meeting anyone. The service entrance would have been the most practical way; he tried to use it, and succeeded once. The second time an employee reprimanded him. One rainy day when the children were running around the house shouting, he decided he could not wait: every day for almost a week now they had been driving by the post office without his being able to stop. He was frustrated, he could not sleep, he felt suffocated by a helpless feeling of rebellion. He turned to his father-in-law.

"How about going out for a drink?" he said. Once they were in the street, he added, "Could you wait for me a minute? I have to stop in at the post office."

"Do you need stamps? I have more than I need. This morning I got a book of them on my way to buy a lottery ticket."

"No," Pierre said abruptly. He found himself at a loss for an explanation. "Wait for me just a moment." He came back a few minutes later, two letters from Laure in his shirt pocket. He had not had time to read them, but that did not matter, he could feel them touching him there like a hand.

The sun was shining again. Outside, under an umbrella, his father-in-law gazed at him, his broad, sad face divided by a shadow. "Why are you keeping secrets from me?" he asked. "Do you think I haven't noticed anything? You're unhappy here, something isn't right. It's obvious."

"No, no, that's not true," said Pierre. "Everything's fine."

"Come, come," the old man said. He leaned toward Pierre, who felt so happy now that he could not keep his face from beaming. "You can trust me. I won't say anything to the women, even if this is about my daughter."

Pierre looked at him without moving. Retired now, his father-in-law was a good man, rather taciturn. "I know what it's like," he added. "I almost left Annie and her mother once. When I came back from Germany, I was in bad shape— problems with my lungs, my heart. I had to spend a winter in the mountains in a sanatorium. Oh, I was in good hands, they took good care of me. And there I became acquainted with a woman, she was married, too, a very fine woman, certainly better than I was. My time there ended, but she had to stay on. I promised to come back. I talked to Marthe about it right away. At first she didn't say anything, she just looked down, and then she said, 'No. I will never let you go.' That was all she said. And I didn't go. I was thirty-five, the little one was eight. I wrote to my friend there, I asked her to be patient. And then time passed. I stayed. Now I've even stopped smoking, though that was all I had left." He was quiet. "You see," he said, and finished his drink in one swallow. "It's hard to be a man without hurting someone. Sometimes it would be better to end it."

"End what?"

"End everything."

After a moment of silence Pierre asked with some effort, "And what happened to her?"

"She died there. I went back once. Wait, I'll show you." He took out his wallet and, fumbling slightly, extracted from it a small photograph with notched edges. It was a picture of a gravestone. Pierre held it and read: Léonie Revoil, 1913–1948. He gave it back to his father-in-law without saying anything. Then he drew Laure's two letters from his pocket.

"This is why I asked you to wait," he said.

"Are you going to ask for a divorce?"

And Pierre suddenly heard the word resonate in a sort of void, a dull emptiness: nothing about his arrangement with Laure corresponded to that word. "I don't know. I haven't said anything to Annie."

"Wait a little longer," said his father-in-law. He had turned to the waiter. "How much do I owe you?"

They stood up and were preparing to head back to the house when Pierre's father-in-law stopped him, putting a hand on his arm. "There's no easy answer," he said. "Either you stay with her and you're unhappy, or you leave her and you're equally unhappy. In any case, time will pass." He was silent for a moment, then went on: "Annie is like her mother. She's a woman with a lot of sense."

They walked all the way to the garden gate without saying anything more to each other. In his letter to Laure that day Pierre wrote at length about his father-in-law, though he did not mention the old man's story about his stay at the sanatorium. He preferred to talk to Laure only about things that would make his time away from her seem innocuous.

* * *

Most often their letters were brief and—Pierre's especially—limited to recalling passionate moments, memories of love-making, or telling her how impatient he was, how he looked forward to seeing her again. For instance, he would write, "Remember when we went to the F. château and I wanted to take you right there, in front of everyone, on the lawn?" What else did they really have to say to each other? It was almost impossible for Pierre to describe one of his days and not risk making Laure suspicious or sad. Everywhere there were traps; nothing was innocent. When he said rather emphatically, to show his good will (as he did in this letter), "I spent the whole day with my father-in-law yesterday," it amounted to saying that he had spent the other days with Annie. When he talked about nothing, his tone hinted at a reticence that Laure was able to divine. If he said he was bored, she either disbelieved him or thought he was saying it to please her; if he was not bored, it was better to say nothing about it. Granted, Pierre did not have a clear idea of the sort of deductions with which Laure had surrounded herself; he understood only afterwards, from the tone of her answers. As far as he was concerned, he would gladly have told her of his swim with Annie and the children the day before, feeling he had not harmed her by what he had done. And he was probably right. But it was also natural that to Laure any reminder of a happy life, or even an ordinary, good life, in which she had no place was an offense, an outrage, a lapse from their faith. So Pierre, feeling he was negotiating a minefield, abruptly changed tactics: he resorted to talking about love, and their letters—like many of their meetings—ended up being exclusively devoted to love-making. This, too, was finally offensive to Laure—she found something forced about it, exaggerated; she was surprised at the monotony of these letters.

"You know I'm not a writer," said Pierre. Laure accepted that excuse, though it was not true. And though she had the greatest difficulty even mentioning parts of her own body or Pierre's, Laure made an effort to reciprocate: some of her letters surprised Pierre. She pushed herself to do it, thinking that women might be less likely than men to talk about their bodies and what they did with them, but that was doubtless because of their upbringing more than their natural inclinations. She was always startled when she heard Pierre murmur certain questions in her ear in his low, excited, voice: "And how is this? And this—do you like this? When I press gently, or when I press hard? When I enter you suddenly?" She would not answer. She would feel herself growing sad. For her there was something clinical about his questions, and they actually dampened her enthusiasm. But Pierre usually did not expect an answer: often these questions meant only that his excitement was mounting. Aroused by his own words, by the gesture or position that went along with them or that they described, Pierre had already gone on to something else and—his eyes closed, closed in on himself—did not ask anything more.

For one whole summer Laure tried to keep up this tone in her letters. Her young nephews would be shouting in the garden, her brother and sister-in-law arguing in muffled voices in their bedroom. Rubbing her tanned legs together, Laure would set to work. And then, blushing a little despite herself, she would fold the piece of paper and put it in the envelope, turning it over to hide Pierre's address.

The following summer, when they had agreed not to write, Pierre tried twice to reach her. The first time it was by telephone, from a public booth by the side of the road.

"I can't hear you," he shouted. Laure could hear him very well, and twice she caught her mother looking up at her from the garden under the windows of the large, cool parlor. He shouted again, "I love you, wait, wait, it's my last token, we're going to be cut off."

Suddenly they were cut off, and Laure felt a great sadness

not to be with him on the dusty roadside, where she had heard the cars roaring past. She saw Pierre frowning, running his hand over his chin, large circles of sweat under his arms. The thought of this last detail only added to the tenderness she felt for him.

CHAPTER 6

IN 1975, Annie decided to rent a house in the country. Her coworkers had been talking about this idea at the office, had passed lists around. Without consulting Pierre, she chose one: a low house surrounded by pines, with a beach not far away— the photograph was a little deceptive, it hid the road that passed in front. Pierre was completely taken aback to discover that Laure's parents lived in the closest village, a little beach resort. Several times already he had written the name of this unknown place on envelopes; now he would get to know it. Though he wanted to mention this to Laure, he did not, uncertain exactly how she would take it. The entire month of June, in fact, he suffered from a strange form of amnesia: when his mother, Annie's parents, or his colleagues asked him the name of the little town, he could not tell them. "It's crazy," he would say, "but I can't think of it." Pierre left Laure without even asking her if she was going to join her brother at their parents' for the month of July, as she usually did; he found it reassuring not to know.

The house was a little farther away than they usually went. Even so, they made the trip in one day. When Pierre actually saw the name of the village spelled out on a signpost, he felt a twinge of remorse. The children, excited, were laughing in the back seat, Annie was dozing, it was five o'clock. As he glanced at them, Pierre felt protected. Nothing bad could happen to him. She loves me, he thought, I will see her again. Something deep in his body confirmed it; and there was a certain male pride in his assurance.

He turned to Annie. "Is it this way?"

"Look at the map," she said, opening her eyes just a crack. "This heat is killing me," she added, hardly moving her lips.

"Hey," said Pierre, "it's good for you, it calms you down."

"Think so?"

In the back the little girl stood up and put her arms around her father's neck. "Are we there yet?" she asked.

"Almost," said Pierre.

"You're hot, Papa."

"Yes, angel, I am. But you're cooling me off with your little arms."

The little girl laughed and tightened her hold.

"Not so hard," said Pierre, "you'll choke me."

She yelled with pleasure.

"No. Stop it now."

They were there.

"And you—" he said to Bruno, "don't read in the car. No wonder you feel sick to your stomach."

For the next two weeks Pierre avoided going anywhere. The heat made that easy, anyway. They swam three or four times a day, staying at the beach until the sun went down. The little girl was learning to swim, Bruno had a mask and would go off on his own without saying anything. Annie was tired, she slept a great deal. Pierre also got into the habit of taking naps, at first on the living room sofa. But he wasn't very comfortable there, and the noise from the road bothered him, so he would join Annie upstairs in the bedroom. He would lie on top of the sheets, trying to find a cool spot for his burning back.

A few days went by. One afternoon as Annie slept with great dedication, a severe look on her face, she put one golden arm across him, and then a golden leg, warm from the sun. She was still asleep when Pierre began kissing her shoulder softly, then the underside of her arm, then the curve of her breast. Gently, without waking her, he turned her onto her back and got on top of her. She put her arms around his shoulders and quickly fell back to sleep. Pierre rolled onto his back again and opened a book. He was not sleepy. He felt unhappy. He thought for a moment, got up, and looked at himself in the bathroom mirror. No, it wasn't true, he wasn't unhappy. Well? He gazed at his tanned face, his hollow cheeks, his red hair already bleached by the sun, the stubble on his chin. He went back, lay down next to Annie, and drifted into a deep sleep.

Yet two days later, having left the house on some vague pretext, Pierre headed in the direction of the village: he wanted to see Laure. With his window rolled down he drove along a broad avenue with gardens on either side. He heard children shouting, sprinklers spinning, a dog barking, the muffled thumps of tennis balls, laughter. Under an arbor an old couple were reading peacefully. His heart beat harder. Where was Laure? A woman looked up when she heard him slow down, and said something, which was drowned out by a radio. He imagined himself stopping, getting out, ringing the bell: "I'm a friend of your daughter's. The bell isn't working"—the dog's barking would force him to raise his voice. "Oh, it hasn't worked for a long time!"

Pierre accelerated slightly. He was already at the corner of the avenue. No, he said to himself, I won't go, I don't even know exactly where it is, and what could I possibly say to them?

Several days went by. The heat gave way to storms, but these passed and were followed by extraordinarily fine weather—bright, clear, mild. This time, Pierre said to himself, I'm going there. Annie had left with the children to do some errands. I can't be mistaken, Pierre thought, after driving around among the houses. Laure had said that from the end of the avenue one could see the ocean. And what if she wasn't there? But he stopped, parked the car, and got out.

On the terrace a woman with delicate features and thin lips was reading. She did not look up. Near her a man with white hair seemed to be dozing. Pierre walked over to the doorbell and pushed it. The dog came up to him without barking, wagging its tail.

"The bell doesn't work," Pierre said.

"Oh," said the old man, "it hasn't worked for a long time."

"I'm a friend of your daughter's," said Pierre.

"I don't know if she's awake," said her mother. "Laure!"

"I'm an old friend," Pierre went on, instantly ashamed, "I was going by, and . . ."

"Please make yourself comfortable," said her mother, "she'll be right down." She was not smiling.

Then Laure appeared next to them. They had not seen her coming. "Hello," she said, holding her hand out to Pierre. She was wearing a bathing suit, and her mother's eyes rested on her bare midriff.

"You didn't get dressed?" she asked.

"So," said Pierre, in an excessively sprightly tone, "how's the vacation going?"

"I've only been here a week," said Laure. One week? Then where had she been before? He felt panic.

"Oh," he said.

"And what about you?" asked Laure, familiarly. He was

surprised, and looked at Laure's parents, her father smiling, her mother impassive.

"But you're already very tan," he said.

"Aren't you planning to get dressed?" her mother repeated.

"Sure, in a second." But she did not move.

"Yes," said her mother, "it's good to go somewhere quiet for a while." There was a note of admonishment in her voice, but directed at whom? Laure smiled and wiggled her toes in her sandals.

"And is the house nice?" How did she know? Pierre wondered.

Laure's father had spoken at the same moment, turning to Pierre. "And you? Where are you taking your vacation? Excuse me, dear, I interrupted you."

"Very close by," said Pierre, "in the little pine wood."

"Ah yes," said Laure's father. "It's pretty there, but we haven't seen it in years. We hardly leave our garden."

"You're very tan, too," said Laure.

"You're both young," said Laure's father. "You like the sun. So did I, once upon a time. Now I'm afraid of it. Look what happens to the garden if I don't water it all the time! Our skin is the same—but she doesn't want to believe me!" He had turned to his wife. "Mother, aren't you going to offer us anything? I'm like my plants, I'm thirsty!"

"Don't bother," said Laure, "I'll go." They heard her footsteps in the kitchen, then the refrigerator door opening, then the tinkle of ice cubes. Honeysuckle hung above them in fragrant strands. Pierre breathed deeply but said nothing.

In the kitchen Laure felt her agitation subside. Pierre is here, she thought. She would have liked to be alone with him in the cool kitchen, to feel his hands on her back. Night would be falling; they would be alone, they would have dinner outside, and Pierre's arm would rest heavily on the nape of her neck. Suddenly she heard her mother's voice—"You're a teacher?"—and Pierre's answer, which she could not make out. Then her father's deep voice rose. Laure had slipped a dress on over her bathing suit. On the tray the ice clinked in the glass pitcher.

"Yes, two," said Pierre, "a boy and a girl." Laure must have missed part of the conversation. She came and sat down next to him in a relaxed way, and handed him a glass. He smiled easily, his tension gone. Idly he turned over a cracker to examine the writing on the other side. "What are you reading these days?" he asked her. Laure leaned toward him. Pierre caught her mother looking at them and drew back. "What a beautiful garden!" he said.

"My husband's responsible for that," said Laure's mother.

"You, too," said her husband. "Don't be so modest. Those are hers," he added, pointing to some beautiful flowerbeds.

"I can never remember their name," said Laure.

"Gloxinias," said her mother.

"A lost cause," said her father. "She will have forgotten again by tomorrow . . . And you—you seem to like flowers?" he added politely, as though to apologize for his family banter.

"Oh, very much," said Pierre. "In R. we have a garden, but I never find the time to look after it."

That "we," it seemed to Pierre, had cast a chill over things. It was time to leave, anyway. He looked at the shadows lengthening at the back of the garden. Laure was not smiling. Under her hair, which was tied back with a light-colored ribbon, her brown neck gleamed. He wanted to put his lips against it. Now, he thought, yes, here, this minute. He stood up.

"Would you like a little more orangeade?" asked Laure's mother.

"No, that's very kind," said Pierre, "but I've already stayed too long."

"I'll walk out with you," said Laure. Her parents stood up, and Pierre shook hands with them. Take a good look at him, Laure thought—you won't be seeing him again.

When they were some distance from the house, Pierre put his hand on Laure's neck and squeezed it. She smiled and slipped her arm behind his back.

"Don't you think you're a little crazy?" she asked.

"Yes—crazy about you. I couldn't go on without seeing you. I . . ." He didn't finish. They had stopped next to his car. "Get in," he said softly. "Please, just for a minute."

Immediately he took her in his arms, then let go of her, started up the car, and drove a hundred yards. He was breathing hard. He stopped under the shade of a parasol pine.

"Come here," he said. He pulled her against him, slipped his hands under her dress, groping. "I want to see your breasts." He leaned over and kissed them gently, one after the other. "They're so soft."

"No," said Laure. "Please. Take me back."

By the time she had returned to the house, her parents were already sitting at the dinner table.

"Jacques telephoned," her mother said. "They're coming tomorrow afternoon."

"Oh, good," said Laure.

"Your friend seemed very nice," said her father. "What was his name again?"

"Seguin," said Laure. But her mother said nothing. Laure had a headache, and went to bed early.

Pierre contrived to see Laure one more time: he telephoned, her brother answered, she came to the phone, they arranged to meet in a café. There they sat in the back room, empty and cool at that hour. Outside on the terrace, couples laughed and called out to each other. The fragrance of coffee and alcohol mingled with the stale smells of sausage and grilled cheese.

"What a stink," said Pierre. He had taken Laure's hand and was holding it on top of the table. "Do you still love me?" he asked. He looked unhappy, it was all his fault, everything was going to fall apart because of him. If only they were in a room alone somewhere! The idea that they had nothing to say to each other frightened him, and he leaned closer to her. Some soldiers walked past and glanced sidelong at Laure—this pretty young woman on the verge of tears.

"You don't love me anymore?" asked Pierre again. Laure shrugged her shoulders. Pierre looked at his watch. "Can I write to you?"

"Yes. Of course."

"You don't seem to like the idea very much."

"No, I do, I just feel a little discouraged."

"So do I," said Pierre. Leaning over the spotted formica table, he pressed his lips against Laure's. "Look at me."

"I am looking at you."

"No, really look at me."

She looked away, her eyes filling with tears. "Come on," she said. "Let's go, it's getting late."

Pierre promised himself not to try to see Laure again that summer. He wrote to her only once before the end of August. When Annie asked him if she should reserve the house for the following year, he said no, they were better off with her parents, weren't they? Annie agreed, though she had been pleased by the place—but she was happy if Pierre was. As for Laure, she did not like the letter Pierre sent, she found it cold and conventional.

Really, the only letters from Pierre that Laure liked were the ones he wrote when he did not have to, just after he had seen her, spent the afternoon with her, or talked with her on the phone. Laure would sometimes do the same, in fact, scribble a note in the middle of the night, and find the crumpled piece of paper among her bedclothes in the morning, along with the uncapped pen, which had left blue spots on the sheets. Pierre would get up quietly and walk through the dark house to the kitchen, where he would scrawl a few lines by the light from the open refrigerator: "I can't sleep, it's so good!" They wrote things they would not say, in a rather poetic style full of adverbs, underlined words, parentheses, exclamation points. Or they would send each other quotations from books, because they found reminders of their love affair everywhere— on television, in movies, in what they read. One day Pierre copied out for Laure a line from Paul's first epistle to the Corinthians: "But the greatest of these is love." The Bible said "charity," but he wrote "love" and he was right. And all their letters ended the same way: "I'll stop here," "I have to leave you," "It's so hard to part," etc.

Laure kept all of Pierre's letters in a box—she soon needed two—along with letters of hers she had not sent to him or rough drafts she had copied over. Pierre had to make slightly different arrangements. He had not kept any of the brief notes the nurse had sent him, but he could not bring himself to tear up Laure's letters. In Laure's case, he knew he had to settle into something that was going to last, the way one settles into a marriage. Right away he decided to throw out the envelopes, despite the protection they offered, because an unfolded piece of paper would call less attention to itself. He slipped the letters into a colored folder, as he did with his class notes. He would have asked Laure to type the address when she wrote to him, but he did not dare.

Besides, she never abused her right—the right he had given her, to her surprise—to send him letters at home if it was absolutely necessary. Often she preferred to keep a letter and give it to him the next day when they saw each other. Still Pierre could not suppress a feeling of pain on the mornings when the soft hand of his daughter or son held out to him a letter on beige paper that he recognized right away, and said, "Here, Papa, it's for you."

Annie did not even look up.

"Again," Pierre said.

"Again what?"

"More stuff from school." And he left the letter on his napkin with feigned indifference. Then he took it into his study and slipped it under a pile of papers to be corrected. His forehead was flushed. When would he stop behaving like a child? Lying, hiding things? But then he opened the letter, and a wave of happiness submerged everything. He was alone: the children had left for school, and Annie was still getting dressed. He had no classes until the next day. A blackbird hopped around in the garden, looking for fresh grass for its nest. Pierre was seized by a sudden need for a purely physical life—he envied that stupid bird, which thought of nothing all season long but a female and her eggs. He bent over the student papers, and when Annie came in to say goodbye, she said he looked so serious! And what a shame his son wasn't as serious as he was. When he heard the car start up, he took the letter out from under the bundle of papers again.

CHAPTER 7

AND SO by July, 1976, when the conference had ended and Laure had returned to R. for two days before joining her parents and brother on the coast, she already knew quite well what a summer away from Pierre was like.

They would not write to each other, not see each other; their relationship was in some sense suspended, hanging there in the monotonous summer sky. For a few days Laure felt relieved. She settled into the large, bright room in her parents' house. Twice she wanted to write to Pierre but did not. Every day she went on long bicycle rides with her nephews. The weather was fine but too cold for swimming. She did not miss Pierre.

When she returned to R. in early August, he was already

back, but she did not know it. The city was hot and empty. The library would not open again until September, so she had three long weeks—even a little more—before she had to go back to work. She tidied up her apartment and rearranged the furniture: she put the bed in a different corner of the bedroom; in the large room she moved the sofa under the window. Her only mail was two cards sent from Sicily by Ghislaine and her friend, a young Englishman, who had written "LOVE" in capital letters in the lower left corner followed by a scribble, probably his name. At some point during her last week of vacation she put the furniture back where it had been, and the next day she found another spot for the sofa. She had bought new sheets by mail, and made up the bed with them as soon as they came. Yet she did not have the feeling that she was waiting.

On Monday, walking along the boulevard, she met a boy who had often come to the library to study the year before, when he was in his final year of secondary school. He was tanned and carried a Greek bag over his shoulder.

"I'm just back from Greece," he said. "It was fantastic. Where did you go?"

"I was on the coast," said Laure.

"Oh, that's nice, too." His arms were bare, his thin neck rose out of his shirt collar, his Adam's apple bobbed awkwardly. "I'd like it if we could get together sometime," he said. "I need some advice."

"Advice? All right, why don't you call me?"

"I don't have your number."

"I'm in the book."

He would be going back to Paris to study, but not for a week or two. He promised to call.

He did not call. Laure thought about it a few times.

Meanwhile Pierre had been back for three weeks. From the moment he returned he had felt full of happy resolutions. On Saturday he washed the car, on Sunday he drove the children to the station. On Monday Annie went back to work, and

Pierre was alone. The garden had dried up: he removed the dead flowers and leaves, raked them into a pile, and burned them. Then, every evening, he carefully watered the flower-beds.

Still, he had to get to work, he felt committed to it. He decided to set himself up in Bruno's room because it was cooler and more peaceful, and after removing the child's notebooks and toys from the trestle table, he found himself alone for the first time in years—alone as when you are twelve years old and have stayed in the house Sunday afternoon to finish your homework. But it was not Sunday, and he was not twelve years old anymore. Through the open window came the smell of the watered lawn. He tried to return his attention to the table.

His eyes wandered over the walls. Nothing was really very different from the way his own room had been: only big color posters had replaced the photographs of soccer players cut out of *Goal and Club*, and Bruno's notebooks had plastic covers with bright stripes. The boy's life seemed to have more gaiety in it than his had had at that age, completely surrounded as he had been—as he remembered it, anyway—by dark things: his dark smock, his leather satchel, the blue paper covers on his books. He tried out the felt-tip pens, the Bics. But then, what did he know of his son, besides the boy's sudden out-bursts of anger, his fits of sadness? Pierre carefully tidied up the various little objects on the table and, when the surface was clear, set on it the small Hermès typewriter he had bought almost twenty years before. Then he lay down on Bruno's narrow bed. His cheek against the pillow, which was not very clean, he fell asleep instantly, immersed in the sweet smell of a young boy, a smell that moved him and transported him unexpectedly back to those countless gloomy afternoons of his early adolescence.

His brother had left home very early. At that point he had made up his mind to "get away." But how? Where would he go? What would he do? He didn't even think about it; he only knew he would not follow in the footsteps of his brother, who was learning a trade, or his cousins (the real ones and the others—his stepfather's nephews) who, at fifteen, already drank and smoked like adults and looked at him with ironic respect when he emerged from his room, his eyes tired from reading too long.

Pierre remembered his sadness during that period, his resolutions, the dining room wall with its flowered wallpaper, and the smell of chicken with celery, which his mother cooked every time his brother came to lunch with his fiancée on alternate Sundays (the other Sundays his brother would spend with his future in-laws). His earliest sexual curiosity, his first explorations of his body, took place in the same small room he inherited after his brother left. He had moved into the more comfortable of the two beds, the one with a lamp next to it. Pierre wondered suddenly if Bruno was already . . .

He sat up, looked around for another pillow, and, not finding one, lay back down. He was about to fall asleep again when he was woken once more by a twinge of some feeling—regret, maybe remorse. The strength he had felt in himself during those years, despite his sadness, had vanished, dissipated, he did not know how. His body was still energetic, still felt young, hard, muscular, but there was no energy left in his mind. How had that happened? What he had expected, when he made the decision to "get back to work" in June, had not occurred, he had not regained his former strength, his impetus. All that effort, he thought . . . the reason for all that effort must have been to free himself from his silent, difficult surroundings, the aura of resignation, compromise, his stepfather's narrow existence, the life models forged in the tiled kitchen filled with the smell of leeks and the tick of the alarm clock.

In a sense, he felt, he had been successful, he had certainly turned out to be different—but what was he? Bruno would be luckier, he could continue something already started, he was taking off from a point already higher and farther along.

After obtaining his degree, Pierre had passed his lower-level state examination, then failed a higher-level exam, to the disappointment of his mother, who would have been almost as pleased to see him pass as she would have been had he chosen to be a physician. Very soon, and without really noticing it, Pierre had settled into a state of simple acceptance, acceptance of an ordinary life. At a higher level, no doubt, than anyone else in his family, but apart from that, there was no difference. It was more comfortable and less precarious where he was, that was all. Given his simple, sweet laziness, then, it was not surprising that a certain portion of his strength had evolved into easy sensuality; when he was an adolescent, there had been "women" (more a dream than a reality), then "young ladies" (the part of the feminine world he had turned to quite naturally, out of an innate respect for convention). It was at this point that he met Annie: he was barely over twenty, she was twenty-two. She was slender, with smooth, even skin that tanned easily, clear eyes, a slightly aquiline nose, and a good deal of determination. They were married in June, just after Pierre had passed the state examination, and then he took his first job. Suddenly the need he had had for books, his confidence in them, vanished. Or rather, he found there was no longer any point to them; he had gotten from them what he wanted. Now he could confine them permanently to a limited role in his life and would not open them except out of necessity or a sense of duty.

He once thought he had chosen a life of books not simply to "escape" but for the secrets or beauty they contained, the access they afforded to a special world. In reality, what had occurred was more commonplace, less surprising. What he had asked of these books was to provide him with a peaceful profession, a regular salary, an orderly life. They had given him all this; what more could he ask? That other world, removed from the everyday world—that special, purer world he had believed in (or believed he wanted) when he was young—had disappeared after a few years of adult life. Its distant glimmer, its vanished iridescence, had left him with some remorse, but he had soon had to give in to the obvious: as with his mother, or his stepfather, who never read, the world of books, which he had entered briefly—and the world that books talked about—would remain forever separate from his own, parallel to it. Even when the events of 1968, at first distant, reaching him only through newspaper headlines and television images, shook the little town where he lived, he was not surprised that, except for a few marches and a meeting or two in his deserted school, they did not affect him, so accustomed had he become to a life separated from the world.

Given this situation, what sense could there be in getting back to "work"? Pierre himself did not really know what he meant by that. Was he going to do some "serious" reading, collect some notes, draft some articles, begin a thesis? Or sit down at a table before a row of books, and so join the great invisible continuum of which these books were the visible sign? But what would be the use?

For years the question had not even come up. Shortly after he was married, Bruno was born. Several streets away were two or three young couples like them, with very small children, old cars of the sort students always seemed to have, and meagerly furnished apartments, always in a mess, their bathrooms invaded by plastic toys and underclothes hanging up to dry. When one of these couples found a larger apartment, everyone got together to help with the move and had a party the same evening, sitting on the floor around an improvised meal. The children were all put to sleep together in the bedroom, on a bed covered with a sleeping bag, and then lifted up and carried away, still sleeping, when it came time to go home. And it was lovely to go on Sunday mornings to one of the houses to paper a child's room or pour the cement floor of a garage, or have a barbecue on the minuscule lawn where they would all gather. Each of the men was very much in love with his own wife, and flirted sweetly with the other wives. Everyone felt the same way, the strength and seriousness of their commitments was masked by the lightheartedness of their behavior; it was as though they were playing at life. Everything was new, everything seemed temporary—apartments found by chance, a first job, early October mornings when they started back to school in a brisk wind that drove the dead leaves before it, greeted by students with faces hardly less childish than those of their own children, and, crossing a courtyard that still smelled of summer, settled down to teach books they felt they had studied just the day before. At noon they would go home to cheerful, messy apartments, crying babies, tired young wives with dark-circled eyes who would tenderly lean against them.

First one left, wanting to be closer to Brittany, where he had been born, then another left for the South, whose climate he kept raving about. Later, Pierre and Annie knew, they would do the same, they would buy a bigger house. Meanwhile they were young and felt daring, carefree. Nevertheless, even in the lightheartedness that seemed to them to distinguish them from true adults (they did not think they belonged to that category yet), they already respected a strict division of ages and roles as ruthless as those of ancient societies. In this way they prepared themselves to pass from youth to middle age, when they would discover that all the barriers they had raised around them as though in fun enclosed a space that was now hermetically sealed.

The groups broke up: André left for Alençon, "his wife's part of the country"; the others tried to replace them with a younger, childless couple who traveled more, but the graft was not successful. Pierre and Annie went to Italy twice and to Greece once with another young couple who also had a baby; and together they discovered the churches of Tuscany, their frescoes loosening from the plaster in delicate, barely faded colors; soft nights in the tent interrupted by the babies' crying; and mild cases of poisoning caused by the sun and unwashed fruit. In Italy, and again in Greece, Pierre learned to adjust to the fact that his encounters with masterpieces of art were always incomplete, in some sense deferred; they were there in front of him, but for whatever reason, he remained separated from them. There was always something in the way: either a little mishap (once Annie scraped her foot on a rock, and the scrape became so badly infected that they had to see a doctor) or an excess of sensuous, earthly pleasure (the desire to stay at the beach rather than climb the Mycenean Acropolis, a long evening sitting over white wine at Orvieto).

Nevertheless, one year Pierre managed to discover Florence, even though their campsite was so far away that trips to the city were difficult. And two or three times he found himself almost equal to the works he saw. It was an odd feeling: not that he could have created similar works, nor even that he understood them perfectly, but that they were intended for him, it was possible for him to be addressed by them. This feeling quickly disappeared. The two young women were determined to head for certain shop windows to look at beautiful leather clothes, silk blouses—all beyond their means—and his friend "wanted a good beer." Pierre was unhappy. He wanted a good beer too, and he also wanted to watch the young women try on dresses; and he sensed, confusedly, that these activities could have gone hand in hand with the contemplation and love of works of art. But his friends' behavior dissuaded him, in the end: they made fun of him for lingering so long in the church that he failed to notice how they were dying of hunger. Still, they did talk about Botticelli for a little while over their meal.

What was the choice, after all? To lose oneself in the past, in the contemplation of art, ignoring the differences between the wines of Frascati and Chianti? Or to play the more practical, up-to-date type, reluctant to "waste time on the past," granting no more than the conventional amount of attention to "works of art," just enough for the obligatory trip to Italy or Greece as a young professor of literature already encumbered with children?

In 1970, Annie had to agree, "for the sake of her career,"

to move to a different town. Faced with a choice of several equally important positions, they decided to go back to R., where Pierre had been born. The bank found them a small apartment in the Rue des Minimes, near the cathedral. Here they soon began to feel cramped; and at first Pierre was less than enchanted with having, every day, to walk past the tall doors of the school he had gone to as an adolescent. Then he got used to it—many of his old teachers had already retired, anyway.

And so the month of August passed. Two weeks went by, and Pierre had not yet settled down to work. One morning, standing in front of the shelves of books, he began to yawn. It was ten o'clock, and he was hungry. He sat down on a formica stool in the kitchen and stayed there for a moment in front of the open refrigerator, surrounded by the smells of vegetables and fish, a piece of swiss cheese in his hand.

Suddenly he saw himself in the glass door: a strong, broad-chested young man with thick, light hair. Was he suited to this work? There was nothing bookish about him, and his hands with their square nails were not the hands of an artist or an intellectual. Yet he was not an athlete, or a tinkerer, either—he did not know how to do anything. The truth was that he did not know who he was or what would have been right for him. He was a craftsman without a trade, a farmer without a plow, a simple man cut off from the work that would have been natural to him and thrust into an artificial environment where he had not put down roots. He was not made for the land—which his family had left two generations before—or for books. All he could do was continue to teach his classes.

He spent the late afternoon reading Faulkner—and here he found something that suited him, a seething, rough core of life far away from books and the sheltered life he led. He spent most of the next morning at the pool and emerged at noon happy, tired, and very hungry. On his way home he went to Annie's office and took her to lunch with one of her young coworkers. While he listened patiently, they argued about the likelihood of their departments being computerized, then changed the subject rather abruptly to fall fashions. They were young, their skin was soft, tanned, Laure would be back soon.

Pierre proposed that the four of them—the young woman was married—go on a picnic Sunday. Annie seemed surprised, but her coworker accepted with pleasure. Pierre worked in the garden the next few mornings, went back to the pool twice, finished his Faulkner, and tried to prepare dinner for Annie when she returned. From time to time he wrote down isolated, enigmatic, brief notes in a little notebook: this fragmentary sort of writing pleased him. Maybe this was the direction he should be going in? He talked about it to Laure in a letter; then, capping his pen with satisfaction, went to have a drink while waiting for Annie. He put on a record. The entire room was filled with the pleasant smell of the cool grass outside. Annie gazed at him. "You look good," she said. Though his eyes were red. Annie bought him goggles for the pool.

At the end of the month a quarrel broke out in the department Annie headed, a quarrel that so offended her that she felt maybe they should leave everything and move to a different town. Of course, there was the house, but they could always sell it. Pierre felt a twinge of distress, but at the same time a vague hope rose in him. Wouldn't this resolve everything? He said nothing either way, leaving it up to Annie. By the next day she had stopped talking about it; she had simply been feeling irritable. This fatigue of hers suited Pierre, because it meant that nights were not a problem. Inwardly he might have been a little disappointed by Annie's coolness, but he had to admit that it was pleasant to be effortlessly faithful to Laure.

CHAPTER 8

SEPTEMBER was approaching, and Pierre had not yet seen Laure. He missed her, but rather abstractly, sure that he would see her again; and at the same time he did not like to think of her mixed in with the resumption of all his fall duties, with the first days of rain, wet raincoats in the back of the car, and the children's complaints over dinner about the "new teacher" or the departure of one of their little friends.

Kept away from the garden by a few days of bad weather, Pierre lay on the sofa, listened to music, and held his notebook open with two fingers, though he had written nothing in it for a couple of days. When the telephone rang, he waited a minute, then got up. But whoever it was had already hung up. He went back and sat down.

The rain, which had just stopped after falling all morning, had soaked the row of hollyhocks, whose yellowing leaves were beginning to rot. Without having planned to, Pierre was already on his feet dialing Laure's number. He waited a moment. He had prepared what he would say to her: "I can hardly hear you." Then: "I want you, can I come by?" But no one answered. He sat down again. The record was over. He did not want to put on another one.

The telephone rang again. It was Annie. "Were you out a moment ago?" she asked.

"No," said Pierre, "I was just about to pick it up, but you had already hung up."

"Everything all right?"

"Yes."

"Are you working?"

"A little."

"I'll be late getting home tonight."

"I'll wait for you."

"No, don't bother. I had lunch with Fournier." She laughed. "I won't be very hungry!"

"Fournier? Is he back?"

"Yes, he got back yesterday. And there were some things he wanted to make up to me, so he took me out for a fancy lunch."

"I thought he was stingy."

"This just proves it . . . Anyway, you go ahead and finish the quiche yourself."

"I'm going out for a while," said Pierre.

In the bathroom he looked once again at the reflection of his tanned, rather rough face—I have lifeless eyes, he thought with a certain pride, the eyes of an inexpressive male—his square torso, the band of lighter skin below his waist, around his hips. He put on a clean shirt, patted himself with aftershave, and unzipped his pants again before he left, to tuck in his shirt more comfortably.

Outside the sun was shining brightly after the rain. The

lane between the houses was quiet: all the neighborhood children were at the pool, the cars were in the garages, the women were either on their back lawns or out shopping. Annie had taken the car, so he headed for the bus stop; the next bus was in twenty minutes. He felt full of sadness and impatience and looked all around him. Nothing, nobody. A bus appeared at the corner, and from a distance he recognized the name of the line. But because he was not used to taking it, he was waiting on the wrong side of the street. There was just enough time for him to cross over.

He had not ventured into the center of town for two months, and it surprised him: in the store windows the displays of summer sales were gradually being replaced by fall clothes; the main window of the Nouvelles Galeries department store displayed a classroom scene, glass-eyed little girls sitting in kilts at old schooldesks before blackboards, stiff boys clutching stacks of notebooks under their arms; giant fake pens were stuck in the wall like arrows from a toy bow-and-arrow set.

He walked a short distance in the warm street, in the soft light of the setting sun. Then, in one window, among some little yellow suns cut out of cardboard, he saw his own face, and a moment later, incredibly, above a blue silk sea and shells holding children's shoes, he saw Laure's face, too. He turned around. She was behind him, her arms bare and tanned.

At a moment like that there was nothing they could have said or done. Pierre merely reached out to Laure and encircled her thin wrist with his fingers.

"Come on," he said. "Let's go to your apartment."

They did not say three words to each other on the way. Nor would they say anything now. She shut the door behind them. In the small entryway they grasped each other roughly, in a confusion of clothes and wet kisses. The very awkwardness of their embrace made them dizzy; their hearts were beating violently. In the bedroom, while Laure lowered the blind, Pierre impatiently threw back the bedspread, and as they lay down against each other they closed their eyes and sighed deeply. Now they were suddenly embarrassed and hardly knew what to do, so great was their emotion, their gratitude: it took away all their strength, they could have cried. They bent over each other and, grasping each other in both hands, eyes closed, gave themselves up to rediscovering each other's bodies. They forgot the time they had been apart: really, it was as though the separation had never taken place. And even when their bodies came together, their hands continued to search for each other, haphazardly, over the sheet.

Afterwards they drank a cup of tea together, the way they used to do, and as Laure leaned against Pierre, he said, "At last I can look at you again."

"How light your hair is!" said Laure.

"I was lonely. I went to the pool every morning."

But time was passing, and Pierre did not have the car with him.

"I'll drive you home," said Laure.

For once they dressed together in the small bathroom and, in the soft late-summer evening, felt as if they were on vacation, preparing to leave the hotel together to go out to dinner. In the car Laure looked over at Pierre's happy face, and she felt fully content. He had put his hand on her thigh and from time to time, without looking at her, pressed it gently. They had left the center of town and were approaching Pierre's neighborhood. Was she at last going to find out what Pierre's house looked like?

The signs of a shared life she saw all around, in front of all the little single-story houses, pained her. A woman was watering a neat lawn. She let go of the hose, which recoiled and sent a spray of water as iridescent as splinters of glass up toward the sky. Another woman at some distance called out to someone, lifting a basket that was too heavy. Over and over the same ordinary family scene repeated itself almost exactly: children circled on orange bicycles; a little farther off, a tablecloth was laid over an iron table.

"If you like, I can come tomorrow," said Pierre. "You're not angry that I came, are you?"

How relieved Laure felt to hear those words! What did those neat lawns matter to her, those dogs the children were hugging tenderly, those dinners outdoors? They had found each other again; they would sleep together again in the damp afternoons. Of course, they had to separate afterwards. But could people who never separated love each other more than they did?

"Stop here," said Pierre, "so I can kiss you."

"Here?"

"Yes. We're very close." And with his chin he pointed toward something, a garden, a roof she could not distinguish from the others. It seemed to her that a stormy light had suddenly darkened the sky.

"Come here," said Pierre. "Let me kiss you again." And he clasped her to him. Laure, who could not close her eyes, had seen a shutter being lowered in the distance, had heard a child shout, a dog bark. Was it there?

When she was back at home, the telephone rang. "It took you a while," said Pierre. Once again she felt a burst of unalloyed, happy affection for him.

"I'm hungry," she said.

"I am, too. I'm eating some leftover quiche . . . I'll see you tomorrow. I love you so much."

When she hung up, Laure felt thankful that Pierre was not with her—he would have made it hard for her to think with all the intensity she needed to, about their rediscovery of each other that afternoon.

By two the next afternoon, he still had not come. The telephone rang: it was Pierre.

"I'll be waiting for you near the bus stop, where we said goodbye yesterday. I want to show you my garden."

She recoiled a little and did not say anything. What? There, in his house? She felt a large empty space in her head. Then she heard his voice again: "I'll start waiting for you in forty-five minutes."

Once again he was with her; she had seen him from a distance, standing near the rows of arbor vitae, frowning, and twice he had passed his hand over his chin.

He looked at her but did not touch her. "You're here," he said. He got into the car next to her. The trees parted, the street turned, Laure was filled with happiness.

"It's here," said Pierre.

Laure got out of the car, tense, chilly; she could not have managed without Pierre's hand on her wrist. She crossed the lawn without seeing it, walked through the entryway blindly, too, then into a large room, where she saw stacks of magazines cluttering a vast, rather battered sofa, and a pack of English cigarettes on a low table—Pierre smoked Gitanes—and was confronted with the smell and the silence of the house. Here and there stood beautiful bouquets of dried flowers. Both the order and the disorder bore witness to an attentive but alien presence: it was impossible to know anything, all the signs were false, deceptive.

"Don't look," said Pierre. "I hang around these rooms all day, I don't put anything away. Follow me. It's this way." He pushed open the door to a small room in the back of the house: there were rows of children's books, toys, a narrow bed.

"Is this where you work?" Laure asked.

Pierre was leafing through some of his notebooks. He put them down again. "This is where I sleep, too," he said. He was not really lying: the past few nights he had read in his office and, so as not to wake Annie, had stayed here and slept on Bruno's bed. He gently pulled Laure against him and sat down on the edge of the bed. She did not resist. Through the window came the sounds of the wind and of a stream of water from a neighboring house. She closed her eyes, giving in completely. Her heart was thumping, the shutter threw a broad shadow across the wood floor, the wind rattled it noisily.

When she opened her eyes again, Pierre, lying on his back, was breathing fast, his face turned to the pillow. "Come over on top of me," he said. "Yes, like that." Then he sighed hard, almost moaning. "I'm sorry," he said. "Oh, please forgive me, I'm an idiot. I've already come. I don't know what happened to me. I was so happy you were here. I could see the small of your back in the window, it was magnificent!"

She hugged him harder; then she stretched out next to him. Beyond the door she could see a hallway, other closed doors. Somewhere out there, "in back," in what direction she did not know, there was a larger bedroom, and a large bed. She closed her eyes.

Pierre had stood up and was coming back to her holding some small notebooks. "This is all," he said. "Two months, two small notebooks. But I'm happy."

"Will you show me?" she asked.

"I don't know. I doubt if it's even worth looking at."

He was on his feet again. "And I have a present for you," he said.

"Show me!"

"No, you open it when you get home."

In the rearview mirror she could still see him: he raised his hand twice to the height of his shoulder, waving goodbye. A woman was watching them from a window in the house next door. When Laure got home, she filled the tub with hot water and stayed in it a long time. She was too tired to think about anything.

CHAPTER 9

AT THE END of September a brief return of summer alternated with brusque hints of winter, sometimes in the same week, sometimes in the same day, as though the season were undecided and had to make several attempts before fixing on a choice. The mornings were foggy, this time it was really the end of summer, and in the dull air the smell of the rubber factory began to be perceptible, a terrible cold smell that would hang over the city all winter. The colorless morning seemed to stretch on forever; the sidewalks and roofs shone, as after rain; and the trees, still green, curled up their leaves under the dewdrops, hard and shiny as frost. But at eleven the sun came out; by noon it was so hot indoors, in front of the windows, that Laure had to lower the blinds.

Though she usually did not like to go out at lunchtime, these days she left the library every day and had a cup of coffee with her coworker in a café on the Place du Vieux Théâtre surrounded by other young women who, like the two of them, savored the remaining minutes of ease and rest. They sat leaning back in their chairs amid the traffic noise, eyes closed, turning their faces and arms one last time to the weak sun, and hitching up the skirts of the thin dresses they had shivered in that morning on the bus as it made its way through an unfriendly landscape plunged in dense grayness pierced only by yellow headlights and the steady beating of the windshield wipers. And more than one said to her neighbor, as her mother and grandmother had once said: "It's impossible to know what to wear. The mornings are so cold."

At five o'clock, by the time people were leaving offices and stores, the sun had warmed the squares and shadowless streets just as if summer had returned. Strolling around after the shops were closed, they would have believed they were in some town in a warm climate, their daily tasks a form of vacation activity, interrupted by long periods on the beach, under the palms.

When she reached home, exhausted by the brutal return of the heat, Laure would collapse into a chair or under the shower; she thought about the people who had "a patch of garden," people who congratulated themselves for the thousandth time on having left "the center of town," as they drank their cocktails and ate their dinner outdoors, between hedges of arbor vitae over which floated the neighbors' chitchat and the sound of their radios, the noise of an argument, the gentle clatter of dishes, and the smell of fried potatoes. By nine o'clock everything was put away and everyone was settled in front of the television. The sky was cloudy again, and tiny drops of water covered the arms of the lawn chairs. Shutters were closed against the steady din of other television sets and against a night that was already cold.

People who lived in town had closed their shutters much

earlier, and no one was left on the streets, as though it were winter, except on the newly constructed pedestrian area, which consisted of a few concrete tubs filled with petunias in summer, pansies in winter; streetlamps with asymmetrical globes; and dirty benches where the Moroccan factory workers from the lower part of town lingered before going back to their hostels.

On one of these days, Laure crossed the theater square at about 8:30—it was already choked with morning traffic—ran up the steps of the library, noticing the expanse of delicately tinted clear sky over her head, then entered the large room, which was chilly because the heat had not yet been turned on. She was not wearing socks or stockings, and she was cold. At noon it began to rain. Strong gusts of wind struck the reading room windows, and one of them broke. While waiting for the repairmen to arrive, she put a bucket underneath it where the water came in, and stuffed some packing cloth into it to muffle the steady drumming of the raindrops. Laure took a hard-boiled egg and a container of yogurt out of her bag. She would do without the coffee.

"I have my thermos," said her colleague. "I was so cold the day before yesterday, and then last night they said it wouldn't last. There's the proof," she added, looking at the black sky.

My feet are icy, thought Laure, I'm definitely going to come down with a cold.

Their relationship, too, seemed to be governed by the uncertainty and changeableness of the weather. Some evenings when Pierre arrived, he said, "Don't touch me, I'm all sweaty, I'm going to take a shower."

"Me too," Laure said. "I'm hot."

They lowered the blind, threw the covers down to the foot of the bed, and lay bathed in a soft, thin, deceptive light, as if they had just woken up from an afternoon nap in Venice or spent a long morning at the beach. Even their smell was a summer smell: under Laure's cheek Pierre's arm immediately broke out in sweat. But meanwhile the sky had darkened, the rain had come; leaving her, Pierre checked his watch twice, thinking he had been mistaken. Night was still far off—and Laure was in pain and close to tears as she found herself alone again in the square room, seeing a few lights on the other side of the street and, toward the west, a strip of clear sky where the storm had broken, allowing a little extra daylight to return.

One evening as she went out, she passed two men in the stairwell on their way home. They greeted her indifferently, and then, for a moment, through an open door, she heard a dog barking, silverware rattling as a table was set, then the whistling of a pressure cooker. She felt no regret, no sorrow, no envy—neither her life nor anyone else's seemed right to her. But once in the street she felt at loose ends, aimless. Somewhere else, in another, larger town, it would have been different—she would have gone to see friends, or to a concert. Other years she had sometimes gone to movies in the evening with Ghislaine. Could she go now, alone? The sight of some soldiers approaching from a rather shabby movie theater confirmed her hesitation. The ticket-seller watched from inside her harshly illuminated glass case as she walked away.

(She remembered how, for years, her parents had taken her brother and her to the movies every Sunday, to the two o'clock show. Around five the empty street would fill with people again; the cars parked a short distance away would start up one after another, piercing the mist with blue smoke; through the rear windshield one would see the faces of children, the face of a man bundled up in an overcoat turning around to back up, one hand nervously wiping away the steam. Her family would walk home. Soon the boulevard was empty.)

She walked along calmly. It was nearly seven. The street was emptying. She could hear the clacking of iron shutters being lowered to the sidewalk. Lights were going off; only the shop windows remained bright, with their hunted-looking mannequins. On the street it seemed to her she was free, that she had escaped some great imposture, and yet her heart was heavy. No one could see her, no one thought of her as she walked along. She was drawn by some lights in the distance, but the shop window was oddly empty behind its black grill. Sitting on a bench, surrounded by bulky sacks, a toothless woman smiled and made a sign to Laure that she did not understand, then turned away and went on rearranging her things.

By now Laure was hungry. She went into the last open charcuterie and stood in line behind some tired women ordering one container of celery salad, two of diced ham and vegetables, and some egg custards in disposable aluminum molds. When her turn came, she bought rice pudding and potato salad.

She walked back home slowly, between ghostly displays of shoes and lingerie on cold, sometimes maimed bodies of women, blue eyes encircled by stiff eyelashes looking out at her. At the bottom of the avenue the square in front of the station still glowed with a little movement, a little traffic, taxis arriving in time for the last train. Here children had fallen asleep among the suitcases, under the tables, at the feet of soldiers. A man was watching her, and she could see that he was about to cross the street toward her. She walked faster, turned the corner, and he did not follow her. What if she let someone accost her some day, what if she took home some unsmiling stranger? Or followed him to his little room, where the dirty wallpaper was peeling off the wall at the head of the bed, where a broken washbasin stood in the corner on a square of linoleum?

She went home by way of the Place du Vieux Théâtre, alongside the empty terrace of the Grand Café between its tubs of trimmed boxtree. One story up, the restaurant was open, though half empty; slowly and gently around the few couples still sitting over their meals, waiters moved back and forth, rolling carts, lifting covers, revealing plates from which steam coiled up. The bus stop was quiet; schoolchildren had left their traces in the gutter—crumpled tickets, broken pens, pages torn from a notebook and covered with awkward letters in felt-tip pen. Suddenly all the lights at the crossroads were turned down for the night, as in a hospital corridor.

She went into her apartment, carefully holding the containers of food upright, without really trying to sort out the feelings that were troubling her: regret at not being with Pierre, a longing for a more ordinary life, and, deep down, the confused but undeniable sensation of being where she should be, of doing what she should be doing, of having no regrets or desires; and once again she thought it was a strange feeling for someone not yet thirty to have. At these times she tried, she forced herself, to see herself from the outside, as others saw her, as she imagined others must judge her, as others must picture the life she led: then she felt a little sadness, even anger, the desire to reproach Pierre, to complain. But when she told him about it the next day, she felt unconvinced by her own words, and also ashamed to see him disconcerted, silent, crushed with remorse as he confronted a claim he found even more legitimate than she did.

At eight o'clock she turned on the television. When she had moved away from R., Ghislaine had left Laure a small, old set. At first Laure did not want it.

"Good for you," Pierre had said.

"Why do you say that? You certainly watch television." In the end she had it serviced and then installed it in her bedroom on a cube of lacquered pine with the antenna out the courtyard window. She got into the habit of having dinner on her bed, where she would lie down fully dressed during the local news and watch footage of strikes in tractor factories, an exhibition of photographs in a converted mill, a flood with animal corpses floating in the dirty water among the round tops of poplars, a press conference with a priest just returned from Central America.

Then she would get up, take her tray back to the kitchen,

and get undressed to watch the evening film. In the courtyard people were doing the dishes, a window banged shut, a child shouted; steam covered the kitchen windows. She would look for a cool spot on the sheet and often, after the film, go on to watch a documentary about raising basset hounds, or wolf hunting in the Ardennes. She would fall asleep with a heavy head and a feeling of distress and shame.

The next day she would talk to Pierre about it. "Did you watch that, too?" he would say. "It was stupid, but I couldn't resist." There was some consolation in that, at least, and a tenuous link between them. What she did not tell him was that she had thought of him several times during the evening. The best moment, the least painful, was the moment of falling asleep, because she knew that while we are asleep, wherever we happen to be, we are always alone. And it was a real comfort to imagine herself and Pierre slumbering in the same oblivion, for even if they could not be together there, they could both still evade what separated them. The hardest time was already past by then; that was around nine o'clock, when she knew Pierre and Annie would become irritated over getting the children to sleep, when first one and then the other would decide to go to bed. For a long time, curiously, it was important for Laure to know—though how could she find out?— if they went to bed at the same time. Did she have to imagine them standing up at the same moment? One carrying the glasses and ashtrays to the kitchen, the other turning off the lamps, checking the shutters? And one saying, "You go ahead and use the bathroom, I'll go after," the way couples did, the way she had seen her parents do, and Jacques and Nicole?

Then Laure would turn off the light and, laying her head down in the darkness, in the hollow of the bed and her own smell, fall asleep over the same monotonous and unresolved questions, finally carried down into some formless and merciful place by the sound sleep of youth and the hope of seeing Pierre the next day.

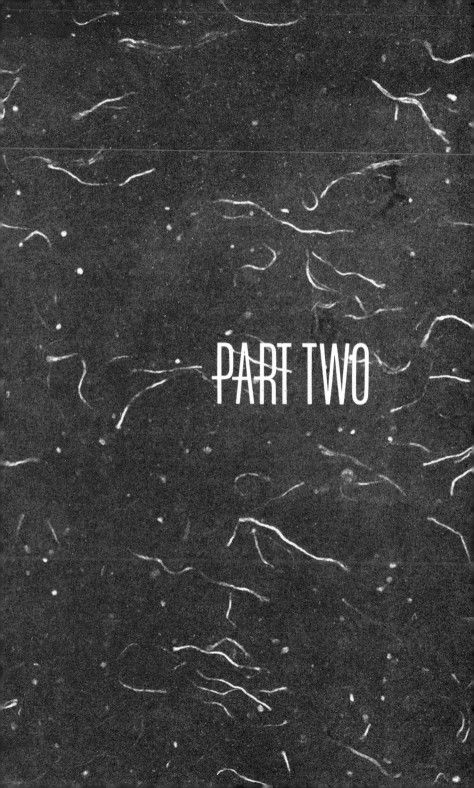

PART TWO

PIERRE had been the first in his family to get a higher education. His maternal grandparents had been farmers. His mother had been born on their little farm in Saint-Saturnin-sur-Leuvron, which already could no longer support them. Pierre's grandfather had had to take a job as an unskilled laborer at the factory, while Pierre's grandmother sometimes worked by the day in the village gardens. Yet until the grandfather's death they continued to live in the low, one-story house whose large, square room was lit by a single window in the back—because the front door was solid, they had to leave it open in the summer if they wanted more light; and the walls were spotted with saltpeter halfway up.

Pierre's mother and his two uncles left school when they

were twelve. The little girl was apprenticed to a dressmaker; in 1930 she became a salesgirl at the Marché Bonnetier, which was a shame, thought people who knew her, because she was "getting on so well" at school and "could learn anything if she put her mind to it." The older of the two boys stayed to help his father with the farm; the second failed the examination for the teachers' college and did not take it again. That same year Pierre's mother, Louise—or Louisette, as everyone called her—married a colleague of her brother's. Pierre's father was killed in November, 1939, and Pierre was born in January, 1940.

Because he was a frail child, he spent every winter in the country with his maternal grandmother. He was studious and quiet. When his mother remarried after the war, this time to a hosiery salesman, everyone agreed that Pierre would be a primary-school teacher or—who knows? said his professors— even a professor himself. Pierre said nothing. He liked Saint-Saturnin: he liked to watch the ducks hatch, help bind the hay into sheaves, go hunting with his grandfather.

But then his grandfather died, his grandmother could not stay on in the village alone, and so the house was sold and she came to live with them in their small apartment in R.: two rooms on the street, a kitchen (which doubled as bathroom) looking out on the courtyard, and a toilet on the landing. The house was not very tall, and over the rooftops the bishop's palace could be seen on one side, on the other, fields. Pierre liked this house, which was so dark that the brothers had to turn on the lights to do their homework. The older boy worked sullenly, but Pierre, like his mother, "could learn anything if he put his mind to it."

Being sons of a soldier killed in action, they had no trouble obtaining scholarships, so Pierre and his brother—who was to stay in school only until he was fifteen or so—became the first in their family to go to a lycée. The famous D.F., later a brilliant student at the School of Paleography, and Maximilien D., who became head of the cabinet of the Minister of

National Education, were in the same class, but there were other scholarship students, too, sons of state employees or local merchants. Of all the students the most highly esteemed, and the most envied, were the sons of other professors, the ones the math teacher would turn to, just before class or recess began, saying, "By the way, how is your father (or your mother)? We haven't seen each other since the orals for the general certificate."

After a difficult period in which he tried to imitate his brother, smoking and nurturing the same passion for soccer, Pierre began bringing home books, borrowing them from the library and even buying them. These were the first books ever to enter the family home. His grandfather had managed to read *Les Misérables* and all of Alexandre Dumas; his grandmother cut the serials out of women's magazines every week. As for his stepfather, he had never even opened a book. Until Pierre turned fifteen, he had no objection to his reading, but after that he sometimes had to suppress an outburst of bad temper at the sight of Pierre sitting in the kitchen, knees up, deaf to everything around him, a book lying open on his thighs. Still, he loved the two children very much, and later they would both say that he had been a real father to them, had never made them feel they were not his children.

Pierre learned to swim with the mayor's son, and his literature professor, Maurice Lautier, became a friend. His stepfather no longer talked to him in quite the same way he had before. Gradually, the presence of books became a necessity, which everyone accepted with a kind of supportive resignation: he would go on with his studies. He always came down late to the family meals, pale and drawn, and for a while he even had to wear glasses; he was "always buried in his books," they would say. "And what about Pierre? Is he buried in his books?" And they were surprised that he should excel at soccer, like his three cousins, simple boys who had failed out of school at the age of sixteen. It was obvious that books would always be a part of his life—costly but indispensable tools, like a doctor's instrument bag or a sailor's sextant and compass. So Pierre entered a career he thought he had chosen—because his mother wished it, since she wanted him to have the security of a civil servant's job, and because he loved "books" and did not know what someone who "loved books" could do, except become a teacher.

Teaching was certainly "the best of the professions," the highest of offices: a clean job allowing for much leisure time and long vacations, and procuring a pension and a degree of respect that put one, within the space of a generation, almost on a level with the prominent people in town, those who had inherited a position, a fortune, an office. At the same time, it was not a self-centered sort of occupation, like business or commerce, concerned solely with a mundane kind of profit (it was almost a guarantee of disinterestedness that salary was not directly connected to the amount of work done). Rather it contributed to the general uplift, by loosing the tight knots of obscurantism and ignorance: the day would come when everyone would have a secondary-school diploma, just as a century earlier one had looked forward to the day when everyone would have a primary-school diploma.

Among shopkeepers, salesmen, and mechanics, however, there was a secret but common belief that a teacher's profession was not really a man's profession: it was too clean, too involved with children and adolescents, whose education is traditionally the province of women, and teachers were believed to have narrow shoulders and weak sight (not true in Pierre's case). What redeemed them in everyone's eyes was the notion that they had chosen the job only for the long vacations that went with it. As for books . . . For a long time the library had occupied one floor of the château, after the municipality had gathered together various bequests and made them available to the public two days a week. (The archives attracted a few more people.) But who would ever go there, except, perhaps, a notary's son, who had to sit for one of his law exams again? No one in R. would have thought of going there to read something: and in those days the books could not be borrowed. Then a former colonial administrator, now retired, made a gift of his works; other gifts joined his, including those of a homosexual landowner crazy about travel and photography. In 1955 a public reading room was opened on the ground floor, and first one, then two librarians were hired. Pierre went there from time to time; every Thursday evening Lautier gave an informal talk on modern literature. His talks on Gide made a deep impression on Pierre.

There was also a theater in R., but it was closed most of the time, opening only for operettas and performances by traveling theater companies. Here Pierre saw *Le Cid* in September, 1953, and *Tartuffe* in 1955. Christmas parties were given in the lobby for retired civil servants and the children of municipal employees, and sometimes people danced under the yellowed posters for *Cavalleria Rusticana*. The theater was a building without elegance, dating from the early nineteenth century—the winner of a Rome Prize, born here twenty-five years earlier, had been summoned back to R. to decorate its ceiling, and in 1870 one of the two boulevards was named after him. In actuality it was an uncomfortable place with pretentious architecture—a mirrored, colonnaded lobby and nymphs on the ceiling. The acoustics were excellent, but they served mainly for the amusement of the visiting schoolchildren. The theater was supported because it was one of the town's glories, yet none of the town councillors, who regularly renewed their subscriptions, had set foot in it more than twice; even so, when a proposal was made to erect a statue of the painter who had decorated it, the monument was unanimously approved on the first round of voting.

Otherwise, there were the newspaper serials, the radio, then, rather belatedly, television, which won out over everything else. The two bookstores in R. did not really have much business except when classes resumed in the fall and when it came time to buy Christmas presents. Some exposure to books was obligatory: in order to enter a profession, it was necessary to pursue one's "studies"—a very vague term that covered the whole of one's life after primary school. Just as it is customary in the Trobriand Islands for adolescents to spend their nights in the "bachelors' house," it was normal for boys—and girls now, too—to go to elementary school, to lycée, even to college, though few enough went to college so that everyone knew who they were. But between this and living with one's nose "buried in books" there was a world of difference.

And so Pierre allowed his life to be determined for him, all the while believing that he was determining it. It doesn't matter, he thought, I'll have some peace, vacations. Wouldn't he have all the time in the world to develop a special vocation for himself? Anything was better than working in a factory, on the farm, or even in an office, he thought. Little by little his sense of curiosity diminished. He had peace: that peace suffocated him. All that was left for him was the secret satisfaction of somehow being involved in the world of books, art, creative works: his profession would still bring him closer to all that than anything else would. But though it might seem otherwise, nothing really set him apart from the people he thought he had distanced himself from—and who thought likewise, regarding him with an intimidated respect after he earned his teaching certificate. Physically he was like them— broad-backed, red-haired, square-faced, short-nosed. They marveled at it, finding it hard to reconcile his strong hands with the distinguished image his profession had automatically conferred on him. But at heart he was like them, and they did not know it. True, he no longer had their mistrust of "books," but he had preserved a feeling of dispossession that resembled it a great deal. At the same time he had lost the confidence they expressed, with an almost animal unselfconsciousness, in their own strength, their virility, by the way they lit a cigarette, leaned back in their chairs—in short, acted like men. He was dispossessed and unhappy about it; he had lost the protective ignorance of his forebears without gaining any certainty. And he came very close to sharing the doubts of his

brother, Georges, who would ask him what use it all was—
everything he was stuffing into the heads of those kids. "Not
much, I'm afraid," Pierre would say, but they would not think
he meant it.

Beyond that, he continued to love soccer, the outdoors, long
meals. Often he was astonished to see the scholarly editions
of the Greek and Latin classics lining his office: "When I think
that I read all those," he would say, "and in the original, or
almost."

His marriage to Annie had completed the separation from
his family: she came from a "better" background than his,
though no one in her family had ever held a position in administration or banking comparable to the one she had earned
through ambition and determination. Annie did not read much
besides an occasional detective novel, the literary prize-
winners her father gave her for Christmas every year, and the
Nobel laureate collection bound in white imitation leather,
which she and Pierre arranged in a small bookcase in the
entryway.

Sometimes on weekends, Pierre felt a certain emptiness,
which would not go away of itself, but the week would quickly
come around again to dispel that useless feeling: there were
classes, the children, exercises to correct, pleasant evenings at
home. In his family it had been such a luxury to have a moment
to oneself, a little breathing space, a Sunday now and then,
even an hour at the end of the day! In the end Pierre was
really no different from Annie, despite the useless books he
no longer opened, which had accumulated to such a degree
that he had had to order high-tech-style bookshelves, which
greatly impressed his mother and also, privately, his stepfather.

When he came to know Laure, however, something
changed. With her, for her, he rediscovered his love of books.
Laure had begun studying for her doctorate, and that brought
them closer together: like him, she had known the anguish of

the month of May and the anxiety of facing her orals—for she preferred the written part of the exam, not being very talkative and not liking people to pester her with questions. Together they rediscovered their adolescent penchant for prolonged conversations in which nothing was held back. Love gave them strength: though they never said it, together they conceived of a form of life in which art, travel, and theater were the natural complements of love, as in the writers' biographies or collections of letters which they lent each other.

Laure, for her part, had no regrets about stopping when she did, not becoming a professor. But her mother, who was the daughter of a noncommissioned officer, had never worked, had married an insurance agent at the age of seventeen, always regretted Laure's decision. According to her mother, Laure should have a "woman's" job, not as a nurse or social worker, though, but as a schoolteacher or university professor. At the age of fourteen or so Laure had shared this opinion: she could very easily imagine herself following in the footsteps of her German teacher, a lively young brunette who had three children close in age. With unfailing good cheer this woman combined the cares of running a household with those of teaching: she was not embarrassed to come in Monday morning and explain to her pupils that if she seemed tired and her eyes had circles under them, it was because one of her sons had the measles. Laure liked to see her walk by, down the hallway that was off-limits to the students, on her way to the teachers' lounge, in her comfortable shoes, her beige loden coat, her printed scarves, and the pigskin bag from which she would pull out bundles of student compositions banded with strong brown paper.

Things did not go quite the way Laure, or rather her mother, had imagined. She completed her third year of university at Bordeaux, was disappointed by the enormous lecture halls, the tiny classrooms, the seminars at which students who did not know one another met only once a week with an aloof professor who had still not learned their names by the end of the year. So she took the librarians' exam, received her qualification, and was appointed to R. She was pleased. Yet it seemed to her that the teachers from the two schools who came to borrow books on Wednesdays looked at her with a certain condescension. They said they envied her because she did not have to correct Latin translations, but it was obvious to her that privately they found her occupation inferior and her skills limited: they almost never asked her advice, always seemed to know the titles, editions, and even locations of the books better than she did. In June they felt sorry for her: school was closed, but she had to stay. "I have to admit I'd rather be surrounded by kids," they would say to a colleague as they went out. "Books always smell of dust."

"At least you have time to read," they would concede.

"Not as much as you think," Laure would say.

She was not bored. In her second year there she undertook to see that the reference library was expanded and improved, bringing in such books as Diderot's Encyclopedia and the Dictionary of the Académie Française. She cleaned them up and gazed at them with satisfaction. The mass of dead pages came to life, and the sun tinted the old leather spines soft colors. She felt she had done something useful.

CHAPTER 11

A FEW months later she met Pierre. She had just celebrated her birthday, which came in mid-December, and at Christmastime the two lycées came together for a theatrical evening followed by "refreshments," as they did every year. Laure could never remember the exact circumstances very well.

"I remember perfectly," said Pierre. "You were standing a little apart from everyone else, chatting with that brunette—a rather vulgar woman, not bad-looking."

"Ghislaine," said Laure. "You see? Ghislaine was the one you noticed, not me."

"Not at all," said Pierre. "I was looking at you. Really."

But it was Laure who remembered their second meeting much better than Pierre.

"It was on the terrace of the Café de la Mairie," she said.

"That was the second time?"

"Absolutely."

"But I remember going to the library sometime in January to look something up in the Dictionary of the Académie . . ."

"Oh, yes, maybe you're right."

From that point on in their history they were in complete agreement and retrieved every detail together. They had met by chance and had a cup of coffee together, and then Pierre had gotten into the habit of working at the municipal library, which he said was quieter than the school library, and of taking out books. Gradually, as one meeting followed another, as one chat followed another, without realizing it they had become very interested in each other. Without a word being said, without a move being made, a sort of understanding had arisen between them; they talked to each other like old friends. If this was love, there would be plenty of time to find it out, so what was the point of hurrying?

Then Pierre's feelings for Laure began to intensify at an amazing rate: he dreamed about her, he imagined waiting for her in the street and walking up to her apartment, but he did not do it. He marveled at this, believing that his capacity to wait indicated the depth of his feelings. It seemed to both of them that something was inevitably going to happen, something that would compensate them a hundred times over for having waited so long.

Anyone seeing the two of them sitting companionably with their elbows on the table at the Café de la Mairie—which they later avoided—would have had no doubts about what sort of relationship they had, yet would have been wrong. Pierre would gaze at the tops of her brown arms, wishing he could press his lips against them. He would smile. "I have to go," he would say. "It's time." With a feeling of joy Laure would leave him, returning to Ghislaine or the other woman she worked with. What restrained them was a feeling of fear, of heedlessness, of certainty. They already had the sort of friendship that sometimes follows the end of an affair, yet they both knew they would not remain at that stage, though they did nothing to hurry things along.

One day Pierre happened to drive her back to work—it was raining, or she was late, or he had to go home, he could no longer remember when he thought about it now—and while saying goodbye to her, he clumsily took her in his arms, yet let her go without kissing her. Though he knew nothing about her, at the same time he had the feeling that Laure was unlike any woman he had ever met.

Suddenly the love between them exploded, and it was no longer possible to contain it in that indefinite expectation where it had remained up to now, perhaps ripening. In fact, it had not really ripened: what they felt for each other had suddenly changed form and in the space of a few days had turned into a passion that completely absorbed them. It had become indispensable for them to meet often, and regularly; in addition, they both felt driven to make unexpected dates, and Pierre to call her in the middle of the night.

At the end of May the weather became so hot it seemed impossible that it could continue; yet it did continue, and the nights were hardly cooler than the days. When they left each other, they remained conscious of each other, seeing, hearing, almost touching each other: their skin did not for a moment forget the contact of that other skin—its warmth, its flavor. They saw everything through the golden haze of their love; the other's face, shape, way of walking threw each of them into a state of oppression and anguish that abated only when their bodies were once again so close that they could no longer see each other, when, silent, out of breath, speechless, sightless, they would seize each other's body avidly, as though to be closer to what was hidden by that outward appearance.

And when they left each other, their fatigue colored everything: the trees on the boulevard shone, and in the thickness of the dark-green, dusty foliage they sensed a presence, a summons, almost a menace appearing in response to what had awoken in them. It was as if behind the visible world the bond between their bodies had discovered another bond, deeper or higher, more radiant, black.

Even so, they did sometimes go outdoors together, take a walk in the old neighborhood behind the Place Biette. Springtime tinted the fronts of a few old hotels, there was no traffic here at all, a cat sped away under the branches, the front doors of the small houses stood open to the street in a friendly way, and inside one could see old people sitting around tables that were covered with oilcloth. Pierre stopped to clasp Laure against him, drew her under an awning to kiss her lips. Only a few hundred yards away was the boulevard, the lycée, friends, acquaintances; here they were alone and protected. Pierre gently raised Laure's face to his and looked at her for a long time before kissing her again on the lips.

Yet they had less and less desire to go out, because they were so eager to be back in each other's arms that when they walked side by side through the streets, the obviousness of their passion scorched them, made their hands magnetic, so that they had to carry themselves in a rigid, unnatural way that betrayed them as much as their smiles, their looks. When they met in the street by chance, they would stare at each other motionless, surprised, as time slowly drained away: mouths dry, knees trembling, surrounded by strangers, hearing them on all sides like a warning and a threat, like an alarm announcing a war, a fire, they could not move. The revelation that had dawned in them without anyone's knowledge, almost without their own, formed a secret connection between them and every sign of metamorphosis in the world: pregnant women standing in line at the bus stop; young poplars bending together in the wind; the early-morning songs of the awakening birds in front of the town hall when Pierre met Laure before she went to the library.

Laure, like Pierre, found herself suddenly deep inside something she had not chosen, something that had swooped down on her, giving her no chance to accept or reject it: this was simply the way it was. She had not wanted it, but there was no going back now. She loved Pierre, Pierre loved her. Of that they were sure; this truth, confirmed every day in a tremulous haste, and the certainty of not being proved wrong wrapped them in a protective cloak. Surprisingly enough, Laure barely noticed that Pierre had to leave her every evening to return home; she was almost relieved to be free, for a few hours, of this relentless tension.

Ghislaine did not question Laure, though she saw her less often now; instead, she feigned discretion and waited for Laure to say something. "Just be careful" was all Ghislaine said to her, once. But careful of what? Of Pierre? Pierre was the one who seemed to need protection, though Laure could not have said from what. As for her, whatever she needed protection from, it was Pierre himself who shielded her best.

Everyone who had known Laure since her childhood thought she had a "good character"—she was calm, rarely became angry, did what she was told without protesting. But there were also some contradictory traits in her: a stubborn adherence to a few simple principles, which she was not always even aware of. Even in her earliest photographs her face, ringed with curly, light-chestnut hair, had a certain gravity, and her small mouth smiled very rarely, though her expression was sweet. She would be holding a doll, though without much tenderness, or her brother's hand. In each picture she was careful to look straight ahead.

Her mother tended to point to her as an example: "I have to say," she would remark, "that with Laure there were no problems." And it was true that Laure had gone through all the stages of her earliest childhood without any problems: she did not cry at night, was not sick very often, quickly learned to read, and asked surprisingly sharp questions. She could draw and paint prettily. Her constant calm was broken by occasional outbursts of joy when her brother chased her, shouting, down the garden paths. She dirtied or tore her dress only once, climbing an old apple tree. Her neatly parted hair shone.

Her brother's childhood had been rougher and more chaotic. Laure's family felt this was because of the difference in their sexes. For a long time he was afraid of the dark; and when he cried, he would exhaust himself with the violence of his sobs— for instance, on the terrible day he caught his hand in the attic door—until he was made to feel ashamed: "Look at your sister," he was told, "she never cries, even though she's a girl." That remark impressed but did not cure him.

Laure would sometimes look at him reprovingly when he was scolded for some futile act of rebellion, some endless argument with their mother. To all appearances Laure accepted everything: her parents' advice, her teachers' advice. She was very seldom reprimanded, being a competent student, though weak in mathematics. But what she really thought, no one knew: specifically, no one was sure whether she unprotestingly did as told because she thought it was right or because she found it useless to argue. Her parents certainly did not keep after her as they did her brother, who was always urged to be "first." One day he foolishly copied the work of the boy next to him, a plump fellow much less gifted than he was. This sin stupefied his parents, and Laure even more. "No problems with her," commented their mother, an authoritarian woman, once again. "Jacques is another matter." There was pride in her voice when she spoke of her son; with some satisfaction, "she saw herself all over again" in him, down to his insubordinate attitude.

By the time she was fifteen Laure had formed an idea of the world that was not going to change. She went on to secondary school and so lost her best friend, who dropped out and entered the postal service. Laure observed very early that by not attracting the attention of others, one avoided finding oneself at war or in competition with them. So without ever having to struggle, Laure always achieved her goals, which were modest. In this, as her family said, she was certainly the opposite of her brother, who was by turns proud, irritable, gloomy, and very high-spirited. Things were the way they were. Which was not to say that one accepted them, still less that one liked them; but what was the good of rebelling? The fact that the world was what it was did not make her responsible for it: it could continue very well without her help. Laure knew right away that open resistance would change nothing and would probably get her hurt. When a generally accepted rule did not suit her, she did not make an issue of it: she got around it without saying anything. Perhaps she was different, but she did not feel at fault. And she would continue to recognize the legitimacy of a maxim she personally took exception to. Never coming into direct conflict with anyone, never trying to win anyone over to her point of view, she met little resistance; she and the world went on their ways, ways that were often parallel, sometimes diverging, Laure never dreaming of complaining, the world never becoming offended at her. Just after she passed her last exams—with a small mention of "Very Good" in philosophy, just the thing that would make her mother happy—her brother, Jacques, was certified as a civil engineer. The following summer he got married.

"I really like her," Jacques said, speaking of Nicole, his fiancée. "This time it's different." What did it mean, to "really like someone"? Laure wondered. For Jacques it meant having a house, children, "building" something together. Laure saw things the same way, except that she was not certain how she would fit into it all. She went out with several friends of her brother's, with one of them for longer than the rest, who squeezed her very hard when dancing with her and asked her to spend her vacation with him that summer.

"But I see it as a real commitment," he said. "It's important. You should think about it."

These words made an unpleasant impression on her. In other ways she liked the young man a lot: he was fair, rather pale, accommodating and delicate in his manners. He was a

serious boy—"too serious," said Jacques—from a modest background, who had become convinced at a very early age that
men "did women a great deal of harm" by thinking only of
their own pleasure; he did not want to be that sort of man.
Several times at student dances, when they were dancing in
the long, overheated rooms with rows of chairs along the sides,
an orchestra in front, and tables in the next room for refreshments, she had felt his breath quicken against her neck, his
body harden against her hip. This had disturbed her; she had
held him tighter, more tenderly, but she resisted going farther
in that direction, thinking it would end in burdensome, immutable constraints. She felt that by talking to her that way,
by looking at her so seriously, the young man was seeking to
make his first real beginnings in life, his apprenticeship as
father and procreator, and that all their games would inevitably
lead to that end. (Later, when they had broken up for good,
he retained friendly feelings for Laure's parents, whom he had
managed to meet: he even sent them an announcement of his
marriage, either thoughtlessly or out of true affection. Laure's
parents talked about him together and wished him happiness
and success, the way certain parents-in-law do a former son-
in-law.)

The following year, the same year Laure decided to take
the competitive exam for librarians, they saw more of each
other. One night he stayed over. He was urgent, frantic,
quick, Laure was not sure why, yet he was careful and made
sure she was protected. He already behaved with a certain
tender authority: took it upon himself to advise her in what
she read, chose the movies they went to see. Afterwards they
would go have a pizza, laugh crazily, run after each other.
Laure almost preferred those times to all the rest. "What he
needs," said Jacques, with false innocence, "is a happy home.
He's smart," he added. "He'll do research."

When Laure was assigned to R., she did not discuss it with
him until the last moment. He understood, but he was so

disappointed that he cried. Laure cried too, but that did not change anything. She had made up her mind.

"So," said Ghislaine one day—it seemed that the silence was beginning to weigh on her—"when is the divorce?"

"I don't know," said Laure, shocked by the words. "We've never talked about it." Ghislaine shrugged her shoulders.

Ghislaine had been appointed to R. one year before Laure; they had become friends right away. She was slender and nice-looking, with an animated face and bright eyes, and she dressed with a boldness that stupefied Laure; in fact, there was great freedom in everything she did. Laure's first months at R., when she was still suffering from her breakup, necessary though it had been, were brightened by Ghislaine. From her Laure acquired a taste for drinking large glasses of Bordeaux and listening to music over dinner.

One evening, to her surprise, Ghislaine asked her to stay over. This was something one never did where Laure came from, for fear of intruding. During the night she heard Ghislaine crying. "What's the matter?" she asked. In a small voice Ghislaine told her. She was sure "he" was seeing someone else. "Give me something to drink," she added. They finished the bottle of Bordeaux together. In the morning Ghislaine had circles under her eyes and a strained look on her face. She spent hours over the washbasin putting cold compresses on her face. "I don't want to cry over that man," she said, and this alone was enough to start her crying again.

The following summer, when Laure and Pierre had such trouble separating from each other—it was the first time— Ghislaine went off to Mexico. She came back comforted, but with her skin yellow and her eyes hollow: she had caught an intestinal parasite that was very common there.

"And what about you?" she asked. "How is everything?"

"All right," said Laure peacefully. Ghislaine shrugged her shoulders. "You're happy?" It was obvious. Ghislaine shrugged her shoulders again. For Laure the feeling had revealed itself in all its purity, pushing aside, once and for all, the prickly questions of life: commitments, a house, children.

She tried clumsily to explain this to her friend. "I don't know. Maybe," said Ghislaine. Laure thought her grudging attitude came from an attack of the fever she had brought back from Mexico. And anyway, Ghislaine kissed her emphatically when they left each other that evening.

CHAPTER 12

LAURE'S friendship with Ghislaine, their talks together, soon showed her that there were really two kinds of women and that perhaps she was neither kind. First, there were the patient, resolute young women like her sister-in-law, Nicole, the ones who laid traps for men with a skill that was completely unconscious, and who would have been offended had their wiles been pointed out to them. There was no cynicism in them, no calculation; calm, joyful, they were only applying a law in which they had complete confidence and that legitimized what they did. If there was a trap, it was a trap common to the species. And both men and women got caught in it, voluntarily, with their own consent, and in so doing merely bore out a general rule larger than they were. And they would find themselves once again facing the questions this rule involved, questions that dozens of couples before them had attempted to solve in virtually the same way.

Ghislaine was something completely different: right from the beginning she had chosen an adventurous, chaotic, passionate life that led her from one painful "episode" to another, no less painful, even when it came along just at the right time to console her for the one before. With a fascination somewhat tinged with repugnance, Laure had watched the courtship of Nicole and her brother, Jacques, as it headed invincibly toward marriage, just as she would have watched some orderly ballet or the mating dance of a pair of peacocks; in the same way she watched Ghislaine's fits of discouragement, her attacks of rage, her ecstasies, as though observing the actions of a creature driven by instinct and fate, actions that required neither intelligence nor free will.

Ghislaine would get up in the morning, her skin blotchy, and immediately swallow a few aspirin; she spent too much money on expensive clothes, which she treated carelessly; she washed perfunctorily, and the warm musky smell she gave off did not quite make Laure uncomfortable, but had an unpleasant effect on her—could this, she wondered, be how men identified "that kind" of woman, the kind her friend was? Ghislaine colored her hair, sometimes garishly, her painted toenails were not always very clean, and even her hair smelled of sweat, cigarette smoke, and patchouli, which she kept in syrupy, disgusting little bottles.

Throwing herself back in an armchair with a sensual grace that revealed the underside of her brown knee or her badly shaved armpit, she would laugh, opening her mouth wide and showing her pink gums, her perfect teeth, and the moist back of her throat. At the same time, despite appearances, Ghislaine was not sure of anything except her power over men, which she wielded immoderately—even with men she found "unappealing" or "too old" or "too ugly" or "vulgar": the butcher's boy, the man who delivered telegrams. Ghislaine felt that something was missing from her day if, as she was getting out of a taxi, her knee did not catch the attention of the driver or a man walking past.

This lack of confidence showed up in her sleepless nights, her attacks of indigestion, her frequent exhaustion, and prolonged depressions, whose causes and consequences she debated endlessly on Laure's couch, stretching and lighting another cigarette. But she was also charmingly attentive to Laure. She never came to dinner without a little bouquet of flowers or a vase, various gifts that she would find a place for, impatiently disrupting the careful order of Laure's apartment; it reminded her too much of somewhere a postmistress might live, she said.

Actually, Ghislaine's young life—she was about to turn twenty-six—already counted its share of "betrayals," which had left her with a simple and repetitive philosophy. The young men she had met had all been flighty, vain, fickle, had not kept their promises, sometimes had not even made any. And yet each time she had "believed in it." A year later, when she saw the faithless man pushing a baby carriage to the supermarket with a pregnant secretary, she would claim to be over it: "I know he was sorry to let me go, I'm the best he ever had. Him, too," she added softly to Laure, nodding toward a stout young man who stood aside to let a woman enter the Hôtel des Postes in front of him. Ghislaine made another, barely perceptible gesture with her head; the man had deliberately turned away when he noticed them.

It was therefore quite in keeping with Ghislaine's character that she watched the awakening of Laure's passion with a mixture of curiosity and various feelings of distrust: defiance, pessimism, incomprehension, and a little envy. This was a passion such as she had never experienced, one that seemed likely to sweep away everything before it. But Laure said nothing. Here, too, she maintained the silence, the restraint that had been bred into her. What had arisen between her and Pierre—if that was the right way to put it; both of them had the feeling, instead, that it had flooded out of them—had no name. She could not compare it to anything she had ever experienced. And however vast Ghislaine's experience may have been, it could not help Laure. Not, for instance, with the "mishap" that soon occurred (the first one), something that Ghislaine surely could have predicted but not cured—no better than Laure, in any case.

It came about a year after they had met. Though they did not usually do this sort of thing, Pierre had gone with Laure to a large store on the outskirts of town. They were looking at a display of curtain material, his arm around her shoulders. It was then that it happened. Pierre walked a short distance away from her to speak to a saleswoman, whom she clearly heard him ask the price of some bathroom carpeting. She joined him. "I don't understand," she said. "Why should I have a rug in the bathroom?"

"No, no, it's for the house," Pierre said calmly.

The house? A black veil fell in front of Laure's eyes, she felt something crumble inside her. She saw underwear drying, an open tube of lipstick, soap spots, hairs, she heard the throbbing of a washing machine, a voice saying, "Hurry up, I need to hang some things up to dry!" Around that intimate, private place an entire house was confusedly organized: in the morning the untidy rooms, in the evening the weak glow of bedside lamps and the voices of the sleepless children softly telling each other stories.

Pierre had not noticed anything. They left the store, though he had not found out what he wanted to know.

At home again, Laure could not calm down. It was raining, cold, night had fallen, but she went back out. She had to know, she had to see. In her car the mist on the windshield blurred her view; the wipers beat time to her unhappiness. She did not know the way, changed direction twice and, driving through streets far from the center of town, her heart thumping harder and harder, reached the neighborhood where Pierre lived. Why had she never made the effort to picture it to herself? How could she have imagined that he disappeared into a nebulous, magically shapeless world? The reality was there, ruthless, in those small houses, all alike yet all marked with signs of real life.

She wiped away the mist with the back of her hand, leaving the windshield even more smeared, and turned on the heat; now she could not see out at all, and she opened the window. She was suffocating. Driving slowly down streets she did not know, whose names she could not make out, passing houses with closed shutters, she felt her heart heavy inside her and her palms moist. A gust of rain came in through the window; she closed it, calmed down, and then saw Pierre's car parked along with others by the newly finished curb. Was it on the left? On the right? Behind the slanted curtain of rain she saw a yellow porch light and the gate to a small garden. She stopped, feeling herself commanded to do so, addressed by an imperious force that said, "Look!"—as when, during a trial, one attends the reconstruction of a crime in the dawn cold and sees the action played through. "Look!" a voice inside her said in a pitiless tone, a voice without kind intentions. Where were the sweet images they had fed each other? The calm room where she would have liked to wait patiently for him as the sun went down?

She rolled the window back down; the rain whipped across her face and hair, mingling with her tears. The strong wind bent branches and snapped them against a housefront with open shutters—in the middle of the housefront, a pair of french doors stood brightly illuminated. The front door opened, and a man walked out of the rectangle of yellow light, listened to something, took a step or two, then went back in. She had started up the car again, in a panic, her heart beating in her throat, and she circled back at the intersection. When she passed in front of the same car she had stopped next to a moment before, she saw that it was not Pierre's. Had she been mistaken, then? All of a sudden her tears came twice as hard. She got home without knowing exactly how.

*   *   *

Strangely enough, Laure immediately forgot this episode, either because of its very violence, or, perhaps, because she had to obliterate the message, the warning it contained, as quickly as possible. But when a similar episode occurred, Laure recognized it immediately—the way one recognizes the second attack of a disease one thought had disappeared, and so realizes it will be around for a long time. The pain was the same. All this time she had buried it, but without making its cause disappear.

One Thursday afternoon when she was sitting in the dentist's waiting room, she suddenly felt oppressed, tired, remorseful. She put down the magazine she had been leafing through. The sensation diminished slightly but did not disappear. Where did this suffering come from? It was absurd, there was no reason for it. She picked up the magazine again, and a picture leaped out at her. It was an ad, a drawing that showed a lawn where three small children played with a dog while a woman stood not far behind them, in front of a house, waving cheerfully to a man Laure could not see at first, then made out at the wheel of a car—he was either parking or just leaving for work. A lawn mower leaned against the garage door. Laure closed the magazine and waited patiently for her name to be called.

The pain would return, and then the wound would heal over, but less and less quickly; and with time the sore spot did not deepen, but neither did it heal. It was like a muscle that was stiffening, losing its suppleness. With time, too, Laure noticed that more and more things hurt her with the same pain: she did not know what this meant. Was it a sign that their love was growing stronger, more demanding? Or the opposite—proof that it no longer secreted the balm that soothed and healed immediately? Sometimes she thought it was the first, sometimes the second. In the meantime what predominated was an intoxicating feeling of happiness. I could never have imagined, she said to herself, how happy we are now.

When they held each other in the soft late afternoon, appeased, satiated, lips together, foreheads together, in the same pose as so many medieval representations of lovers, the time passed imperceptibly, without taking anything away from them—they had no strength left. Pierre sometimes brought a little work to do or a book containing a passage he had wanted to show her or read aloud to her, but he would not do the work and they would not open the book. They would remain there motionless, eyes closed. What harm could come to them, once Laure enclosed him in her arms and he enclosed her in his? In the newspapers there were reports of deaths, car crashes, wars, catastrophic railway accidents, all sorts of events occurring in the world; but between them there were only the events determined by their love. Laure forgot the pain of their brief separations, the torments, her fear of indifference, the bad omens—she was completely carried away.

Later, much later, she would not always enjoy recalling this time when almost nothing had jeopardized the illusion. On the contrary, she would take a certain pleasure in laughing at herself, at her capacity for blindness. Her only satisfaction, then, would be in destroying even the beauty of her memories, her only remaining enjoyment a determination to prove she had been deceived.

CHAPTER 13

AS TIME passed, there came more and more signs that made her uneasy: a curious reversal threatened to occur, one that would transform the happiest moments of their early days together into a source of pain. Moments, for instance—like those delicious ones that occur in illicit relationships, most prized by clandestine lovers—when Pierre managed to "escape."

It was with an extreme joy that during their first spring—about a year after they began seeing each other—Laure greeted Pierre each time he managed to "escape," to "dash in and out," as he said, naturally adopting the language people use in such a situation. Laure had not yet acquired the suspicious and spiteful turn of mind that might cause her to say, with heavy irony, that anyone who had to "escape" was not really free, and that his rather breathless joy only proved how little leeway he had. But, although they did not know it, they were in their golden age then, a period that exists in the history of each person as it does in the history of humanity, a blessed period that can never return. Laure confined herself (wisely, it would seem) to believing this: Pierre's finding a way to "escape" proved, quite simply, that he wanted to escape and therefore to come to her. She even managed to conceive of a future in which those times would be not an exception but the rule: their golden age, she believed, was still ahead of them. But in fact it was soon behind them. Here, too, it was the same in the history of the individual as in the history of humanity. And she would have been wise to enjoy the respite—disenchantment would come soon enough.

When the era of suspicion came, it swept everything up before it. She saw, or thought she saw, signs of caution even in Pierre's slightest gestures: his refusal, for instance, to use a soap that was too perfumed, or his precipitous return when he had left his tie behind at her house. Why, she would ask herself, did he brush his teeth and clean his nails so carefully before he left her? The age of regrets had imperceptibly followed the age of hope.

But for now Pierre had "escaped": Laure accepted all his reasons, in fact did not ask for any, but greeted all his excuses with joy. He had gone out to buy paint, or some wood to finish a bookcase or a cupboard. Likewise, she accepted all the arguments he depended on to make the excuse appear flimsy. "Me! Handy! I don't even know how to hammer a nail!" She would laugh.

The reason was not important. All that mattered was that he was there, and she would hug him to her, breathing in the smell of his skin. He was there, he had knocked at the door, not yet daring to use the keys she had given him. Anyway, he had already called ahead; she opened the door immediately, the light was still on in her bedroom, it was just before nine.

"The hardware store doesn't open until ten on Sunday morning." And he hugged her, crumpling her nightgown.

"Do you want some coffee?" she asked.

"No, yes, in a little while. What I want right now is you."

She gazed into his face, which was filled with a childlike happiness and the relief he felt whenever his love for Laure magically fit in with some change in his family's plans—an outing postponed because one of the children had a cold or Annie was tired.

They were together for an hour, maybe more. They forgot everything. Pierre threw off his clothes, slipped into the bed, which was still warm, and closed his eyes.

"Come here," he said. "Come quickly."

"I want to show you something."

"Later. Come quickly."

Afterwards they went back into the larger room, faces still flushed, limbs tired, skin irritated, the same smell on them, the same fatigue around their eyes, half-dressed, she wearing Pierre's shirt, he wearing Laure's dressing gown, which did not cover his muscular legs. Breathless and happy, they sat down for a moment at the round table, still half-entwined in each other's arms, to drink a cup of coffee, watching the time. "Not too much," said Pierre. "If I drink too much coffee, I can't sleep later." And Laure tried to push out of her mind the image of Pierre's fits of sleeplessness.

They were tired, and they rested. Their minds wandered among the impressions left on them by this peaceful Sunday, the quieter noises, birdsong under the window, the ringing of church bells . . . they imagined vast stretches of countryside, green rivers, trees moving in the wind.

Pierre broke the silence. "A cupboard! Do you realize? There isn't a single cupboard in the whole house."

Laure had not heard. Spring light was flooding in with the sound of the great bell from the cathedral.

Then Pierre stood up. "I have to hurry to get there before it closes," he said. "I need wire fencing for the garden."

"The garden?"

"Oh, it's very little, but I like to sit there in the evening."

Sit there in the evening? Laure closed her eyes for a moment, opened them again, and it had passed.

Without really understanding the reason, but guessing from a few signs—as sensitive children do, and dogs—that something had darkened her mood, Pierre became anxious and tender: he must have done something wrong, but he did not know what, or had he said something he shouldn't have? He was afraid of venturing into the dark labyrinth he saw she was lost in.

"My love," he said, closing his eyes and holding her tight against him. His voice, naturally deep, dropped another half-tone. He caressed her shoulders, her hips. "Give me back my shirt, I have to get dressed." She took off the shirt. "I think of you all the time," he added, and she felt calmer. Yes, all this time things were easy for him. Pierre guessed that it would not last, it would not always be enough to comfort her with a gentle answer and a clumsy caress.

She lifted her eyes to Pierre's face, where a short, reddish beard had begun growing again, irritating the skin around his eyes and temples.

"You're prickly," she said.

"Already?"

Pierre had disappeared into the bathroom. Laure, who had recovered her serenity, was tidying the bedroom. What they had had, what she could still feel in herself, on her skin, that warmth—wasn't that the most important thing? How much could what separated them matter compared to these powerful bonds, secret though they were? Before parting they sat down again for a moment side by side, holding each other's face, their weak lips out to each other. They could not take their hands from each other, they wanted to go on indefinitely being a sort of soft, pink, weakened extension of each other's flesh.

* * *

Then, when the door had closed behind him, Laure would question herself at length: a long Sunday stretched ahead of her, and soon she would wonder if she did not, at heart, wish that Pierre had not come. She lay down again for a moment, leafed through the book or magazines Pierre had brought her. Sometimes she fell asleep again. Then, when she woke up, she would think about what he had told her. "I'm going to arrange the house a little differently," he had said. "I'll have a room to myself." That phrase came back to her. What could it mean? That he wanted to "get down to something finally," to "work." She accepted that without asking any questions.

And he was so warm, so attentive: he took an interest in everything that concerned her, helped fill out her income tax forms (giving her the benefit of Annie's financial expertise, though she did not know it), straightened a shelf, talked about repainting the kitchen, though he did not do it. He became freer, approached dangerous areas, was not overscrupulous about respecting limits—it was enough to have to respect them unfailingly at home. He risked alluding to some walks in the forest, quoted something his little girl had said, talked about an interest of his son's. No doubt he thought Laure would accept this as proof of his confidence in her, and also as a sign that in his life away from her nothing important happened, nothing that had to be hidden. Laure accepted this reasoning, even felt thankful for it.

Nevertheless, she flinched, one January day, when he gave her an engagement book issued by Annie's bank, bound in beautiful green leather and monogrammed. That was too much. She said nothing, put it on the table, turned it over twice, caressed the soft leather. Suddenly she felt so indignant she could hardly breathe. It was four o'clock. She ran and shut herself up the kitchen. With the door closed behind her, her anger grew even greater. She paced back and forth, picked up the kettle. The pain that stung her was so sharp, so oppressive, that she felt she was suffocating. Her cheeks burned, her hands were icy. She tried to find words for what she felt, but all she could think of to say was something quite strange that nevertheless satisfied her, for the moment: "The fool, oh, the fool!"

When she did not reappear, Pierre in turn felt uneasy. He paced back and forth, trying to understand, parted the curtain and looked out at the street as if something might come along to save both of them. He did not even try to find out exactly what had made her so angry: he was sure of her, of himself, too. First of all he had to calm her down—and then try to understand, but that was not the most important thing. First he had to soothe her, because he did not like to see her suffer, and also because he felt remorseful even if he did not see why she was so upset.

He turned around, his heart thumping, when she finally came out of the kitchen. He had only half-guessed what was wrong and would not commit himself. It was probably the engagement book—maybe she would have preferred a real present? "What a brute I am," he said, which meant nothing. But Laure heard this as the wonderful, unexpected admission of a guilt she wanted him to acknowledge though without being crushed by it. It was her duty, she felt, to forgive everything.

Later, when she thought back over that scene, she judged herself severely and condemned her "blindness" and her own "weakness"—she was quick to apply excessively harsh words like these to herself. She even felt some disgust for Pierre, who could not keep a sharp enough boundary between his life as a married man and the life he shared with Laure. It was as if he had come to her steeped in an alien atmosphere; when this occurred quite literally, when she could smell the kitchen odors on Pierre's jacket, she felt great revulsion, though he would only shrug his shoulders and say, "But I have to eat something now and then."

"What a brute I am," he repeated, his head on Laure's shoulder, his mouth against her neck. And now it was she who had to comfort him, run a soothing hand over the nape of his neck and the stiff hairs grown back since his last trip to the barber. At the same time the gesture calmed her, and she rested, leaning against her lover, who was so relieved to see Laure's sorrow and tears fade away that he could have cried in turn, shaken by the pain he had caused, a child's pain, as quick to burst out as to die away.

Without opening his eyes, he lifted his head and ran his lips over Laure's cheek. Laure's hand had moved down Pierre's side to his waist, where it lay still. During this time their bodies had taken the initiative again, making small, brief, barely perceptible motions, small calculated adjustments quite outside their direct consciousness, and of their own accord rejoined in the union their souls had temporarily broken. And it was already a relief and consolation for them to feel each other's hip against their own and abandon themselves to it. When Pierre's lips reached hers, Laure opened her mouth and Pierre gently bit her lower lip. It was one of their favorite games, and as she recognized it, Laure smiled without moving. They were so tired that they remained motionless for a moment in that tender position. And then it was time to leave. In the end Pierre forgot to take back the troublesome engagement book, which Laure threw into the bottom of a drawer. When she found it again a few months later and leafed through it, her pain was gone. Eventually she came to miss the time when such a sharp pain could be caused by something so slight.

Yet almost exactly the same incident occurred again one morning when Pierre came and knocked on her door without warning around eight; he did not have his keys with him. She opened the door without mistrust, barely awake. His arms were loaded with dahlias. Then he was already in the kitchen looking for a vase or a pot and running the water so hard that his shirt was spattered.

"What did you do with the paper they were in?" Laure asked.

"They're from the garden," Pierre said. "Beautiful, aren't they?"

But Laure did not want flowers "from the garden." She put one up to her face, and it smelled dreadful to her, like the smell of underwear drying in a bathroom.

"You're not happy I came?" asked Pierre.

"Of course I am," said Laure. She felt a stubborn, sticky sadness she would have liked to banish—but that day she could not. She kept seeing a cool pathway in the evening, children playing, a radio, a young woman sitting on a doorstep. Tears sprang from her eyes.

"My sweet!" said Pierre, "What's wrong?"

She listened to him, then moved away.

"Is it the flowers?" He, too, was making progress.

"I'm being unfair. Forgive me." But that was not what she really thought.

"A little unfair. You know how little importance I attach to the place where I live." Could she believe him? What had inspired him to say that? True melancholy, sincerity, a desire to calm her? She bent down, gathered up the fallen petals, and arranged the stalks in the vase. Then she carried it over to the window and put it down. When Pierre called her a few hours later, she was feeling much better.

CHAPTER 14

AGONIZED as he was by Laure's pain, tormented by her tears, convinced that he must do everything possible to spare her from suffering, Pierre was bound to a second resolution, no less exacting, no less firm, and that was to keep Annie from suffering, too. So it was out of the question to think of separating from her, or talking to her about Laure, or even letting her guess anything.

How had Pierre managed to keep this relationship secret, in a town of less than fifty thousand people? The answer was simple. It was no secret—either to Laure's neighbors, who did not know who Pierre was, or to the concierge of her building, who knew him by name. But Pierre lived on the other side of town, and Annie was away at work eight hours a day. Besides this, Annie was by nature not in the least suspicious: not that she had any special confidence in Pierre, but that for her these things simply did not exist.

Pierre's colleagues were just the opposite, but they had so few opportunities to let Pierre's wife know what they thought that the risk was completely negligible. The men among them, when they met Pierre on the library steps, sometimes alluded to the "little one" who was "not bad-looking," but generally it was Ghislaine they were talking about. The only frankly hostile one was Mme. Feider, the English teacher, who had seen him with the nurse and said, "I don't like his face. He's the sort of man to get into trouble."

"What sort of trouble?" asked her husband placidly.

"Woman trouble, of course."

But she was the only one. The other women on the faculty liked him very much, especially Mme. Rougier, the literature teacher, who, when she learned about his trip to Florence, was eager to share her love for Italy with him.

If he was incapable of leaving Annie, it was, he admitted, for his own sake as well as hers. The feeling that joined him to Annie, however much it had changed with time and the shock of his love for Laure, involved the larger entity they composed: there were Annie and the children, and behind them her family, his in-laws, their vacation house, furniture, plans, habits—all of this forming such a tight-woven fabric that he saw no way he could free himself from it and find any version of himself capable of living an independent life. His love for Annie? What also had to be included was the love that Annie and his children and his in-laws and even his dog had for Pierre. Taken separately, each of these elements could be given up; after all, he could live with another woman, could tolerate spending only Sundays and vacations with his children, could with even less difficulty move to a different house or town. But these elements were joined together in such a way that he could not manage to untangle them, his life had grown up in their midst, so mingling its branches with theirs that he could no longer imagine tearing himself away. What would his life be without Annie's fatigue? Without her sudden Sunday morning resolutions? Without the children's bicycles in the entryway and their old sneakers in the closets? Without the joint bank accounts, the visiting cards with both their names printed on them?

When he had met Annie, he was barely twenty, educated but without much knowledge or experience of the world: he was unfamiliar with any life but the student life, which was not really life at all, and he had not traveled. They decided very quickly to get married. At forty she would be a manager in her bank, Pierre would be preparing his students for the university or—who knew?—teaching at the university itself. Once again Pierre accepted everything, including the plans that were made for him, without feeling that he was really committing himself.

In their early twenties they had made it their common goal to discover physical love together, in all the enthusiasm of their awkward young bodies, without torment, with a need, an untainted legitimacy that was not merely the legitimacy of marriage. The time for love had come; they devoted themselves to it. Annie gave herself to it with seriousness and decisiveness, with the formidable determination of a young woman that changes with time—even when the body no longer plays more than a modest role in it—into a staunch attachment. Neither of them was ignorant, but they were absolutely inexperienced. They therefore also wanted to learn, to read books that gradually revealed to them the possibilities their bodies held.

The question of children posed itself right away—not that it was the reason they had wanted to get married, though the conventions they had inherited would have led them to that as much as their love. But in the end there it was: children were the goal of marriage, though they might be deferred; they were its ultimate justification and in some way its consecration, however little religious feeling the couple might have. The notion could be thrust aside for a certain length of time—everyone certainly recognized their right to do that. And if at first their use of contraception managed to dissociate their youthful eroticism from its consequences, they were determined that this time would not last forever. Finally, deep within them, a shared and tacit conviction came into being: at that point, once and for all, the certainty that one day children of theirs would be born lifted all guilt from their love and their desire.

In the unconscious division of qualities they had made, it had fallen to Pierre to fantasize and be irresponsible, because he was the man and it was up to him to disobey the couple's rules, even those he had helped to lay down; also because he was still a student and really the younger of the two and, destined as he was for the vocation of teacher, always would be the younger in the eyes of Annie and her family. These qualities came into play especially in the forms of sexual transgression, modest as they were, that he always promoted. For instance, he would persuade Annie to make love in the afternoon, or even elsewhere than in bed—though not without first taking some prophylactic precautions. Then, Annie would be the one to steer them back to the path of reason—and Pierre would also accept all the tiresome tasks he had to perform, such as filling out their income tax forms or fixing leaks.

Still, essentially, they shared everything, money first of all (in the beginning Pierre had almost no income, except his earnings from private lessons) and household tasks, including doing the dishes and even making the bed, which he always did better than she. Contraception was something else they undertook together, even though it was Annie who was protected, inside her body that the contraceptive was placed. But he submitted with good grace to the terms Annie's body imposed, its little ailments, its vague pains, difficulties of all kinds—for instance, when she rejected the diaphragm, or could not tolerate spermicidal jelly. It was as though they had only one body between them, and they talked about Annie's body as though it were a shared piece of property, a heavy responsibility entrusted to both of them, a delicate and fragile unit of production whose optimal functioning in their interests and for their pleasure they both had to ensure. Each of their bodies belonged to the other, who had the right to use it but also the duty to maintain it, to manage it, to take its weaknesses into account. In this shared machine the role of Annie's body was obviously the more important, and she took a natural pride in this. This was exactly what she expected from life: to be respected for all the formidable power of her female organs but not to be limited by them. Pierre, naturally, supplemented with other women the basic knowledge he had acquired with Annie; but the discoveries he made never altered his conviction that a woman's body was infinitely more complex, and to be handled more delicately, than a man's body.

They had lived in L. for a year before marrying. They married, then Pierre was appointed to R. and Bruno was born. Love, eroticism, physical existence, then childbirth fitted effortlessly into the social and professional scenario of their life. Marriage had only added greater legitimacy and more financial conveniences. They could borrow money and apply for loans.

A permanent bond was created between them by this mutual education which had taken them, together, through the last stage before adult life. Thus, they had a certain camaraderie, like the feeling one always retains toward those who went through the same apprenticeship at the same time. For this reason their life was somewhat predictable, but it strengthened them, their notions of themselves and each other. Pierre learned to discipline himself, to put the needs of someone else's body first—his own needs always seemed to him more ruthless but finally subject to control. He thus saw himself as he had always imagined men to be: less refined than women, more savage, more demanding, but capable of learning, of being tamed. For her part Annie felt the gradual appearance in her of the characteristically female satisfaction of having secured her life to another life and attached both lives to a solid, though relatively mobile, axis, as she saw it, the way one moors a boat to a floating buoy. Thus, they could confront minor changes—an improvement in their situation, a move to another house, the birth of several children—without having to question the very nature of their union. A union that, Annie felt, could only become richer with time, since it had been conceived as something that would be "built together." For a long time—in fact, until he met Laure—Pierre felt the same way.

Pierre had passed the lower-level state exam and failed the higher-level one, while Annie rapidly moved ahead in the bank. Pierre hesitated to take the exam a second time. He had enrolled in the university again and was taking correspondence courses. They had a regular daily routine, and Pierre knew how to plan out a life that was not too demanding. They rose at seven. Annie fixed their breakfast while Pierre gave the baby its bottle. At this time of day they were gently attentive to each other in a way that kept alive the memory of the night: as they walked past each other, they never failed to give a delicate caress to whatever part of the other's body was within reach, even while kissing the child's fat cheeks. By ten, two mornings out of three, Pierre found himself alone again, and on the other days he went off to teach his classes. But he always had lunch at home, and every day except Friday he settled down at his table around two o'clock, filled his pipe, and applied himself to the textbooks on his curriculum. When Annie came home with the child, picked up from the baby-sitter at five, Pierre was still studying. They would have a glass of wine together, then he would heat up a can of ravioli.

But this period did not last long. When the child was bigger, they became skilled at preparing their own healthful food, rich in green vegetables and in yogurt, which simplified shopping and cooking, and was good for children, besides.

This went on for ten years. At the end of those years Pierre and Annie were true adults, over thirty, all trace of childhood gone. Each had been so completely formed by contact with the other that they could have separated, lived apart from each other for a year, stopped talking to each other, and nothing would have changed. Without knowing it, they had completely fulfilled the Gospels: the two were one flesh.

When Pierre was alone—and, soon enough, alone with another woman—he felt Annie's presence in an almost dizzying way. Even when, in his own eyes, he was betraying her utterly, in reality he had not left her. That fusion was not only the psychological consequence of a physical, emotional, erotic understanding: it was an entity that had grown up alongside them, outside them, which had to be taken into account. Paradoxically, it was the very strength of that union that enabled Pierre to meet another woman that year.

Pierre was thirty, their son seven, the little girl two, when the affair occurred that was to complete Pierre's education. One Friday in December, during the eleven o'clock recess, he took a student who was vomiting to the infirmary.

"Is something wrong with you?" asked a voice. "Did you get a student to come with you? You're pale."

He stood up. "No, it's him."

"Go in there," the young woman said to the boy.

"Actually," Pierre said, following him, "I always feel weak about ten in the morning."

"Have some sugar," she said. "You're a little hypoglycemic."

The young woman had poured some drops into a glass, which she held out to the child. She walked back and forth quickly, wearing a rather short white smock that revealed two beautiful, strong brown legs with delicate ankles. A blue vein beat in the hollow of her right knee—Pierre recalled that detail.

Two or three weeks later they met again by chance in front of the school. She was waiting for the bus. Pierre walked over to her. "I have my car," he said. "Can I drive you home?" She looked up at him with reddened eyes, swollen lips, a chafed nose. "What a cold I have!" she said. "Those rotten kids, it never fails."

They headed for a part of town Pierre had rarely visited since that distant time when he used to go for long bicycle rides. They left the town behind altogether, and she pointed out to him a row of yellow buildings in the distance, in the fog. "There it is," she said. "Cheerful, eh?" He let her off in the parking lot. "I have to hurry," she said. "My boys must be home already." They shook hands, and Pierre drove off without looking back.

In the following days he thought of the row of projects two or three times. Ideas came to him that he had never had before. For instance, the idea of climbing the narrow concrete stairs: he would ring the doorbell, she would be alone and would open the door into an entryway with flowered wallpaper and a barometer on the wall. He would not say anything, they would go directly into her bedroom; he would take off her white smock—like an adolescent, he could picture her only in her nurse's smock—and soon his legs would be around her, he would be against her, in her, he would breathe her slightly pungent smell, her smell of sweat, she probably did not shave under her arms.

And this was exactly what happened. He had looked at the staff bulletin board and seen which days the nurse was off duty, and one afternoon in late February he parked his car in a rectangle outlined in white on the dirty asphalt of the parking lot. ("I saw you," she said later. "You looked pretty uncomfortable surrounded by all those motorbikes.") Children ran past him laughing through the noisy, dimly lit front hall of the building while he searched the row of mailboxes for her name. The stairwell was permeated with a vaguely unpleasant smell.

He rang the bell, and she opened the door. She did not seem surprised. Everything was the way he had imagined it— even the barometer on the wall—except that she was not wearing her white smock. She smiled at him without speaking, a rather sly look on her face.

"Come again whenever you like," she said later as she walked him to the door. "My kid doesn't get back till seven. My husband picks him up on the way from work."

Pierre returned home exhausted but happy: she was tanned, strong, and muscular, just as he had pictured her. The hair between her legs was thick, as it was under her arms. Toward the end she had sat up in bed, arms outstretched, heavy breasts uplifted.

"Feels good, doesn't it?" she had said. And then: "I saw you, before, in the parking lot."

Her name was Elisabeth, but she wanted him to call her Babeth, like everyone else. She demanded nothing, asked no questions, simply smiled, and immediately she was in his arms, and he felt her tongue in his mouth, a fleshy, cool tongue, supple, mobile. Her abundant saliva drove Pierre to a pitch of excitement.

Her husband was a conductor for the national railway, and she had been married for ten years.

"Like me," said Pierre. That was the only time they alluded to their marriages. She had had an "operation" after her son was born, and knew that she could not have any more children.

"Come here, come to me," Pierre said, and once again he bent over her breast, its nipple so dark it was almost black.

They ran into each other once at the Carrefour, where they were shopping with their families. She came over to him and shook his hand, introducing her husband with no sign of embarrassment. The husband had a case of liquor in the shopping cart.

"Who was that?" asked Annie. "I didn't catch her name. A colleague?"

"No," said Pierre. "She's the school nurse."

"Oh. She looks Italian."

Pierre had not thought of that. That black hair, those rather short thighs? But he thought he remembered that she had been born near Toulouse. He forgot to ask her.

Thus ended Pierre's years of apprenticeship: he had experienced two kinds of love, and this might have been sufficient. All the other encounters he was to have could have been modeled on the one with Babeth: passionate but short-lived adventures that mingled silence and sensual pleasure in satisfying proportions. The pedagogical course of the early days of his marriage had been perfectly complemented by an almost diametrical experience, in which he had found out that not everything can be learned, that unexpected encounters are always possible, that two people can understand each other with a mere hint, and above all that there is no need to try to build anything.

In a sense there was something completely predictable about that very unpredictability, though not for Pierre, who had thought he was safe from physical surprises or fated, for lack of opportunity, to experience them seldom. In the end Babeth left him with few memories—or, rather, nothing really personal: only the image of a musk-scented body, a thick mop of hair, very red lips. She had liked him, she said, because he seemed to have his head in the clouds, and also because she felt he needed it, for health reasons, like everyone else. She never read anything, had not traveled, had never set foot in a museum. She had a narrow, pessimistic—and therefore fairly accurate—view of life: she knew she was stuck in an uninteresting job, tied to an unexciting marriage. And so, she liked to say, they had happened to travel a stretch of road together. When these images came back to Pierre, they had something pungent and scarcely proper about them, like those exquisite, odd, hard-to-describe foods one tastes on a trip, then congratulates oneself for having done it, but also for having avoided being poisoned.

He did not really regret anything but certain very powerfully physical moments, as he liked to think of them: the tangled sheets, not always very clean, in which he once or twice thought he detected signs of the conductor; Babeth's habit of always making love a second time, and the way she didn't wash right away afterwards. He would think of this whenever he saw Annie leave their clean sheets almost immediately—sheets they never dirtied; Annie did not like that—and wash herself with loud noises in the bathroom. The idea of Babeth herself (who left town a few months later) never preoccupied him. Nevertheless, two or three times he recalled the sadness of the parking lot and the varnished wood barometer on the entryway wall.

CHAPTER 15

PIERRE met Laure a few months later, at the end of 1972, imbued with an innocent sense of security—he felt henceforth protected from the more dangerous, ungovernable forms of love by his idea of himself as a man who had short-lived sensual encounters. This was why he did not experience any urgency: what he was confronting was too new, too unexpected, to place in any of the usual categories. Had he wanted to, he could easily have found another woman for a relationship such as he had had with the nurse. Everything about Laure, therefore, surprised him, everything was new: she could also be a friend to him; even, he thought—why not?—merely a friend, no more than a friend, someone he could talk to, meet on a café terrace as though they were still students, lend books to.

It was probable, in a sense inevitable, that sooner or later she would become his lover. But the fact was, there was no urgency. Later he was excited by her seriousness, her meticulousness, her enthusiasm, which extended to the details of her love-making—curiously like Annie's—as well as by a youthfulness he had not conceived of before.

"When I see you in the street," he said, "when I watch you at your desk, I can't believe you're the same."

"The same as what?" asked Laure.

"The same woman I'm holding in my arms right now." And he leaned over her, kissing her face or her breast. Laure's hair with its neat part, her Scottish kilts, her small heels, her measured step, and then this: her with him inside her, her on top of him, disheveled, flushed, teeth clenched; her way of locking her thighs around him like a vise, smooth white thighs beaded with a few drops of sweat—a child's sweat, he thought, the sweat of a little girl who has been running too much in the garden. Her skin was delicate, her sensitive cheek turned rosy under Pierre's rough, reddish beard, as he watched, incredulous.

Walking between the bookshelves or returning a volume of the encyclopedia to the central table, Pierre would glance secretly at Laure with a jealous pride; he would look at her face, and think of her lips on his sex, and he would be afraid of blushing. His eyes would dim, his heart would beat harder, once again he would see Laure lying on her back, her sex half-parted, spotless and pure, a faded violet color.

He never said so, but he had always loved this contrast in women, the contrast between their faultless appearances and their secret clefts. He had actually felt the lack of it in Babeth, who, he thought, "showed her hand" right away with her too-short smock, her rounded calves, her teasing eyes. Laure, on the other hand, seemed to him a perfect example of the mystery that suddenly blossoms around the most reserved women once they enter the intimacy of their bedrooms. He had enjoyed it in Annie, the contrast between his wife's beautiful, confident demeanor—her claret-colored suit, her little glasses, her perfect nails—and images of their intimate life together: Annie going back to sleep Sunday morning after pulling over her head, inside out, the nightgown he had pulled off her a few minutes earlier; Annie in the dining room, her tanned, unshaven legs showing, holding the little girl, who wore a bathrobe spotted with chocolate, laughing loudly with her daughter and saying, "Now tell the truth, rabbit, didn't you make a little fart?"; Annie in the upstairs bedroom of her parents' house; Annie on her back, eyes closed, legs wide open, and he, leaning over her, endlessly slipping his tongue and his lips into the sweet wetness of her secret folds.

No doubt one could find such contrast in all women, in the women he worked with, in the women Annie worked with, in the stern postmistress; and also in men. But to Pierre men seemed completely blunt, naïve, transparent, without mystery. And their way of giving themselves to love, besides not interesting him very much, seemed to him so rough—and, when all was said and done, hasty—that he was amazed women could put up with it.

But with Laure it was not the same—everything was different with Laure. His breath failed him when he thought how, because of him, for him, Laure lost all control and ceased to look like an untroubled young girl. He burned with desire and pride, at once rejuvenated and cleansed by the violence of his love and this discovery. Laure amazed him. Because she fit none of the conceptions he had formed so early, he told himself her nature was richer, more mysterious, more complex. He imagined, since Laure said so little, that all her attitudes, her decisions, her refusals were the effect of a will that was maturely deliberate, free, superior. He therefore felt some shame in her presence, as well as admiration. But then Pierre was always prone to admire women.

There was something else: that a woman could attach herself lastingly to a man who was "not free" had always seemed to him to result from one of those silent compromises or "make-do situations" women endure for a while when they are very young, or when they are older and obliged to accept this "last chance," even in a degraded form. Pierre may even have felt some scorn for such women. But that Laure, being what she was, could have become attached to him without any assurances, any promises from him—and he would have been hard put to it to know what to promise—seemed like a miracle to him. He was also surprised at himself, because he had always thought that only libertines (and he did not consider himself one) enjoyed maintaining a number of secret extramarital relationships, some of them quite long-lasting. Nor did he feel he was as unhappy as the others were said to be, those who were not libertines.

In fact, Pierre and Laure corresponded so little to their respective notions of the usual partners in their situation that they would look at each other with an astonished gentleness, a true delight, a true, and perhaps justified, satisfaction: nothing would happen to them but what was good. They alone would be spared the meannesses, the worries, the difficulties attendant on adulterous love affairs; all that would remain to them would be the joy—and the pain too, of course, which was noble.

Pierre took full advantage of this situation for two years, even a little longer. He and Laure actually felt they were changing in a permanent and profound way under each other's influence, and it was true that their most conspicuous failings had disappeared, or at least diminished: Laure's coldness, irritability, squeamishness; Pierre's slowness, his ponderous view of things, his didacticism. They loved each other, learned from the experience, took pleasure in ignoring what they had learned, and also harbored feelings both had thought unworthy of them: anger, violence, jealousy, vindictiveness, and, in Pierre's case, tormenting delight in clandestinity. Their relationship cleared everything before it, purified everything, scoured the cloud-encumbered sky with strong gusts of wind. Their sole remaining enemy was "what people would say"—

and so they no longer met in public. The perfection of their relationship was such that it stopped short, as though of its own accord, of where their other obligations began: it did not affect their professional lives, or Pierre's family life, or even the rhythm of time itself. But when they were together, they did not even think about this; it was as though all obstacles had been magnificently dissolved, and that from this fusion was born a perfect, incomparable love. How much could obstacles count in the face of this unrivaled harmony? It was truly a pure love, since its strength derived from its intrinsic power alone and not from the power of obligations, contracts, constraints—indeed, from its very capacity to resist these. In the early part of his love life Pierre had believed, like Annie, that love was something that accumulated, that was built; with Laure he discovered a sublime gratuitousness. For Laure, of course, this was harder to admit, and Pierre's discovery would have struck her as a very convenient one for him—how hard was it to exalt a love without commitments, without contracts, when any sort of commitment or contract was out of the question? Yet it may be that with her Pierre actually came closer than Laure did to the truth of love.

Because for Pierre love was there, complete, in Laure's little bedroom—nothing lacking, no regrets, no yearning—as he laid his clothes on a chair and quickly went to join her in bed. What he had discovered there and could not tell her about was so new and dazzling that it blinded him. In a sense, the obstacles that had been overcome soon reappeared: as in films projected backwards, the collapsed wall came together and rose again from the reintegrated dust. He was not lying (contrary to what Laure was later tempted to believe) when he declared to her, somewhat contradictorily, both how little importance he attached to his daily life—the family gatherings, the Sunday morning walks—and how relieved he felt to be rid of it when he was with her. But precisely because she had none of those things, Laure believed that love necessarily resided in such concrete manifestations. She was also right when she sensed, inside Pierre and all around him as well, the thousand invisible bonds that, whatever he said about them, tightly joined his whole being to his family life. Because of this, if Laure's love was something like a revelation for Pierre, Pierre's love could not serve the same function for Laure. The wonderful gratuitousness of this passion was for Pierre staggering in its newness; for Laure, since she had no hope of a change, it was always the sign and the consequence of a fact undetermined by her and continuing despite her: that Pierre was not free. Not that Laure would necessarily have wanted to "build something" with Pierre: perhaps that idea was alien to her. But she should not have been forced to accept the opposite.

Thus, they had embarked on parallel paths, and surely, under these conditions, nothing would ever change. For, besides the certainty that, whatever he said, Pierre would have been incapable of giving up the bonds that he and his family had formed, his amazement at being so "free" with Laure kept him from contemplating any other solution: what would be the good of losing, by living with Laure, what he gained precisely from their not living together? During this time Laure's concerns were quite different: she had to develop a system of rules governing a "life apart," since it was impossible for the two of them ever to know any other kind.

Things seemed this way to Laure: On the one hand, she had to accept living apart from Pierre and therefore coping with the inevitable pain of it. On the other, she also had to adapt to a daily routine she would never be able to control. Finally, if she wanted to experience true happiness and not merely a series of consolations, she had to submit to this law so willingly that by an odd reversal it would be possible to think she had wanted it. But first she had to acknowledge this: whatever the strength of their ties, each was unquestionably kept away from the other's separate life, Pierre scarcely less than Laure even though he visited her in her apartment, since he could share no part of her evenings, Sundays, or vacations, just as she could never share any part of his. So the question of what place to assign any sort of normal, everyday life was forever unanswerable; naturally, their situation led Pierre to minimize the importance of it and necessity for it, Laure to exaggerate it. This was the source of endless discussions.

"We've never once," Laure would say, "had breakfast together."

"Breakfast!" Pierre would say with unfeigned exasperation. "If only you could see me then! Unshaven, grouchy . . . I don't eat anything, I just make myself a cup of coffee, and anyway . . ."

"Still," Laure would say. For her the quick meals they sometimes ate together often seemed like caricatures of the "real meals" she would have liked to eat with Pierre, whereas for Pierre they were pleasant, entertaining snacks, a comfort, a chance to show even more his admiration for Laure and her capacity to keep herself from becoming "locked" in the heaviness of "obligations," schedules—ignoring the fact that it was he who forced this on her.

Laure eventually forgot that she hated family meals and fixed hours, as well as shopping and doing the dishes, while Pierre forgot that he heartily appreciated regular meals and lingered at the table for a long time in the evenings. In Laure's severe opinion a life apart could never be more than a semblance of a life: what would have been a day and a night for a "normal" couple, they would sometimes compress into half a day, sometimes less, going back to bed at three, making the bed again at five, and having dinner during the next half-hour. If for Laure their life apart too often resembled a simulacrum of a life, for Pierre this simulacrum would become enchanting, especially when they had lived through the equivalent of a whole day in several hours, finishing with a childlike tea, eating orange marmalade right out of the jar. Of course, after Pierre left, Laure would gaze rather sadly at the pile of damp towels in the bathroom, the rumpled bed, the remains of their semblance of a meal, and contemplate her images of the "real life" she would never know. Pierre, on the other hand, would return home delighted with this day of vacation, whether out of necessity, convenience, or a real taste for secrecy, game-playing, drama. And when he thought about it, that day had been a radiant one, capped by a tender separation on the threshold of Laure's door, and his real fatigue would effortlessly lead him to sleep.

What more could a *real* day have given them? An occasion for quarreling, worries, troubles. Besides, what did they lack that would have made them a real couple? Pierre knew her birthday—and her menstrual cycle—inquired after her parents, reminded her to pay a bill or have her car serviced. She worried about him when he had a cold, and they often ended up eating what was left of a tart they had started the day before: an infallible sign of continuity. Though Laure sometimes rebelled at having no choice but to give in and try to understand, still for a long time she did not ask herself what Pierre might be doing after he left her. Perhaps, when all was said and done, he was more preoccupied by her than she was by him when they were not together, because he could picture her to himself, know the spaces she was moving through. And many times Laure was quite unaware of when he missed their calm afternoons—when the children had colds, Annie was tired, or the house was too noisy. All in all, Laure put up with this divided life better than she thought she did, better than she had to—and she had to because she did not want to place many demands on Pierre.

Pierre, who took her at her word, nevertheless showed annoyance at some observation she had made when he had to postpone a meeting at the last minute. "If only you would put yourself in my place!" he said.

She looked at him. He was right, she was not thinking of that. But he made the mistake of going on. "Yes, if you were married, like me, it would obviously be very different."

Laure glimpsed all sorts of unpleasant ideas lurking in the darkness like wood lice under a damp stone. If I were married, she thought crudely, you wouldn't have to feel any remorse.

But Pierre was looking at her so tenderly, with such a wondering light in his eyes, that it was contagious: she gazed back at him. He could not be guilty. His eyes were so trusting! She guessed that silence was preferable, because it was the tacit sign of an agreement, the covenant one accepted, not to change what both parties did not want to see changed. By saying nothing, she spared Pierre troubling questions that he could have confronted only with silence or some kind of lie. But she spared herself much suffering as well.

From time to time he forgot the contract, as for instance on the day when he left Laure with this painful and resonant remark: "The children . . . you know, I didn't really want them." What had made him say that? Why bring her, even if only for a moment, into the intimacy of a love he had known and shared with another woman? Wasn't it worse for Laure to imagine that his union with Annie had had no other basis, no other reason for existing, than love? She was too distraught to think of anything to say to him.

CHAPTER 16

THE question that Laure never asked—and for a long time refused even to ask herself, either for fear of what the answer might be or because she was ashamed of her curiosity—was whether Pierre was faithful to her. In the early days, naturally enough, she was carried away by an emotion that banished the usual array of rationalizations, fears, hopes, suspicions, and she did not think of it, she was too exclusively absorbed in her physical love for her lover's body to think it could be any different for him.

When they left each other, they were so tired that it almost seemed to them they were tired of each other—certainly they wanted to "catch their breath," to "recover," and it never occurred to Laure that in fact he was going back to a house where not only his children, his dog, and his dinner were waiting for him but also a companion who did not have their reasons for falling asleep at eight o'clock. During this whole period, even if she had thought of it, and even if Pierre had proven unfaithful to her, this might not have caused Laure very much suffering, consoled as she would have been by the violence of their reunions. It is not at the height of passion that jealousy causes the most pain; the pain very often increases as the passion diminishes, and is in some sense the last proof of love—or the guarantee one clings to that it has not entirely disappeared.

Nevertheless, once they had entered a more stable and lasting phase of their relationship, the question could no longer be completely avoided. Other women than Laure would perhaps have arrived at it directly, women who were more cynical or more used to sharing feelings. In any case Laure went through every degree, experienced the subtle variety of secondary jealousies, which have a life of their own and are not, as one might think, merely guises of the main jealousy: jealousies over family meals, over rambles in the woods, over long dinners in the garden. Yet finally she had to confront that larger jealousy without turning away. She approached it head on, or rather in this way it attacked her; but she did not talk to her lover about it. She therefore immediately found all sorts of reasons for believing Pierre to be innocent: he loved her, he was tired, they were both so fulfilled. When she had the vague suspicion that this proved nothing, she clung to something he had said one day: "I slept so badly last night that I got up and corrected exercises." Or: "These days I get up early, the little one is sick." Yet there was a black hole, hours of the night she knew nothing about, though she could usually get past them by sleeping. Was it ten o'clock? He's watching television, she thought, or he's preparing his classes for tomorrow. Then: "It's midnight" (in the meantime she had been absorbed in a movie, in reading, in a telephone conversation with Ghislaine), "now he's sleeping, he was so tired just a little while ago!" And when she woke up at seven or eight: He gets up even earlier than I do, she would think. And the shadows of the night would be gone.

But in the face of the obvious these rationalizations had no power, could give her no certainty, and she was well aware of it. Suddenly an argument would come along to contradict the reassuring considerations, an argument dictated by that second creature inside her, that malicious creature always ready to harm her or her image of Pierre. She had thought only of Pierre, his desires, his fatigue, his daily routine; and if he was faithful, it was only because of his sincere love for Laure.

Then what about the other woman, the one he went home to every evening? What rationalizations could Laure find to apply to her? What responsibility did she have toward Laure? Laure was horrified by this thought and defenseless against it. Never before having contemplated the flesh-and-blood body of a "rival" she had never seen, Laure had thrust away all the images that affirmed the basic nature of the marriage, its crudity, its cruelty. She had accustomed herself to seeing it as a series of commitments and constraints for Pierre, an austere order, a collection of duties, sometimes even tiresome duties, but never the expression of a physical relationship. When she had thought of Pierre's life as the life of a married man, naturally it was always "before they met," and the loving intercourse of married couples, if she imagined it, had appeared to her as one of the many shared activities of marriage, like doing the dishes, the shopping, something indulged in out of habit, routine, necessity, never inclination.

They had had two children, and that was surely the "goal" of their marriage, but it had already been accomplished and the idea did not really draw attention to the reality of the desire, the attraction, the pleasure. The children resulted from the marriage by its very nature, just as a woodworking shop produces windows and chairs. So Laure could, if forced to, allow that Pierre might continue to exercise this inferior degree of desire, which led almost abstractly to procreation, on condition that he still reserve for her the ardent, audacious, irreversible forms of an attraction free of all commitment, infertile, ruled only by desire. (This was why his remark that he "had not really wanted" the children had shocked her.)

However that might be, in this case Laure was forced to do more than imagine Pierre's love or desire for his wife, to look beyond any apparent signs of disaffection or disengagement that Pierre's meetings with Laure instilled in him: she had to imagine—something a man would have done right away, experiencing the presence of another man in the life of a loved woman as a conflict or form of rivalry—the love and desire Annie might have for Pierre's body, imagine that they were parallel to her own, at war with them. Laure was seized by an atrocious pain: she had had some experience of physical jealousy, though the feeling of abandonment she had when she thought of Pierre's pleasant Sunday walks was sometimes even worse, but she was helpless against this sort of jealousy, which consisted in imagining that the object of her love or her desire could not only desire someone else but also be the object of someone else's desire. For in the face of that desire we can do nothing. We can think that our lover will remain faithful out of love, out of principle, out of strength of will, we can even tolerate deviations, exceptions, allow for and understand them—love sometimes makes us generous. But how can we endure the idea that someone else, a third person we may know nothing about yet may detest, can look with desire on the beloved body, can touch it with lustful hands, a lustful mouth, flatter it, seduce it, lead it by every possible action to be unfaithful to us?

In contemplating Pierre's sexuality, Laure for a long time did not go beyond regarding it as the compulsions of his male desire. Although it displeased her to think he might want to act on them elsewhere and otherwise than with her, she could have put up with it; but she broke out in an anxious sweat upon seeing him refuse (or accept) a hug, an embrace, seeing him yield out of sensuality, or weakness, or to avoid making trouble, or to forestall suspicion—or because isolation, a good meal, a secluded bedroom, and a loving woman are very powerful arguments. She thought of all the connivance that could go on, all the odious bargaining; what husbands resort to to appease their wives without too much trouble, since it has always been their habit to celebrate reconciliations, or hasten them along, in bed. But what did she know about all that? Nothing. What did she know about those agreements made so long ago, about those deeply ingrained habits, about those shared tastes, which neither time nor a new love affair could influence at all? She felt defeated.

Whether out of prudence or embarrassment, they never dealt directly with this question; and Laure knew that as to her own faithfulness Pierre could not have the least doubt. This was in some sense another source of inequality, a real injustice, but it was better not to insist on that too much, either. Besides, any deviation on Laure's part from their arrangement would have been understandable—Pierre had put himself in a position where he could not demand anything— but also more serious, creating as it would an additional commitment, whereas Pierre's unfaithfulness would only be honoring an earlier commitment. Thus, the question became absolutely impossible to pose, because one could not ask: Were they faithful to each other? or: Was Pierre unfaithful to Laure? but only: Was Pierre continuing to honor his marriage vows in a sexual way?

For Pierre it was more or less as Laure had imagined. For months his passion for her so absorbed him that he had nothing to resolve in any way, nothing to reconcile. In addition, at that time Annie's work at the office occupied a great deal of her attention; both of them came home exhausted, heads aching, and Pierre would collapse and fall asleep as soon as dinner was over. Annie was not surprised. They had always been respectful of each other. She slept a lot, too. And the fact was that she was not a very complicated woman, and she knew Pierre very well, she was used to his periods of silence, of withdrawal, of fatigue—though now something was happening about which she knew nothing, guessed nothing, sensed nothing, despite knowing him so well. She was very attached to him, and everything was good between them, even when he fell asleep like a child next to her.

To be frank, Pierre felt more absorbed by Laure than truly alienated from Annie: he did not feel distant from her or repelled, as one can feel when a new love comes into being. It was simply that for now he scarcely saw her anymore. Yet he liked to watch her dressing in the bathroom or lying back in an armchair, postponing the moment when she would have to leave for the office. And if the occasion had presented itself, he certainly would have responded to Annie's desire with a similar desire. But he tended to fall asleep instead. What was more, he very soon came to believe that he could easily have made love with her—for two months the question did not come up, but it could have—without being unfaithful to Laure, and also without a sense of taking on new commitments toward Annie or of renewing his marriage vows. And it was entirely possible that they could cease to be lovers for a while without his feeling, or Annie's suspecting, that their marriage was on the point of breaking up.

Pierre was rather conciliatory: he tended to make arrangements that Laure would have judged with the greatest severity. He had never talked about it, but he was sure that Laure would have left him immediately on learning he was continuing or resuming sexual relations with Annie. This implacable judgment he submitted to without really understanding it, though it drove him to a little more dissimulation. That was how Laure was, and he admired her all the more for it, though at heart he did not see things the same way and did not feel bound by such a lofty, rigorous morality: these things were not serious, he said to himself, they meant nothing.

Between Annie and him, he knew, there was a sort of in-

termission taking place, and he would do nothing to prolong
it. Obviously, he would say nothing to Laure about it when
things resumed their earlier course. An evening would come—
or return—when he and Annie felt happy, at peace, embraced
by their own familiar house and the gentle murmurs of the
children in their room, who were not allowed to wake them
on Sunday mornings; Annie would move close to him in bed,
or she would not move and Pierre would reach out and touch
her shoulder, her back, her breasts, which he had always found
so beautiful. Then he would start caressing her, and Annie
would turn toward him with a happy sigh. And when he got
up a little later, Pierre was sure, his love and desire for Laure
would still be intact.

All of this—the accepted constraints, the resignation, the
unasked questions, this mixture of surprising goodness and
daily pain—was what Laure, to herself, called their "understanding." The exceptions and rules in the way people use a
vocabulary seem to serve them as a philosophy or morality.
In Laure's case the choice of a precious and somewhat unexpected word obeyed two laws, the first leading people to reach
into a common stock and draw from it words for their inti-
macies, pet names like "sweetheart" or "baby," expressions
like "making whoopee," and the second obliging them to find
"personal" ways of naming each other, ways that correspond
to their own ideas of the particularity and nobility of a feeling,
unrelated to the ideas upheld by their social circles or their
culture.

But there was also another reason, which Pierre accepted
without quite grasping it: they had to find a word that would
prove the relationship between them was not purely sensual
but had solid intellectual and emotional foundations. For
Laure it was necessary to maintain an equilibrium, which
meant, therefore, not risking the ridiculousness of, say, "our
smoochie woochie"; to be neither trivial nor too openly erotic.
She therefore naturally hit upon the word *understanding*, which
also had the advantage of giving their illegitimacy a higher

legitimacy. Thus, she would write, for example, "Isn't that one of the constraints of 'our understanding'?" At first set between quotation marks, the word had almost appeared to be a quotation. It remained. In Laure's eyes it was a wonderful euphemism, and euphemisms were very popular in their vocabulary: there was "get away," "find a moment," "go to bed," "nothing to be done about it today" (as a way of saying on the telephone that there was a luncheon with the in-laws or that the little girl had to go to the doctor); "family" when he should have said, more crudely, "my wife and children," or more simply "my wife"; "the kids" when speaking of the children, which reduced them to an indistinct, exhausting, and clamorous generality for which one had only the most conventional feelings; or last, "casual friends" when speaking of a couple with whom he had been very close for the past ten years and who would never have been able to acknowledge their "understanding."

This curious mixture of adolescent language and elusive images took Pierre back to the age of clumsy excuses, grudging admissions to his friends, when he would say, "I went out with my parents yesterday" or "with my family" to avoid saying "my mother." Also, Pierre often used the word "I" in an ambiguous, equivocal way. He would say, "I went to the country yesterday"—but did that mean he had gone alone, for a little of the solitude he said he missed so much, or that he had not dared to say "with the family"? Laure never asked. That "I" of his, however hypocritical, sounded good to her, as though meaning that the "I" is never totally dissolved in the unit of the couple, in the heart of the family, but always remains autonomous and distinct.

At home, too, Pierre had to use similar precautions and even vaguer language. "I don't know where I picked that up," he would answer when Annie asked him, feeling no suspicion, where he had gotten the book that was lying on the dining room table and which he had brought back that day from Laure's apartment. That phrase "I don't know" or "I don't know what that (old) thing is" was useful to him in both places: at home it explained a gift, a book, a pen, a notebook given him by Laure, and with Laure a sweater or a watch, a birthday present from his children, his mother-in-law, Annie. In the end he himself lost track and reconciled himself to feeling that his mind was thick with the same mist that had to surround everything he did. "What time did you go out today?" Annie would ask, innocently. He would say he could not remember, and that was true. And yet he had not gone to see Laure. Just in case, it was better to answer, "I don't know, five o'clock, I can't remember." But Annie rarely asked him this. It sometimes seemed to Pierre that as time passed he had become like a series of little islands of detached actions, floating in a contourless ocean.

To go back to the word *understanding*: the choice was really excellent. There were all sorts of reasons for eschewing the odious *living in sin* as well as the insipid *liaison*. But though Pierre and Laure had also agreed tacitly to avoid the contemporary terms *affair* and *relationship*, only Laure seemed determined that the word they chose should not emphasize the erotic aspect. On the contrary, Pierre tended to congratulate himself on the strongly sensual aspect of their union, and to comment on it, in Laure's presence, in terms whose enthusiasm, she felt, barely tempered their crudity. Even when he had burst in on her or had to go home earlier than usual, he liked to pride himself, as he left, on not having come "just for that." This was exactly what Laure did not like.

CHAPTER 17

FOR, however passionate their love-making was, and however strong the desire that each aroused in the other, however brutal their assuagement sometimes was, however attached Laure was to her lover's body, and Pierre to hers, it was most important that, in their actions as much as in their language, their understanding should not consist entirely in that. In Laure there was something very conventional in this point of view, a vestige of an image of women (inherited from her mother) according to which men were more physical than women, more single-mindedly devoted to the sensual aspect of a union. At the same time this could be read as an almost desperate desire to inscribe their union deeper in time, and the hope that being there one or two hours longer would make

Pierre something other than just a sexual partner. It was therefore necessary at all costs that an understanding which was neither an "adventure" nor an ordinary "liaison" should include conversations (all too rare), walks (even rarer), and a meal now and then: Laure was very eager to preserve, even in the words she used, this semblance of a shared life within their life apart.

But what could they do? When they had gone several days without seeing each other, or when they had only a few hours, or when Pierre had been able to "get away" some morning, a chat over tea was certainly not going to satisfy them. So it was not surprising that after many weeks that followed the same pattern Laure was afraid their "understanding" consisted only in making love. Naturally, it was rather unfair to complain about this, since she would have been even sadder and more disappointed if before Pierre left again they had not been able to hold each other, even for a half-hour, deep in her bedroom and her bed, away from everything, and so banish quarrels, doubts, disagreements, resentments in the joyful and passionate rediscovery of their bodies. But Laure would not admit that their meetings could have anything in common with those of "a waitress and a traveling salesman," to use a pejorative example her mother was fond of: to avoid such a comparison, they simply had to make sure that the act of love— the indispensable central point of their understanding—took place in an open space where they could have a snack, talk, read a little. Besides, as a matter of convenience they often talked, snacked, and read in her bed—and Laure loved it.

But the fact was, too, that beyond the obligatory stay in Laure's bedroom, the ever-reawakening passion of their bodies, and the snacks and conversations in bed, they could not really enter any of the areas typically closed to adulterous lovers: going to the movies was out of the question—too little time, the risk of meeting friends, relations, or colleagues—and certainly so were shows (rare enough, in any case) put on only in the evenings. Anyway, excursions such as these, to the theater or a concert, belonged not to the life they each led but to the dream life they had created together, a life they did not talk about very often.

And so, strangely enough, books and conversations occupied a considerable place for them and became a sort of substitute for a better, freer life they would never have, either together or separately. Books filled their silences, their separation, and their clandestinity, bringing in a breath of the outside world by connecting them to the great life of the mind, to the lives of the great lovers whose correspondence they read together. It was a little as though they lived in a country occupied by a foreign army: they retreated into their home, into themselves, into the richness of their intimacy. It was Laure's pride that though their love undoubtedly cut them off from the world, it also separated them from the vulgarity and poverty of ordinary life and gave them access to another world, one certainly unknown to the people around Laure who were content with the social appearances of happiness. This was the world of books, unquestionably, but at the same time it was the world of the countries where they would travel when they could, where they would have traveled if they had been able to—they never made specific plans, anyway. Laure had accepted the idea that Pierre's life was nothing but a succession of tiresome chores, in which she represented not merely a diversion but a gust of fresh air, an interval of real freedom and real life.

Thus, they entered different, complementary labyrinths of "clandestinity." Pierre was not systematic about it, he spoke politely to the concierge and did not hesitate to go on a few cautious errands with Laure in her neighborhood—but he was "careful," and she could not blame him. Little by little, however, she sensed a feeling in Pierre that she did not exactly understand, any more than she had understood his attraction to a love "without constraints," "without commitment"—and this was a profound, real love of secrecy that went beyond what was necessary. He liked secrecy for its own sake, for its beauty: he relished arriving this way, suddenly, without warning, at a woman's home, and drawing her into her bedroom. With Laure he could not often do it, he felt she resisted it, whereas with the nurse there had been no problem. Laure actually became all the more precious to him because it was so hard for him to keep letters or photographs or any other sign of her in his house, or even in his pockets.

The key to Laure's apartment itself presented problems for him. Annie discovered it one day on the shelf in the entryway, where he had happened to toss it while emptying his pockets. He did not know what to say except "I don't know, I must have found it in the street."

"Throw it away, then," said Annie. "We can't use it for anything."

Since she was watching, he quickly threw it in the garbage. Later that night he retrieved it and, shamefaced, wiped off the traces of coffee grounds with a sponge.

He probably also loved the secrecy because it lent a certain romanticism to their love, because it eroticized their meetings, and last, because it led to exquisite reversals: the creation of night in the midst of day, in a bedroom with drawn curtains, a sudden awakening after a few minutes of sleep, in the middle of the afternoon. None of this could be part of his marriage, because of the children, the in-laws, telephone calls, impromptu visits from friends, and also because married life puts an end to young people's impulses. But how could he make Laure understand that? This sort of secrecy oppressed her a little. "It's true," Pierre said one day, "my real life is here"— for once he had brought work and was sitting with some books at the round table—"in the secret we share." In this Laure felt the pleasure of being able to keep a secret, of being happy in silence and discretion, so unlike the ostentation of lovers who hid nothing, which she found almost obscene.

Thus, for a long time she felt nothing was missing, and sometimes she would even glance in a slightly superior way at the other young women she met at the hairdresser's or in the supermarket, women whose faces were marked by a tense mixture of legitimate happiness and family cares. Her "understanding" with Pierre bore her along invisibly—these women could have no notion of what it was like. How could they imagine such happiness? Wasn't this the very situation they were most afraid of? Wasn't this danger itself to them? How else could they describe this secret happiness but as a degrading and shabby thing? At these times Laure felt a mounting rebelliousness, a resentment she felt was justified.

As is usually the case, it took some time for Laure to admit that the picture others had of her, or of her situation (even though that picture might be formed by incomplete observation and so disregard peculiarities that were completely essential to her) was not as wrong as she might think, and that she was far from being the exception she had been so sure she was. Thus, certain ideas and images associated with the word *affair* so shocked Laure that she had substituted an equivalent word that was more precious, more romantic, and above all, she thought, more accurate. The images that others have of us and the names others call us probably tend to make us fit cruder preconceived notions, and this comes as a shock to our inner sense, powerful as it is, of individuality. Our experiences are unique. But in going through them, we rejoin the crowd. Pierre was certainly like other people—hypocritical, tender, weak, and sensual; and Laure was also like others—passionate, oversensitive, sad. Even in her desire to elevate her "affair" above the common level, she still conformed to a common model.

Yet however discouraging the notion others have of us, it is sometimes our only resource, the only thing that saves us: from it alone, in fact, can we derive comfort, through it see our experience in its correct proportions, and discover that we are not the only ones to be victims or perpetrators of a situation that is crushing us.

But what about happiness? For quite some time Laure was

overwhelmed with happiness, because in her blindness the feeling that she was an exception made her endlessly happy. But when she lost this feeling, she found herself defenseless, wounded, drained. She continued to think she had been an exception, but this time exceptionally foolish. In the meantime, however, Pierre felt she was living in a dream state. Something was going on that was not natural and could not last forever. Pierre sometimes became afraid. What would happen when she woke up?

"I'm taking everything away from you," he told her, "and I'm not giving you anything."

She did not understand. "I love you," she said. "Isn't that enough? The way you are, the way we are."

Pierre shook his head. "No, I know I'm hurting you."

She protested, refused to believe him, though what he said reverberated dangerously in her. Deep in her heart she eventually came to agree with him, but it was enough that he had recognized his guilt, that he had anticipated a reproach she did not yet dream of formulating.

She forgave him everything. They lay down side by side, barely touching, eyes closed, then began with a few slow caresses. "I was so unhappy," Pierre said, "so miserable." (They let the water boil away, and found only a little burnt deposit of lime at the bottom of the teakettle when Laure went to make tea.) She squeezed Pierre's muscular legs between hers and gazed at a cut rose in a blue vase. Two days later she put it to dry in a volume of the *Encyclopaedia Universalis*.

When they reversed their roles this way, Laure consoling Pierre for the hurt he thought he had done her, Pierre went back home extremely relieved. On one occasion among so many others—an evening in December, perhaps, or January—he arrived home after the sky was completely dark. When he turned off the engine in the garage, he felt very happy. He breathed deeply. In the entryway he set his bulging briefcase down against the radiator and stayed there in the darkness for a moment, listening to the happy talk of the children and their mother on the other side of the dining room door. An exuberance welled up in him. He was protected, gently wrapped in a warm feeling, carefree and fulfilled. He turned on the light and went into the little bathroom to wash his hands carefully. Both women wanted him, he thought with a blaze of desire and a new cynicism that surprised him. He thought he could respond to both demands without any trouble.

Taking a few steps into the room, he went up to Annie and stroked her cheek, then collapsed as usual into the broken-down corner of the sofa and pulled out from under his buttocks a little plastic car that had slid down there. He was hungry. The smell of chicken roasting whetted his appetite.

After dinner they were alone, the children had gone to bed, and Pierre brought the bottle of wine and their two glasses out of the dining room. His supple body moved easily. Annie had made a fire in the fireplace. The dog groaned in its sleep. The flames, rising and falling in whimsical and reassuring shapes, seemed to say to him, "Be happy, don't torment yourself, be happy." A little later he joined Annie in bed.

"You smell good," he said. From the next room they heard a cry. The little girl was talking in her sleep.

"Go to sleep," he said loudly. The voice quieted.

"You smell good," he said again.

"It's my hand cream," Annie said, but she was smiling. In the half-light he saw that she had turned toward him. He rolled over on his side and put his arms around her, feeling no remorse.

PART THREE

CHAPTER 18

BY Christmas, 1976, Pierre and Laure had known each other four years: the fourth autumn of their "understanding" had just ended. At two or three points this understanding had seemed repetitive to them—even their happiness seemed repetitive. A certain regularity had been established, a meticulous observation of the constraints of their limited time together, and their love had had to conform to this, though they both refused to accept the idea. In early December the cold inspired them with a vague plan to go see Holland, frozen canals, a turquoise sky crossed by birds. But there was not much conviction in it.

Then, one after the other, two days apart, the children came home from school red-faced, eyes watering—it was chicken pox. Laure sighed. She would go to Blois, where her cousin was getting married. She wanted to complain a little, demand something of him, but she thought better of it. She did go so far as to say, "Do you remember Ostende?"

"Of course I remember," said Pierre. "I thought about it constantly those days. I even listened to that song by Léo Ferré. Twice. It was like one more secret between us."

This childish mention of a guilty, adolescent sort of secret irritated Laure; she would have prefered a concrete plan. But she said nothing. As he was leaving, Pierre hugged her hard. "Holland, traveling, adventure—for me, you are all that. You're my real life. I don't need anything else, because I have you."

The year after they met, an old school friend of Pierre's, a professor at Lille, had invited him to take part in a series of meetings to set up a teachers' association. This was not a subject Pierre had thought much about, but he agreed to go anyway, out of curiosity, without talking to Laure about it. Nothing was certain.

"I'll go with you," Annie said. "We can send the kids to Mama."

"All right," said Pierre, disappointed but resigned. After all, he had not gone on a trip in a long time—they could spend two days in Belgium. He did not say anything. Then: "We can stay with Marc—he invited me."

"I don't like him very much. I especially don't like his wife. It scares me to see her looking at me. God knows what she's thinking."

"You know what her ideas are like."

"It isn't that. I don't know what it is."

At the last moment, however, Annie backed out; she so rarely spent any time with her parents, she said. "Since we got married, I've never really been alone with them. They'll be happy to have a visit from me."

"Thanks."

"Oh, honey, one little week alone isn't so terrible."

And so Pierre persuaded Laure to take three days off. "If you like," he said, "you can come Thursday evening, and we'll have three whole days to ourselves. I had told a friend I would stay with him, but maybe it would be better if we went to a hotel."

"Definitely," said Laure. "I can't see myself staying with your friend."

Pierre left before her. He found the first two days tedious. The people attending the meeting proposed a charter, voted on statutes, established a schedule of contributions: it was like a union meeting, and quite disappointing. Pierre turned down the position of treasurer, and Marc refused to be named president, to Pierre's surprise. The third day Pierre waited for his friend in front of the school cafeteria. He had not said anything to him yet.

"I hope you're not too disappointed," said Marc.

"A little," Pierre said, "but I think eventually it will take some kind of form."

"Of course," said Marc, a touch of scorn in his voice. For a long time now he had been very active in the group. "They have no sense of organization, but they have to be left alone—they'll come to it by themselves."

"You should have agreed to be president."

"I'm not so dumb," said Marc, who apparently had contented himself with being responsible, in a vague way, "for general guidance."

"I have to tell you something," said Pierre. "I won't be staying through Thursday or Friday. I'm going on to Belgium for a few days."

"Oh," said Marc, "go ahead. Nothing will be happening on those days—take advantage of it. Your wife is off work?" he added, with an air of severity and innocence that intimidated Pierre for a moment. He shook himself. After all, he did not owe Marc anything.

"No," he said.

"My family is," said Marc, "but too bad—no one's going anywhere. It will make them feel like a real collective."

"The children are with their grandparents near Guérande, with Annie. But I want to spend a couple of days in Belgium with a friend, and I'm counting on you to say I stayed with you the whole time."

Marc pinched his mustache between two fingers and pulled on it gently. "What have you gotten yourself into?"

"Nothing."

"It's none of my business. After all, you do what you like."

Fortunately, thought Pierre. But he felt irritated.

Then, after a moment, Marc asked, "When is she coming?"

"Thursday evening."

"I won't ask the two of you to dinner. My wife and Annie are friends, and it would bother me for her sake."

Friends? thought Pierre. If only you could hear what Annie says about Marie-Paule! "We wouldn't have been able to, anyway," he said. "We're planning to take off right away."

Marc and his wife had met in a Communist youth organization in the late fifties. At that time Marie-Paule was fond of quoting Clara Zetkin—incorrectly—as Pierre well remembered: "Love can't be drunk like a glass of water," she would say. A glass of water, Pierre thought. Laure is my intoxication, my liquor, he added, feeling that the notion was completely ridiculous.

Laure and he dined joyously in an elegant restaurant lit by pink wall sconces and small pyramids of candles on each table. They drank a little more than they should have, and Pierre could not help covering Laure's hand with his again and again. "My baby," he said.

But actually he was uneasy, almost frightened. Around ten o'clock he called Marc, who said coldly, "No, no one has called, but don't worry, I would have found some excuse. Everything okay?" And he hung up.

Pierre had reserved a room in the Hôtel de la Mairie. It was

small, the light from a neon sign flickered through it rhythm-
ically, and they could hear the distant sound of traffic on the
belt highway. Laure had set her suitcase down in the middle
of the room—it was a little too big but the only one she had.
The door to the wardrobe gaped open; they had to keep closing
it.

Pierre had brought his bag from Marc's house that morning.
Without saying anything, they got undressed and for the first
time lay down in a bed that had been prepared for them, their
things tangled together on a chair, their toothbrushes in the
same glass. In Pierre's bag Laure saw a pair of pajamas, which
he did not put on. She had never seen Pierre in pajamas, had
never even seen any of Pierre's pajamas. They were so moved
that they put out the light, clasped each other close, and did
not make love until much later, in the middle of the night,
clumsily. They fell asleep, then were awoken a short time
later by the streetlights and the noise from the highway. Pierre
got up twice to try to adjust the curtain.

In the morning they put their bags in the trunk of Laure's
car, and Pierre got behind the wheel. Laure watched him,
smiling, with the map and the guidebook on her knees. The
first time they stopped to eat something Pierre did not come
back to the table, and the cashier said, "Your husband is
waiting for you outside." By two o'clock they were in Bruges,
by five in Ostende, and from there Pierre called Marc again.
Laure did not ask him any questions.

"I made the necessary excuses," Marc said. "I said you were
at the movies. You went to see a Hitchcock film. I had a
headache, so I let you go alone."

Had he said anything to his wife? Pierre remembered Clara
Zetkin and imagined Marc and Marie-Paule with the lights
out in the darkness of their bedroom. He imagined Marc saying, "I didn't tell you, but Seguin seems to be involved in
some hanky-panky."

No, Marc had not said anything to Marie-Paule. Actually,
Pierre thought he had detected some envy in his eyes when

Marc was walking to the hotel with him. "Everything all right at home?" he asked.

"I think so. I didn't have time to ask, and the connection was very bad. Annie just said that they were all going home tomorrow."

"What do you mean, 'all'?" asked Pierre. "Her parents too?" But the line was already dead. Pierre hung up.

Nevertheless, once outside again, and then all through the evening and the following day, Pierre forgot everything. The cold sun pierced the morning fog, they felt like lovers in a movie, Pierre hugged Laure to him and felt her cold, wet nose against his cheek. "Oo," he said with a happy laugh. He put his arm around her shoulders despite their thick coats. "Let's go see the boats," he said.

They spent the next day in Gand, not staying long in front of the altarpiece because the church was so cold. But they liked the town. What they had vaguely sensed turned out to be the case: their true homeland was a series of towns whose history and language were unknown to them, whose inhabitants were complete strangers to them, except the ones they inevitably came into contact with—café waiters and hotel chambermaids, museum guards, boatmen who spoke a rough French that delighted them or an English they did not always understand.

"How hungry I am!" Laure said. It was already Saturday evening, but they still had all of Sunday before them. They could even sleep in Lille, and Pierre would go back by train Monday morning, as they had agreed. Christmas was two days away, the streets were filled with crowds, and for once Laure and Pierre could gaze at the bustling families together without feeling that what they saw concerned them in any way.

It was extremely cold. To warm her hand, Laure had slipped it into Pierre's, deep in his pocket. Their palms were pressed so tight together, and so damp with sweat, that when pulled apart they made a little sucking noise. "Give me back my hand," Pierre said, "so I can open the door." The café was warm, welcoming, full of people. After their walk in the open air Laure felt her cheeks turning bright red. She was sleepy.

Back in their hotel room, they fell asleep quickly in each other's arms. They were already used to this way of life—this was their second hotel. But they slept fitfully, woke up again and again in the night, moaning, each searching for the other, making sure the other was there. Wide awake at three in the morning, Pierre felt deeply grateful, though he did not know for what.

Monday morning they said goodbye to each other on the foggy station platform. "Don't cry," said Pierre. "I'm feeling terribly sad myself."

"I'm not crying," said Laure. But her eyes were full of tears. That morning she had noticed a closed, absent look on Pierre's face. Was he already somewhere else? she wondered. Was he thinking up excuses or worrying about his children?

He turned toward her. "I'm sorry," he said. "I didn't sleep very well." She did not ask why.

This short trip left Laure with mixed feelings. Naturally, she was sorry that only by chance had they been able to go off together, that it was highly improbable they would ever be able to again. And yet, all things considered, it had worked out well: it had allowed them to confirm the depth of their understanding—there had not been the smallest quarrel, the slightest irritation, in three days—and also the certainty that they would never get along better than in places that seemed made for them. They had experienced "real nights," had woken up in the morning together, had known life in "actual time." Most important, they had had a chance to experience together what they both loved and so rarely had a chance to enjoy: foreign countries, works of art, the past, the beauty of old towns.

Because, in truth, both of them had ended up harboring resentments against their own town, its narrow-minded spirit, its unpleasant climate—even Laure, who had seemed so accepting up to then. But the daily difficulties of her understanding with Pierre had ended by becoming confused, for her, with the straitlaced atmosphere of the town—the stupid shop windows, the boutiques proudly lining the pedestrian area, the new café terraces crowded with schoolchildren—its inhabitants so single-mindedly concerned with the practical side of life, to the exclusion of daydreams, long walks, works of art, books. Pierre, too, having become used to that milieu over the months, now thought it was time to wake up—and he blamed the gray sky over the town, the monotonous parade of clouds over the muddy yellow countryside, for "putting him to sleep," for making him lazy, erratic, too prone to accept things as they were.

Actually, Laure needed only Pierre. And it was in Laure's company that Pierre had discovered his dissatisfaction with his life, though he might have been mistaken about the reasons for it. How convenient: all they had to do was open a weekly paper, leaf through a movie magazine, and they felt excluded. So many obstacles! So far from everything! If they stayed in R., nothing was possible. But they did stay, did continue to lead the same unsatisfactory life.

As it turned out, they lived by two sets of values: the higher values (those which they were "deprived of" in R.) and those which sustained their daily life. Left to himself, Pierre read very little and found good excuses to pass up the few opportunities to go to the theater or a concert, staying instead in front of the television. And taking his students to the local museum, he admitted to himself, was a chore: they were noisy and unruly, and besides he really had no interest in the works of art he was supposed to teach them to like. (Yet in their eyes Pierre was someone for whom these things really existed, who was "moved" by them: "Did you see Seguin?" they would say to one another with mixed respect, irony, and incomprehension, and "Art is his thing, he's crazy about it," as he lectured in a gloomy tone on the Greek vases in the Desparts Collection.) His higher system of values was epitomized, really, in the trip to Italy: walks in Tuscany, his tanned arms emerging from short sleeves, a guidebook open between his sweaty fingers. But the most important part of Pierre's life was the normal, everyday reality of evenings with the family, of a regular job punctuated by a few Saturday nights at the movies. Pierre easily accommodated himself to Annie—who preferred a good movie, "even on TV"—both by inclination and out of a gentleness in his nature that always led him to avoid conflicts with those whose life he was sharing. So it was all the more understandable why Laure was his "pride." Because of her he had to wake up—even though nothing much came of his efforts, and things always remained in the planning stages.

For her it was a little different. She had thought she should go along with Pierre's daydreams—though he had made them up only to please her. They shared the same taste and were easily satisfied. Laure listened to "more music" and had her stereo fixed, but it took her a long time to progress from *The Four Seasons* to opera, and she did not know what to make of Bartók's quartets, which a colleague of Pierre's had recommended to him and which he had given Laure as a present, though without listening to them himself first.

Even if "trips" (especially a trip to Italy) might have reconciled everything, the subject was hard to broach: for Laure to demand it would have burdened Pierre with yet one more grievance, and her complaints tended to come at inopportune times, when she was feeling moody rather than truly desirous of something. What was more, their past experiences in Italy had not been very encouraging, perhaps because they had not been together. Laure had gone to Italy with her brother and sister-in-law, and the two or three times Pierre had gone it was with other young couples. Besides, Pierre felt nothing but scorn for the conventional enthusiasms of his colleagues, for instance Mme. Rougier, a middle-aged woman and a literature teacher like him, who spent every Easter vacation in Tuscany with her husband and returned, as she said, "revived" (a word that had made the rounds of the teachers' lounge). On his own trips he had always been limited by not having much money, by the demands of family life, and by the presence of very young children. Laure, traveling with her family, had found it tiresome to stand and wait on the Ponte Vecchio while her sister-in-law compared the prices of gold-leaf wooden plates. In the museums she quickly grew tired, and she was a little ashamed of preferring to stroll through the streets; but Nicole "was too hot," and Jacques listened only to Nicole and, surrounded by dubious smells and men in unbuttoned shirts, sat drinking white wine on café terraces, even though it gave him a headache.

It would probably have been different with just the two of them. No children crying in the night, no fussy traveling companions debating endlessly when the time came to pick a restaurant. But as the question did not come up in any practical way, they never knew the sweetness of driving down a road in the early morning, a small chapel appearing among the cypresses; delicate, barely faded frescoes; or small hotels on public squares, with the sound of fountains all night long, and siestas behind closed shutters in the stifling Southern afternoons.

In fact, the subject of vacations became distressing for both of them. For Laure it was painful to see the times of the year approaching when they would be separated again, having uselessly discussed some unworkable plan and witnessed Pierre's clumsy excuses and sincere sadness. He had, once and for all, relegated vacations to the category of "family chores"—a phrase he used so readily that in the end Laure took a dislike to it. As for the couple of days here and there out of the year that Laure could have enjoyed, Annie often spoke of "taking advantage of them" to "get away by ourselves," "take a little trip to Italy or somewhere else, Normandy if you'd rather— wherever you like." And then something would come up, some reason for not going through with the plan, which Annie would quickly abandon. She would say that nothing could equal three days at home: "I never have time to do anything."

And during those three days Pierre would also not be able to see Laure.

Some time after their trip, Pierre received a letter from Marc, who, after chatting about various other things, slipped in a few ostensibly discreet but clumsy allusions to "Pierre's situation"—his word for it. "What's happening with that now?" he wrote. "Marie-Paule and I talked about it. The best thing would be to tell Annie everything. We're prepared to help you, if you like, but don't ruin everything."

Pierre's answer was not what Marc and Marie-Paule had been expecting: "I think I really love her. We can't separate."

"Who is he talking about?" Marie-Paule asked with annoyance. "Here at the end he's being intolerable. Is he talking about his wife or that girl? He doesn't know what he wants."

"He doesn't know what he wants," Marc echoed, as though the discovery deserved to be repeated.

Marie-Paule went on, "I never really trusted him much, I have to admit, I couldn't really understand how you—"

"I know," Marc interrupted, "but I like him a lot."

"So do I," said Marie-Paule. "That's why it upsets me to see him ruin his life."

CHAPTER 19

AND SO they were separated by Christmas vacation. Laure decided to attend her cousin Rémi's wedding.

"Listen, my child," her mother had said on the telephone, "do what you like. But—"

"But I'm coming," Laure said.

"That's good," her father said. "Without you, I'd be bored."

"How's your painting?" Laure asked.

"I'm not really sticking to it," he said, "but it's coming along." Ever since retiring, he had spent a lot of time painting in a chilly shed he called his studio.

Her mother got on the phone again. "Everything's ready, we've found a perfect escort for you, a young English teacher. He even taught at Coëtquidan Military Academy." And her father added in the background, "For his military service."

Rémi's father, Laure's uncle, was—like her grandfather, whom she had never known—a former soldier who had left the army at the end of the war in Indochina to open a real-estate agency. His office was in his house—he used the smallest room on the ground floor as a waiting room—and on Sundays, so that the family could have lunch together, they had to remove the construction models from the other room. Laure's aunt was a strong, quiet, calm woman. She had sold the land she had inherited from her family to buy the business. Their two oldest sons were married; the first worked for his father, and the second had opened a small bookstore in Paris opposite a lycée.

"And what about Jacques?" Laure asked.

"I'll be very surprised if he can come," said her mother. "At this time of year it's not really convenient for him." And Laure could hear the old pride, the old favoritism in her mother's voice.

They all arrived close to the same time, a little before nine o'clock: uncles, cousins, friends, parents on both sides, people Laure barely recognized or whose faces seemed older to her, thicker, tired, as though seen through a veil. More and more of them kept getting out of fat Renaults or powerful Citroëns with chrome-plated fixtures. Their faces all had a vague look of having been groomed for the occasion, though the men were gloomy—probably tired, or worried about money, or worn out by a difficult drive—and the women severe, almost hostile—probably also tired, or worried about a sick child, or careworn in general, or upset by an argument in the car, or sorry they had sent a present that was not lavish enough, or afraid of having drawn attention to themselves by sending a present that was too expensive. Over their dressy outfits, the fabric a little thin for the season, the women wore heavy fur coats, and the straps of their patent-leather shoes cut into the red swellings on their insteps. A few of the men wore heavy signet rings on their fingers and cufflinks that showed conspicuously below their coat sleeves. The rear doors of the cars opened first, releasing neat, clean children: rather sour-faced little girls, and boys with ears made more prominent by recent haircuts. Everyone came over to Laure with an enthusiasm, a tenderness, an affection that touched her. Caught in the flood of navy-blue suits and dresses of crêpe and chiffon, assailed by the heady smells of face powder and sweat, Laure felt exuberant and unreservedly held out her face to receive the family kisses. "Ah! Here's little Laure," her uncle the insurance agent said jovially. Recent wives and distant cousins offered Laure a cooler cheek or held out an arm dangling a black patent-leather handbag for a more hesitant handshake.

The young cousin was a soldier on leave. He was determined to get married in uniform, which was flattering to his father. He was carrying white gloves, his cheeks were pink and sprinkled with small pimples, his shaven neck was irritated under his chin. He gave off a smell of aftershave and a light sweat of emotion when he leaned over to kiss Laure.

"Things aren't too bad for you down there?" she asked out of politeness, referring to where he was billeted, near Metz.

"Oh, just fine!" he said. For now, anyway. The army wasn't the worst thing in the world, he came home as often as he could, but the separation had been very hard on his fiancée, so they had decided to get married as soon as possible.

They were trapped, Laure said to herself. The commitment had been made: whatever happened, he would never want to hurt her. From now on, Laure said to herself, he would be deaf to all other suffering, like the male of certain species of birds, attached to his tree, his nest, impervious to all other calls, incapable even of deciphering them.

"Have you met her before?" asked a voice near Laure. No, she did not remember her. Someone came to her rescue: "Of course you do, from Jean-Paul's wedding." Oh yes, that was it. "In fact, that's where they met." The crowd was thickening. It was time to head for the town hall.

Laure no longer knew which of her nephews, cousins, second cousins she had already kissed, and she became lost among the lilac suits, the pearl-colored neckties, the blue blazers, the pink-patterned dresses. Fresh masses of flowers arrived. "To the restaurant! To the restaurant!" said the groom's father with authority. "Hey! What am I saying!" A hand seized Laure's arm and drew her toward a car. It was the oldest of her cousins, her uncle's associate. "I'll drive you," he said. His wife got in back, and Laure was submerged in the heavy scent of her heliotrope perfume. She was a thin woman with dyed hair and a closed, rather hard face. Like some of the other men, Laure's cousin wore a square signet ring on his right hand, and black hair grew on the backs of his fingers. Their two girls had gone on ahead separately, one with a young man her mother **did** not seem to like much, the other with Laure's parents.

I hardly had time to say hello to them, Laure thought. Her father was smiling under his thick, white, combed-back hair, and Laure thought his skin seemed very red. Her mother, as always, looked absently at the crowd: she had refused to wear her glasses and could not recognize anyone. "Your parents are amazing," said Laure's cousin. "Actually, mine don't seem to be getting any older, either."

They arrived, the door of the town hall opened, there was a movement in the crowd, and the car belonging to the father of the bride drew up. The bride got out, a small, delicate brunette, resting her hand on her father's arm as he leaned out with some difficulty.

"He wears a pacemaker," someone said.

"Yes, he's had it for three years now," said another.

The sky was pale, the sun would soon be out.

"We're lucky. Just think of the weather we had yesterday."

"Really? Not where we were."

The soldier had put on his gloves. The bride was trying to look cheerful, but her face was drawn and her dark eyes had rings around them. "Two months," someone whispered, "she isn't showing at all, not yet." But she had vomited a great deal that morning, before getting in the car. Laure gazed at her, hoping she would have a chance to talk to her during the meal.

"She has her degree," the oldest of her cousins murmured to her. How old is he? Laure wondered—forty, forty-five? Maybe less? "She works for the Treasury. Obviously, she'll be leaving there now."

"Why?" asked Laure. There was no answer.

Everyone in the room fell silent as the mayor entered. Laure sat down, contemplating the tired necks of the older people in front of her, and was filled with an emotion that swept everything else away, something like a great wave of acquiescence.

Rémi turned to face the pale young woman, eyes sparkling, chin spotted with little pimples, shoulders square in his uniform jacket. She smiled.

"Later," said a voice behind Laure, "when her children are grown up, she'll be able to go back to work. That's what I did. A woman gets bored, alone at home."

Laure felt herself staggering beneath the weight of obviousness and convention. How tranquilly, with what conviction, that pronouncement had been made! Nothing could penetrate it, one was helpless before it. Laure put her hand to her temple and felt a slight pain. She pressed harder, and the pain sharpened. Two days before, Pierre had come to see her in the early afternoon. They had sat side by side on the little couch, then slid down onto the carpet. When she tried to get up, Pierre had hugged her against him, under him. Her head had struck the table leg.

I love him, she thought, but here those words had no force. She looked around. Wasn't it possible that these strong, healthy men who had procreated legitimately between the sheets of their marriage beds had each left someone behind, too—the wife of a coworker, a young secretary, a typist—and were thinking about her right now with mixed desire and resentment, the aftermath of a quarrel the day before? "My brother-in-law is getting married, I won't be able to come tomorrow," they might have said. Or "my wife's brother," or "Marie-Lou's cousin," or "Jean-François's younger sister"— "what a bore." And soon now they would go telephone her from the restaurant basement or a nearby café, on the pretext of needing fresh air or cigarettes. She felt a pang. She had no ally anywhere, not among these ruddy, heavyset men, who did not look anything like Pierre, and even less among these young women, who looked so festive, whom she now imagined vindictive or unhappy, tense with irritation as they made the same demands over and over again. In the end she did not feel close to anyone, except perhaps the youngest of her female cousins, whose little boy had some sort of blood disease. They're all doing the right thing, thought Laure, except me.

"Your shoes are very pretty," one of her young cousins whispered to her. Laure smiled at her. Was that her "friend," the young man her mother found "vulgar"? And what about these married women, who smelled of well-fed flesh under their fragrant face powder—did they have lovers? But Laure refused to go on asking these sorts of questions, which revolted her a little, and, gazing once again at the group of people, she contemplated the power that emanated from families when they were gathered together. Men with necks squeezed into their ties, already estimating how much time was left before lunch—flushed, sexual, tense. Women who were too thin, or too stout, strapped into girdles too tight for them—all fed with the same food and marked, after fifteen or twenty years of marriage, by an indefinable resemblance to each other, the result of being steeped daily in the same household odors, the sweat of the shared bed, of the bath towels. Her gaze lingered especially on the younger women, with their pink skin, their round bodies, their flesh saturated with semen. Looking at their handsome children, she could already see, in the openings of their collars, in the bends of their knees, the loveliness of the substance shaped by the solid bodies of the parents, and in their eyelids, in their temples, a blue-tinged sweetness that moved her. This is what is real, she thought for a second time, the true path.

Behind her some old relatives whose names she still did not know were already subsiding into vacant anticipation of the meal to come. They speculated about the menu and remembered similar feasts, their own weddings, with real emotion and other, perfunctory feelings. A heady smell rose from the bouquets of flowers. The mayor, an old friend of Rémi's father, embraced the newlyweds a second time. Laure joined the group congratulating the young people. She was hot, and her forehead hurt. Her escort came over to her, and she greeted him with a smile. Meanwhile Rémi had lifted the bride's veil and was kissing her like a well-oiled machine, with a sort of energy that had no tenderness in it, with excessively broad motions of his chin and cheeks, and his bride was responding similarly, as though the two of them wanted to prove publicly their capacity for love, now legally sanctioned. One almost felt like applauding, Laure thought. And in fact, two old uncles had raised their spotted hands and were striking them gently together as they watched the pair.

The couple kissed again in the same way many times during the meal, at moments that seemed expected, planned according to some time-honored script. Methodically, at regular intervals, they would stop eating, Rémi would give his wife a look that was almost harsh and then, leaning toward her, devour her mouth and chin in a long kiss, conscientiously agitating the muscles of his face and neck, to all appearances a difficult and rather tiresome exercise. They would separate slowly without taking their eyes off each other, the edges of their mouths red, and then, without letting go of each other's hand, turn back to their celery remoulade.

During all this the young English teacher made an effort to sustain a conversation with Laure about the books of Rolfe, Baron Corvo, whose footsteps he had traced the past summer on a trip to Venice. The bride's brother was looking at him with visible antipathy. He himself had been teaching commercial English for two years and made frequent trips to Texas. "I never read novels," he said. "They're nothing like real life." Laure's "escort" looked at her with distress. He had a short mustache and wore a gold ring on his finger and a neat pullover. His hands were delicate. Laure felt sympathy for him.

Now people were proposing toasts, laughing, applauding: once again the married couple kissed. This was part of the ritual, and everyone saluted it, raising a glass and marveling, while counting the seconds, at how long the kiss lasted. Laure lowered her eyes to her mushroom tart.

"Nice to see, isn't it?" said her cousin. Then he added slyly, "But the mayor was hardly necessary, was he?" He closed his eyes as though oppressed by some inner vision and sighed heavily. Then he drained his glass, and as he leaned toward Laure to speak to her more softly, she smelled his male odor: a mixture of shaving cream, ironed linen, and sweat warmed by the good wine and generous food.

He glanced at Laure's escort out of the corner of his eye. "I don't think he's for you, if you know what I mean." And then he continued in a louder voice, slipping his arm over the back of his wife's chair, "But there's nothing better than marriage, is there, my little bunny?"

"I don't know what you're talking about," she said.

He went on, for Laure's benefit. "I don't know how I'd ever be able to fall asleep at night if I didn't have my little wife next to me. There's only one thing wrong with her: she snores."

His wife's face had reddened under her carefully arranged blond hair. "That's not true," she said.

He leaned over and kissed her neck. "Hey, I was only joking, little bunny."

Laure gazed at the bent heads, the flushed faces, the animated mouths, then looked up at the walls, covered in frightful wallpaper, then imagined, above them, the flat roof of the restaurant and, farther above, the colorless roof of clouds over them all; higher, even higher, the sun was no doubt shining on a limitless expanse of azure. Her gaze dropped back to the noisy dining room, which the children were beginning to leave: a square of soft light came in from the courtyard, where the youngest were shouting and running around in circles. A dog barked. Laure looked at the people around her again. Nothing but kissing, flesh against flesh, legitimacy on display!

The mother of the bride had stood up and was helping her daughter unhook her dress in the back and detach her veil. Rémi bent over them. "Come, come, children, a little patience!" someone shouted. Rémi, without straightening up, picked a crumb of cake off his young wife's lips with two fingers. Now people were handing around photographs, holding them by the edges so as not to leave smudges, seeking opinions from the people next to them. Laure listened: "Has it been five years already? But that's Louise's son!" Or: "They had it built. It's very comfortable now!"

From a distance her father smiled at her. He was a little flushed. The children were playing among the cars in the parking lot, and the sun was beginning to go down. In the direction of the hills beyond a curtain of trees a flock of birds passed. The librarian looked anxious. He had been trying to attract Laure's attention for the past few minutes. His brother came to his rescue. "He has something he wants to say to you," he murmured to Laure. "You're both into books, you know."

But he was drowned out by Laure's uncle. "So now I have another daughter," he said. "I already had two"—turning good-naturedly to his other daughters-in-law—"and," he added graciously, "soon a new grandson or granddaughter? That'll be the fifth."

They're chained together now, Laure thought, they'll never leave each other. When we all go our separate ways, which will be soon, the families will regroup and the children will fall asleep in the cars. The day after tomorrow is Christmas.

"And what are you doing for Christmas?" asked her cousin.

"I don't know," she said.

They would unwrap presents, toasters in red paper, a barometer for the foyer, necklaces of real pearls for the wives of the wealthiest. Her cousin's wife wore an expensive bracelet on her wrist that jiggled every time she moved.

Already music was coming from the next room, music with a strong beat, a simple melody. "Shall we?" asked her cousin, drawing Laure along with him. Her "escort" did not seem in any hurry to join her. Every image of easy happiness seemed to Laure to be in evidence. Someone laughed, one of the old uncles had asked for silence and was telling a story. Laure walked close by two pairs of girls dancing quietly. A little boy, the youngest of her cousins, had sat down in a corner and opened a book. Laure gazed at the child's delicate, amber-colored eyelids. He looked up, saw her, and smiled. With her cousin's arms tight around her, she began to dance. She felt like crying; she leaned against his shoulder and looked at the little drops of fragrant sweat beading his stout neck.

CHAPTER 20

WHEN they saw each other again in January, Pierre asked Laure nothing more than a brief "What was the wedding like?" which did not require an answer. Usually she would congratulate herself on her lover's questions or urge him to shake off his "indifference" toward "her life." Yet Pierre was surprised when she did not answer.

"Are you mad?" he asked. "Are you angry with me?"

"Of course not," said Laure.

Pierre said nothing. He had taken off his jacket, and Laure rested her head against his shoulder, which felt strong and warm through his shirt. Nevertheless, meeting again was not quite as good as it could have been, and usually was, after two weeks apart. They left each other feeling tired, mistrustful, bewildered.

There was no use trying to hide from each other the lassitude that had weighed them down since the beginning of December. The air was cold, the sky overcast and monotonous, a flat and contourless expanse: the image of their future. And every day the early nightfall made them feel gloomy. Pierre stayed with Laure a little longer on Tuesdays and Thursdays, Annie's busiest days at the bank. Sometimes, too, he came to have lunch with her on Fridays before his classes started and Laure went back to the library. But now Pierre no longer liked to go home too late, after dark, when his little girl was already in bed and Bruno in front of the television. He would have liked to be with them for their afternoon snack, their dinner, to chop the wood, clean out the fireplace, have a drink by the fire while waiting for Annie to come home.

When he did return home, he was tired and often in a bad mood. The children certainly noticed it but did not say anything. There were silences at the table. Later, when he was alone in his study again, his head ached, yet he did not want to go to bed. He would open a book, sit down at his table, doze off. Annie would come looking for him. "What are you doing? Come to bed." He would get up and follow her to their bedroom. Once or twice he fell asleep in front of the television and woke up feeling ashamed. The next day things would be better.

Then it would start again. He went to see Laure at four o'clock, and when he left her at six-thirty, she was angry that he was going so early, whereas for him it was already late, too late to have "a little time to himself." Annie was already home, taking off her wet boots. "Did you remember the bread?" she would say. It didn't matter; they would eat crackers instead, not for the first time. That was why it had been easy for him—even a relief—to accept the obstacles that rose before the prospect of "finding a few days" for "a little trip" with Laure, and her decision to attend her cousin's wedding.

Vacation began the twenty-first, Pierre stayed at home alone the whole day of the twenty-second. At first he listened to music, but he soon turned it off in favor of the television and listened to the programs from the kitchen, the screen out of view—like a housewife, he thought, like a woman alone at home—while he made a chocolate mousse. ("The only thing he knows how to make!" Annie would say, smiling. "Oh, but he makes it very well!" "And how about boiled eggs?" Pierre would retort. But it was more than ten years since he had boiled an egg.) Rinsing the bowl in the sink, he gazed out at the garden. Gusts of wind tossed the small bushes, stripped leafless by winter. The children were back, squabbling on the sofa. Once or twice he thought of Laure and, strangely, of a walk they had taken along the boulevards, past the bright café terraces.

Christmas soothed him, reassured him, infected him with some of its melancholy sweetness. Laure was gone. He bought a tree and pushed back the sofa to make room for it. Every evening of the week the candles had to be lit. "Oh no," Annie would say. "Not the candles. It's too early."

Pierre's mother had to be persuaded to come. She was so comfortable at home in B., but on the other hand how could she spend Christmas without the children? She agreed to come for two days. But she was sad, always dressed in black, and refused to let the young woman who came every day to help with the housework do anything for her.

There were nine of them at dinner Christmas Eve, including two of Annie's coworkers and two of Pierre's. At about ten o'clock Pierre's mother went to bed, but the children stayed up, begging, "Just a little longer!" Pierre felt something re-awaken in him that had been there ten years before, or even longer, when they would get together with a few other couples the same age, but the feeling died away and could not be summoned back. He left the room, returned, talked a little too much, a little too loud. He had opened the oysters, bought the best wines. Annie was wearing a pretty black dress with only one jewel, a gem pendant that Pierre had given her—in Florence, as a matter of fact. One of the men, a coworker of Annie's, had opened his vest over a beige nylon shirt and was telling a story about a mishap on his vacation, some business involving customs and false declarations, which made everyone laugh. "In the end I got around them, though," he said. Pierre had just stood up to make a toast when his mother prepared to leave them and go to bed. "Stay a little longer, Mama," he said. But she would not listen to him. The children said goodnight to her warmly, in anticipation of the presents they would be getting the next day.

When he woke up in the morning, Pierre felt some shame, a vague disgust, at finding the dining room just as they had left it a few hours earlier. He tried to banish the feeling, and it helped to see his children in their nightshirts, hovering over the unwrapped packages. "Don't open them right away," he said. "Wait for Mama and Grandmama." It was barely eight o'clock.

"But I've already opened my present," said the little girl.

"Too bad—back to bed, and don't make any noise, Mama's sleeping."

Pierre returned to bed, slid in next to Annie, and, turning her over without any tenderness, seized her roughly. She moaned, "I'm sleepy." He tried, but it was no use. Finally he rolled over on his back and slept again.

At noon they ate a meal of leftovers, surrounded by opened presents, the noise of a whistling robot, and Françoise's frightened cries. Bruno nearly cut himself with the new electric knife, which he had been forbidden to touch.

All week long Pierre was alone again, as he had been during August, but now the bad weather made it impossible to work in the garden. He was waiting for Annie's parents to come and did not open his little notebooks. He felt unhappy, let down, foolish. Laure would return soon, and he did not know whether the prospect comforted him or revived the sad image of days filled with difficulties. In the end Annie's parents did not come. He looked after the children: they, at least, did not disappoint him. He cut out pictures with his little girl, together they tossed Japanese paper flowers into water and watched them open; he bought ice skates for both children and patiently taught them to skate; he chose records for the little record player in their room; he began constructing a model airplane with his son, startled by the robot's sudden comings and goings through the dining room—it emitted a sharp whistling noise every time it encountered an obstacle.

It seemed to Pierre that he had been missing far too much where his children were concerned, neglecting them far too much, that he had been blind to everything. He looked through their notebooks, felt the importance of taking an interest in their studies, in their work, in their development. When they were playing, he interrupted them to examine their teeth and their hair, and measured them against the doorframe twice. "But Mama already did it," said Bruno. Mama? He felt good with them, justified, calm. He did not have to explain anything, he was simply there, they loved him. They had never doubted him. He might be distant, neglectful, cross with them—yet everything was forgiven. His life seemed brighter. Leaning on Bruno's shoulder, he showed him how a sextant and compass were used. They watched birds flying over the cold earth, and he took photographs.

"You're a strong guy," he said to his son one day, squeezing the robust little shoulder.

"Not as strong as you, Papa," the child said.

Were they proud of him, too? Pierre was confused and grateful. All this had been here the whole time, so close to him, and he had almost failed to see it. Françoise sat down at the piano, Pierre followed her little attempts lovingly and watched her braid move against her back. More than once he had to redo her braid, tie the ribbon on again—so now he was even learning to fix her hair.

* * *

After her cousin's wedding Laure went to stay with her parents, waiting for her brother and nephews to come. Every morning she got up late, and one morning she did not get up at all. Her father knocked at her door at about ten o'clock. "Do you want your breakfast?" He brought it up to her. A pot of jam that he had put on the tray was too heavy, and a little coffee had spilled. "I'll clean it up," he said. "Your mother would scold me." And he came back with a damp washcloth and rubbed clumsily at the spotted sheet. "Don't bother, Papa," said Laure. She was moved by the sight of his white, wrinkled hands. "Leave it."

The cat came up to sleep on her bed. She read *Great Expectations*. The night of the thirtieth—they had spent Christmas with Nicole's parents—the "little family" arrived. Laure gave them her room, not without regret, and took over the sofa bed in the dining room. The two children slept upstairs in a comfortable sort of attic with sloping ceilings, where beds had been set up for them. In spite of everything Laure was happy and filled with good will. She helped her mother prepare New Year's Eve dinner—her mother always asked her to help rather than Nicole, who "deserved some rest" and "didn't know where anything was." She wrapped everyone's presents prettily and graciously joined in her brother's jokes during dinner. In the pictures he shot with a flashbulb she stood between her parents, her arms around their shoulders, looking happy, or held the smallest boy in her arms while he pressed her cheek with a mouth ringed by chocolate from the yule log cake. Looking at the pictures later, she felt the touch of those tender little lips again and was moved. During the visit she had a few long talks with Nicole, who "had no one else" in whom to confide certain things, who complained a little about Jacques because he "thought about nothing but his work."

When she returned to R., there was nothing from Pierre waiting for her, not a card, not a message. Oh well, too bad, that's the way it is, she thought. But only two days later when she heard his voice on the telephone, she dissolved in tears. She was overcome by a great relief, a feeling of confidence, too: he was there, he had not left her. "You haven't left me," she said. He took it as a question. His heart swelled. "My darling! I love you so much! You can see that I'm here, can't you? You know I'm here." These words comforted Laure despite the strange contradiction they entailed: after all, she and he had not seen each other for two weeks.

They saw each other again, life resumed its course, and a certain monotony set in once more. They could not get rid of the feeling; though they said nothing about it, it was there even in their sleep, even in their anxious, preoccupied expressions.

In the doorway of the teachers' lounge Pierre was stopped by one of his colleagues, who said he looked a little "out of sorts." "What's up?" asked the young man, a mathematician Pierre liked a lot—he had always preferred the "scientific types" to the literary ones, especially the women, whom he found pretentious, complicated bluestockings.

Pierre was surprised. It was probably true that he wasn't feeling very well. But what should he say? How could he talk about it to this man, who, however open and genial, wasn't really his friend? Anyway, thought Pierre, do I really have any friends? He had to say he did not. How was that possible, how had that happened? Could one really go through life without any friends? He admitted to himself that even as an adolescent he had had only casual acquaintances, boys whose conversation and companionship were always less important to him than a date with a girl; then that period ended, too, and now he had nothing. But I have Laure, he thought—we're friends as well. Nevertheless, that friendship would not be of any help to him if their "understanding" ended: both relationships would vanish at the same time.

As for the other part of his life, he had not gone beyond exchanging the most conventional remarks—easy jokes, witticisms—with his colleagues and, except for this young teacher, had never gone out with any of them after school for, say, a cup of coffee. They addressed one another familiarly, they knew everything about one another (marital problems, tobacco addiction, a case of cancer in remission), but they never really talked about anything. They were all so used to keeping their personal lives well hidden that a genuine confidence would have disconcerted them. Anyway, what would he have wanted to tell them? Sometimes the news went around that So-and-so "wasn't very well," that he had not come in to teach his class, that his pupils had been divided up among several other classes; when questioned, the headmaster and his assistant would answer with evasive gravity. The other teachers would visit the hospital once or twice, welcome their colleague back with broad smiles and hearty handshakes, and behind his back comment on how he looked, how thin his face was. "Did you see his neck? From the back it's frightening."

But what about Pierre? What could he say to them? "No," he told the young mathematician, "I'm fine." Very few of them were so blunt as to ask private questions, intrude on a situation such as Pierre's: their expression for it was "He's gotten himself into some kind of a mess."

One afternoon the following week, on a Monday, he decided to telephone Lautier, his old literature professor. Lautier had retired nearly ten years before, and Pierre saw him from time to time in town, at the market. People said he had begun drinking since his wife died; certainly, he looked rather unkempt. No one answered, and Pierre went back to correcting exercises.

He tried to remember the last time he had seen Lautier: last spring—no, the spring of the year before, and he had not even sent him a New Year's card. He had seen him at the market in the Place Saint-Georges. Pierre had left Annie and Françoise to put a basket of vegetables in the trunk of the car. From a distance he had recognized Lautier bending over his open wallet, a large black imitation-leather bag in his hand. Pierre had started slightly: was he wearing slippers? Yes, those were slippers, and moving closer, Pierre saw that his pants were badly spotted. Strange—after all, it's not raining, Pierre thought.

Lautier had turned around and recognized him. "Seguin! Good to see you." He put down the apples he was picking through and looked at Pierre's little girl, who had come up to him. "Is that your little girl?"

"Good morning, Monsieur Lautier," said Pierre.

"Good God, Seguin," he said, "will you always be so cruel as to remind me that I was your teacher eons ago?"

"How are you?" asked Pierre, noticing the sagging face, the pale cheeks crossed by tiny red veins, and the too-bright, washed-out eyes.

Lautier shrugged one shoulder fatalistically. "Don't ask— but really I'm fine, I'm fine." And he rolled the apples around in his bag.

"I haven't called you since . . ." Pierre started and then stopped.

"It doesn't matter," Lautier broke in. "I know how it is. And it was nice to get your note."

My note! Pierre thought. How far back was that? He felt bad.

Lautier continued, ". . . especially your allusion to our old class! I must say! Those were my last years, but in my whole career I never had a class like that one."

"No thanks to me, certainly," said Pierre. "I was an absolute dud in Latin composition."

Annie drew Pierre's attention to her heavy bags, hefting them with discreet exasperation. "Go to Mama," Pierre said to the little girl. "Tell her I'm coming right away."

Lautier turned and waved politely in Annie's direction. "Am I holding you up?"

"No, no," said Pierre.

Lautier leaned down to the little girl and stroked her cheek. "I seem to remember you have other children as well?"

"Yes, a boy."

"Anyway, what a class that was, despite your Latin, which, I grant you, wasn't your strongest subject! But come see me one of these days."

"I certainly will," said Pierre. "Definitely." He shook his hand.

"Actually," Lautier added, "try to call me during the morning. Or the evening before. I sometimes go out for a short walk."

"I'll do that," said Pierre.

He watched Lautier hold his hand out to the boy giving him his change. "Fourteen francs fifty? Oh, I'm sorry. I didn't hear you." His right arm trembled slightly. Pierre looked at him once more, from the back: he really looked pitiful, he thought.

Pierre tried to call Lautier again in the late afternoon. He had put aside his pupils' exercises and reread his notebooks with discouragement. The winter fog had come down, heralding nightfall. Nothing would be spared him. He stood up, went into the bathroom to wash his hands—for some time now he had been doing this—and ran a comb through his hair. Wasn't he beginning to lose his hair? Surely there was more in the comb each time. He went back to his work table.

At seven o'clock, when he called again, Lautier had returned, but Pierre could not hear him very well. Bruno had put on some music in the children's room and left the door open, as usual. "Damn it, Bruno! The door!" he shouted, then said, "Excuse me, Monsieur Lautier, I can't hear you. The kids are making an infernal racket."

"Come tomorrow at about two, or let's say three. I let the phone ring before. I was out on my balcony. I was bringing in the geraniums because it's probably going to snow. Hello?" His voice sounded older but still imperious.

"I can hardly hear you at all," Pierre said, "I'll have to go put a stop to that noise." He hung up and went off toward the children's bedroom, furious. But on the way there he stopped. He thought about Lautier. Putting his head through the doorway, he looked at the child. Bruno had stood up and leaped guiltily toward the record player.

"Okay, Papa, I'm turning it off, I'm turning it off."

"It's all right," said Pierre. "It doesn't matter. I'm not working anyway."

CHAPTER 21

IT WAS October, 1959, Pierre was about to turn nineteen, and he was walking with Lautier through the schoolyard.

"You're going to prepare for the exam, you'll try for the best school you can, won't you you, Seguin? You're not going to be as foolish as I was?"

"I don't know," said Pierre, "I don't think so."

"Is it your parents? Is it that you don't have a scholarship? What a shame we were never able to start a second-year prep class, even though it never would have become one of the great ones."

"No, it isn't that," said Pierre. "I'm getting married."

"Ah" was all Lautier said. There was a short silence. "And then?" Lautier went on. "What will you do then?"

"My wife—I mean my wife-to-be—is going to work in a bank."

"Here?"

"No."

"I see," Lautier said; and then, after another short silence, "And how old are you, Seguin?"

"Twenty, or almost."

"Twenty! Well, do what you like, but at least pass your exam . . ."

Pierre said nothing.

"Ah, it's time," said Lautier. "Let's go back to our beloved Gide." He turned toward the windows of the classroom, his small dark eyes shining in his flushed face. In those days he dressed elegantly, at least in Pierre's opinion, extracting his books from the deep, rather misshapen pockets of his tweed jackets. Pierre admired Lautier, who had read everything and who knew everything, even though he had not traveled. "Throughout my career," Lautier would say, then as now, with a tone of merited satisfaction, "I have believed that . . ."

His career, Pierre thought. Now that he is retired, a widower, and probably an alcoholic . . . Today was there a single one among them, Pierre and all the others, who would dare speak the word *career* without a smile of derision? For them, that word referred to nothing more than a career in administration. The time had passed when for men like Lautier—despite his wearing socks and sandals in the summer, which somewhat detracted from the famous "Lautier elegance"—it had designated a sort of destiny: the merging of a life and a plan, a thing you did not choose but which was nevertheless truly your own. I myself have no destiny, thought Pierre. I have a life, and I'm not doing anything with it.

That day, he thought to himself, Lautier taught us about the infinitive clause in Gide, I'm almost sure. But I should ask Jean H. . . . . What a pity we don't see each other anymore.

Or was that another day? And Pierre remembered Lautier's red lips setting forth the terms of his exposition with the precision of an archeologist, the satisfaction of a scholar who has discovered a vanished species or a bone that evolution has rendered superfluous in a skeleton. His hair was white, but his eyebrows were still very dark, and his face was red. He was probably already drinking, Pierre thought. But after all, he had good reasons to drink.

Pierre chose to walk to the part of town where Lautier lived, had always lived. It was the oldest part of town: between beautiful, grassy esplanades stood grand houses with carriage gates in front as well as other more modern buildings—depressing, squat—like the one in which Lautier lived. The real cold had come, Pierre felt good, he rubbed his cheeks to bring the blood back into his numbed face; then he pulled his scarf up over his mouth, and soon the wool was damp and fragrant.

A few years before, he had met with Lautier in the Golden Ball, one of the cafés in the center of town, at an hour when it was empty except for a few whispering couples and some teenagers waiting for the afternoon to be over. Lautier had chosen the table farthest back in the room, in front of a speckled mirror, and, as soon as Pierre arrived, had emptied his glass of rosé and ordered another. "You'll have a glass of rosé too, won't you?" (The next year the entire front of the café was torn down to make way for a terrace, a false ceiling was constructed, and the swinging door disappeared. At that point, invaded by students from the lycée, the place echoed with their intense conversations, their laughter, and their music—only the back rooms were left to the couples who "had something to discuss.") Lautier had put his glasses down on his book. "These are my reading glasses," he said, and took another pair from his breast pocket. He had never gotten used to wearing bifocals, which, he said, were not flattering and made one look old.

After that they saw each other once or twice in Lautier's little apartment, where Lautier had taken care of his sick wife for twenty years and then stayed on after she died. For twenty years, in that small apartment, he had been her nurse, sleeping two hours at a stretch, often in an armchair near her, washing her, dressing her as long as she could still get out of bed, then feeding her by spoon and living the way she wanted to live: in the dark. Her illness had become steadily worse; toward the end she could no longer move anything but her eyes, and everyone who knew them marveled that they understood each other so well. But Lautier could not have any guests or even listen to the radio; she did not tolerate the presence of anyone else, not even a cleaning woman. Lautier would go out only to teach his classes, stop by the library, and bring back something for their meals.

Lautier was looking out his window at the street, where a bright, cold sun shone. Pierre had raised his head. "One cannot have a great soul or a penetrating mind without some passion for literature": Pierre remembered that Lautier was fond of quoting that sentence. How had this great soul lived, in the Rue Sainte-Croix, with his penetrating mind and love of literature? He could hear the birds chirping in the courtyard. The tall chestnut trees swayed. Lautier spoke in a steady, quiet voice. A gentle torpor overcame Pierre and the other schoolboys. "Pelletier!" came Lautier's voice. "I'm waiting!" But Pelletier had dozed off. Everyone laughed. Oh yes! It was a sentence from Vauvenargues. Lautier lifted his arms toward the sky, then went on with the class.

The house was brick, three stories high, with balconies on the front—Lautier grew geraniums on his—and, at the very top, broad zinc windowsills on the mansard windows. Preparing to cross the street, Pierre saw Lautier signaling to him. Was he watching for me? Pierre wondered. They met in the stairwell. "I wasn't watching for you," said Lautier, "but I happened to see you coming." They went up to the top floor together, slowly. The door was open.

"Pshsht!" said Lautier. "Don't come down here!" A large, gray, frightened-looking cat turned back when it saw Pierre coming. "He's always trying to go downstairs," said Lautier. "Maybe he wants to run away. I don't know. An old cat like that—he should accept things. But he doesn't accept things." At intervals light came into the stairwell through bay windows bordered by colored tiles. Pierre had forgotten how small the rooms were, how old the walls, how yellow the ceiling. "This way," said Lautier, quickly closing a door.

". . . tell you, after twenty years it needs work!" Pierre had missed the beginning of the sentence. "But I'll leave that to whoever lives here after me." The main room was scarcely larger than the others. The cat leaped up onto a round table that stood in the middle of it, crowded with books. A ray of sunlight fell across the remains of some bread and cheese and a few oranges lying in a pretty fruit dish that had been broken and clumsily glued back together.

Pierre picked up a book. It was one of the two volumes of Gide's journal. "Yes," Lautier said. "Just think. I've begun rereading it for the nth time. There are still some things in it that make me stop and think, that even irritate me, I would say, but what tone, what exactness of tone! You should reread it, Seguin. Truly a master, a master of French prose." He had sat down opposite Pierre, who noticed that he was still wearing slippers. His face was pale but smiling.

"And the infinitive clause," Pierre said.

Lautier's face brightened. "You remember? But who, today, would dare teach a class on that? And why? Because he would be afraid of boring the youngsters! Did I bore you?"

Without waiting for Pierre's answer, he went into the kitchen and came back carrying two glasses in one hand, in the other an uncorked bottle, which he set down carelessly. The cat opened its eyes. "Did I scare you, Oscar?" he said. Pierre smiled.

"Tell me frankly," said Lautier. "Was I a tyrant?"

"No," said Pierre.

But once again Lautier was not listening. "I never asked for your opinion, true, but that's what a teacher is! Someone who shouldn't try to please."

He sat down and filled the two glasses, handed one to Pierre, and drank a mouthful of the other. "Would you have preferred something different?"

"No," said Pierre. "This is fine."

"You see," said Lautier, "I have a grandniece at Alençon, and they invited me to spend last Christmas with them, no, the one before. They have a two-year-old child, a devil! But they're constantly asking him 'what he wants to do this afternoon.' At the age of two! 'What he wants for lunch!' At the age of two! He doesn't want anything, the poor kid, he cries, he throws tantrums. What else would you expect? But," he added after a silence, "it's the same with adolescents. *Mutatis mutandis.*

"*Mutatis mutandis,*" Lautier went on, "because nothing is harder than making choices at that age, when one knows nothing. That is the cost of one's intellectual development"—he pronounced the two *l*'s separately—"one's intel-lectual development. What a young man needs is for someone else to choose for him, for someone to show him the way, someone who knows better than he does, at that time of his life, what is suitable for him. Afterwards there will always be time to choose, because someone will have given him the means to choose. At least," he concluded with a sigh, "someone will have tried. Wouldn't you like to sit in the armchair?" he added abruptly.

"No," said Pierre, "but please go ahead."

"No, thank you," said Lautier. "I sit there all day, with that creature on my knees, and the days are long. You see, I'm not sitting there and he's cross with me, he's sulking. Are you sulking, Oscar?"

The room smelled of dust, cat, unwashed clothes. In the hallway Pierre noticed a closed door. That was where it was, he thought. Now everything had been tidied up, the bed made. Where did he sleep? On this cold sofa, no doubt.

Lautier had stood up. "Coffee?"

"I'd love some," said Pierre, who had a headache from drinking rosé at three in the afternoon.

The cat mewed, stretched, and followed Lautier into the kitchen as soon as it heard the clatter of pots and the sound of a dish rattling.

Pierre picked up a pencil from the floor and put it on the table. "That animal!" said Lautier, coming back into the room. "What he likes best of all is to take his paw and sweep things off the table. It used to be my pipe, but I don't smoke anymore. When it isn't my pencils, it's my glasses. I have to search and search for them."

Pierre crushed some paper into a little ball and threw it at the cat, who pushed it around with a gentle paw, then flattened its ears and began to play. "So you're not all used up yet," said Lautier with delight. "Just look at that, will you? An old creature like that, almost fifteen years old!"

Steam rose from the coffee. Pierre set down his cup and gazed silently at his hand as it rested on the table.

"Well?" Lautier said softly. "I don't suppose you came to see me just to hear me talk about my cat or the infinitive clause?"

"No," said Pierre, and felt suddenly very embarrassed. The cat had jumped up onto Lautier's knees, and Lautier was gently running his hand down its fur with a familiar gesture. The animal responded by lifting its chin and thrusting its chest out.

"No," Pierre said again. Behind Lautier beautiful china pieces were arranged in a glass case, which Pierre had not noticed when he first walked in.

"What's wrong?" asked Lautier. "Do you mind if I speak frankly? You don't look very well."

"I don't know what to do," said Pierre.

"What to do?"

"Yes, with myself."

"I went through that when I was about forty," said Lautier.

"I'm thirty-seven," said Pierre.

"How young you are," said Lautier. "When I was thirty," he continued, "I thought I had a vocation as a scholar, I even thought I had a talent for letters, as we like to call them." ("One cannot have a great soul . . ." thought Pierre.) "I soon lost my illusions, put my meager attempts away in a drawer— though I must say I never threw them out. Never reread them, either," he added with a smile. "And then I was offered that position teaching the first-year preparatory class at R. I must say—how strange these words sound today!—that I experienced the greatest joys of my life there. But all the same, when I was forty I went through a bad period, an empty period."

Pierre felt grateful to Lautier for not making him talk. He also thought Lautier was neglecting to mention that his wife had become ill around that time.

"I had the feeling I had gone beyond something, or had let my chance at something slip out of my hands—really, those stupid, all-too-convenient things one tells oneself in order to disguise the truth from oneself, rather than admit one hasn't missed anything, one has done exactly what one was supposed to do, what one was capable of doing."

Pierre shook his head.

"I'm not saying this for your sake. At thirty-seven you're still young, you can still get hold of yourself. But I beg you— no bitterness, and especially no self-deception! There's a person inside us who knows much better than we do what is right for us: as a general rule, whether we like it or not, it is this person we obey. And if we later find that our destiny was only a mediocre one, it was still meant to be ours, no doubt about that."

"It isn't that," said Pierre.

"Of course," said Lautier, "no two cases are ever alike! And I tell you, you're still young."

"No," said Pierre. "It's my private life, as they call it."
Lautier's face had imperceptibly closed.
"I married young, you know."
"I know," said Lautier, "and, if you don't mind my saying
so—though I was no doubt wrong—at the time I thought you
were in quite a hurry."
"I did the right thing," said Pierre. "We have a thirteen-
year-old boy and a little girl. We're very happy. But . . ." He
paused, then plunged on. "But I met another woman. There
it is, it's all about that, I don't know what to do anymore. I
don't know why I'm telling you this, either."
"Recently?" inquired Lautier. This question, asked more
out of embarrassment and politeness than any true curiosity
or perspicacity, soothed Pierre.
"No," said Pierre, "almost five years ago." Lautier's face no
longer radiated the same warmth, the same attention. I'm
boring him, Pierre thought, or shocking him. "I'm tiring you,"
he said.
"No," said Lautier. "Is she . . . married too?"
Pierre thought of the housing project and the nurse's hand
on his belt as she unbuckled it. No, he would not mention
that. "She isn't married," he said. "She's very young. She
works in the library, she's a librarian—an archivist, as they
call them now."
Lautier shrugged his shoulders. "People will say anything.
The word *librarian* expresses the idea perfectly. Are people
ashamed of books now?"
"She's only twenty-six," said Pierre.
"I see," said Lautier, and remained silent. Pierre felt he had
to go on. "I never thought this sort of thing would happen to
me. I thought I was protected, protected by our way of living
and by . . ." He hesitated. "By my wife's trust in me."
"Naturally, you've talked to her about this?"
"No," said Pierre. "She still trusts me."
Night was falling. Lautier pulled a cord, and the ceiling
lamp went on. Then he stood up, walked around to the back

of his chair, and rested his arms on it, bending toward Pierre. "Look," he said, "it may surprise you to hear this, but I have not really lived. Not in the sense you mean. I'm listening to you, but I know nothing about such matters."

Pierre went on. "Her name is Laure—as you see, I've never left the realm of literature."

But Lautier was not listening to him. "For twenty years I was content to be the . . . companion of a sick woman. She was demanding and bitter, and not without reason. We had had a little girl, who died from diphtheria at the age of one. After that . . ."

"Please excuse me," said Pierre, "I shouldn't have bothered you like this."

Lautier went on. "I never looked beyond my life here." Suddenly the declining sun shone in on them. "I lived here, among my books, I looked to them for everything. I lived in a sort of companionship with the great works of literature. This may have alienated me from everything else, but it also took the place of everything else for me, gave me the strength, the desire, to . . . to go on. Once . . . once . . . I want to tell you something." He sat down. "One day I had to go up to Paris. I hadn't been there for thirty years, since I was in school. All the people I had admired then were dead, there were even streets named after them! And I also saw that no one was reading them anymore. It was then, as I looked up at one of those street names, that I understood how happy I was to have stayed away from it all."

Pierre gazed at him. He was a little irritated. "I really love her."

"All right," said Lautier, and added, though without much conviction, "All right, be brave, leave your family, marry the young woman. After all, she hasn't done anything to deserve this."

"I really love her," Pierre repeated. Then he shrugged his shoulders. "In my wife's eyes," he said, "I'm . . . an adult, someone with plans, a future, some talent, perhaps. If she were to learn about this, she would be, more than anything else—how shall I put it?—disappointed. Yes, disappointed. As if she had found out, for instance—" He stopped just in time. He had almost said, "that I had begun to drink." Instead, he said, "that I was stealing from supermarkets."

CHAPTER 22

LAUTIER was playing with his spoon in his empty cup and
no longer looking at Pierre, who continued, with some effort,
"Annie is—how shall I put it?—so innocent! I mean about
that sort of thing."

"And what about the other . . . young woman?" asked
Lautier. "She probably thinks you're unhappy, that you made
a mistake? That's what they usually think in these cases."

"She doesn't," said Pierre. "She doesn't think anything. She
loves me. She's waiting for me."

Lautier's face had closed again. "Women wait for men to
marry them," he said. "And they are entirely right, we have

nothing better to do, we are nothing compared to them. Except that one can't marry two women."

"Not at the same time, no," said Pierre.

"That's not what I meant," said Lautier. "Not even one after the other."

"I would have to be free again," said Pierre, "magically free. That's how she . . . how Laure sees things. Magically free, without having to leave anyone, without having to hurt anyone. But I can't."

"No," said Lautier, "you can't. I have always mistrusted physical love, it asks too much of us. We have only one body, therefore only one soul: we must recognize this."

"But I'm not what is known as a libertine."

"Of course not, but for me to have lived as you do—I was never able to do that—would have required a strength or a lack of awareness that I did not have."

"I don't have those things either," said Pierre. "To everyone else, at least everyone who knows about it, I'm a divided man, a man leading 'a double life.' But it isn't true. With each of them, in each part of my life, I am whole—myself, entirely whole. Like those pictures in which the background forms one image and the foreground another, and the images keep shifting." He was becoming confused. Then he thought of another image: "Or in photography, the positive and the negative of the same man."

"You can see I'm right," said Lautier, "but what's the good of telling you? I repeat, I know nothing about these things, I haven't lived. But I have no regrets about it."

Time was passing. Pierre felt he should be going. "Please forgive me," he said. "I'm ashamed of unburdening myself like this, letting you know how weak I am."

Lautier shook his head. "Think of me: everyone saw me as an admirable person, a man who had sacrificed himself. That wasn't true. Not at all. I was perfectly happy here"—then he gestured with his head toward the other part of the apartment—"and there. One must be patient. Patient," he repeated. For the first time he laid his hand on Pierre's arm. "But can one say such things to an ardent young man?"

Out in the street again, Pierre wondered, Am I an ardent young man? He shrugged his shoulders and pulled up his scarf, shivering. It was almost completely dark outside.

Late the same evening Pierre tried to call Laure. But she was already in bed, sound asleep: by the time she got to the phone, he had already hung up. She thought it had probably been Pierre. Back in bed, eyes open in the dark, she did some calculating: during that whole month of January she had seen Pierre only six times. Even counting generously, that added up to a little less than fifteen hours in all. In ten years, she thought, they would have spent about two months together. This calculation discouraged her, but she went back to sleep anyway.

Pierre remained standing in the dark for a moment near the silent telephone. Then he sat down at the table and put his head in his hands. Electric light fell over the dining room, the magazines on the couch, his son's little cars. After a moment the door opened. "Can't you sleep?" asked Annie.

"Yes," said Pierre, "I'm coming." And he stood up and went back to the bedroom with her, after turning off the hall light.

That night Pierre had two dreams. In the first he was in Saint-Saturnin, his grandparents' village. It was night, the moon shone bright on the streets and gave them a cold, menacing look. All the doors were closed, the shutters fastened. An old man was coming toward him, leaning on a cane. As he approached, Pierre saw his face: it was extremely delicate and still young, bathed in a strange light that illuminated his features, his hollow eye sockets, his ecstatic smile, even though the source of the light was behind him. Pierre woke up sweating.

Then he dreamed about Lautier:

"I spoke to your wife," said Lautier, putting down his coffee cup. "She agrees to everything."

"So she knows?" asked Pierre.

"Of course," said Lautier. "I didn't tell her anything she didn't know already! Oh yes, and we talked about a good many other things, too!"

Pierre's heart was thumping. "Well, what?" And he looked at Lautier. "You have always been a model for me," he added.

Lautier burst out laughing. "A model!"

"I mean intellectually." He pronounced the two *l*'s separately, as Lautier did, and he repeated, "intel-lectually." Then he felt ashamed, fearing that Lautier might have noticed. He'll think I'm making fun of him, he thought. Pierre woke up with the impression that he had forgotten a large part of the dream.

Several days passed, and Pierre did not telephone again. His silence did not surprise Laure, who could think of various possible reasons for it and even imagined she shared them. A sort of ill-defined confidence tempered the pain of being separated, soothed the fear that he had decided to leave her. Actually, Pierre had not decided anything: he was simply not calling her.

At night Laure would look at herself for a long time in the full-length mirror in her bedroom, lifting her nightgown to uncover her belly and the tops of her thighs, seeing her body intact but sensing how it was imperceptibly aging—imperceptibly and uselessly. Then she would lower her nightgown and go to bed. She would fall asleep quickly.

All this time, by not telephoning, Pierre was already subjecting himself to her judgment of his silence, his absence, his "attitude of resignation," as he thought she would call it. Anticipating her severity, he accepted it in advance and even saw it as an occasion to manifest and strengthen his admiration for her. With a secret pride and a feeling of guilty, overwhelming happiness, he thought to himself, She is so completely there for me—forgetting that Laure had no obligation to be "there" for someone else at the same time, as he did. She had an "upright" notion of life—even her features seemed to suggest this, her eyes a little too close together and her hair low on her forehead—which consisted in rejecting "compromises"; it did not even occur to her that they might sometimes have to be overlooked.

Pierre himself was no more fond of compromises than she was, yet for him they were indispensable, since he could not keep his commitments to one woman except at the expense of those he had undertaken toward the other. He envied Laure her ability to breathe so effortlessly the rarefied air of purity, while his own life, it seemed to him, was governed by division and the establishment of makeshift truths. At times like these Pierre, guilty, unhappy, watched Laure get up out of their bed and—as in certain ancient Greek texts where a mortal sees the woman whose bed he has shared take on a terrifying appearance before his eyes, her face filling with a dazzling light and her body growing to gigantic proportions—cover with a bathrobe the cold, merciless forms of an allegory of total abandon. In reality, however, Laure would be on the verge of tears and doing her best to hide it.

Laure's cruelty was torture; her gentleness, her indulgence even worse. Because whatever he did, Pierre felt he was not doing something he should or could have done. If he left earlier than he had on other occasions, he felt he was in the wrong; if he stayed longer, he was showing Laure that on those occasions he had been in a greater hurry to leave her, or more compliant with the demands of his family. Either way he clearly demonstrated that he was not free to do as he wished. All at once the scope of his actions would shrink, diminish— and Pierre sensed the indeterminate space that made them possible growing smaller and smaller every day. A sudden desire to work or read would occur at the very moment he had to leave to meet Laure or pick up his little girl at the pool or drive Bruno to the doctor. Every part of his life was regulated, predetermined. There was Laure, of course—but there were also student conferences and teachers' meetings, dinners at home or with friends, the children's afternoons. The slightest change in his daily schedule would have not only upset Laure but also risked attracting his family's attention, arousing suspicion—"Why are you at home this afternoon, Papa?" his children would say, for instance. And when he actually found a free hour in which he could "escape" to see Laure, as he had used to do at the beginning of their relationship, he did not: he remained sitting at his table, unhappy, his courage failing, scanning the same page of a book ten times over without understanding it, knowing very well that by staying at home alone he was losing both the happiness of seeing Laure and the benefit of having sacrificed something for his family that they would never be aware of.

Despite this, when they saw each other again in February after a timid phone call to Pierre—Laure believing her attitude still had to be one of wariness and mistrustful observation, Pierre unhappy, dissatisfied, and sure he would continue to be—everything started up again. It was possible for everything to resume, what they had together was not over. And it was as though, without their knowledge and almost against their will, their "understanding," rather than faltering, dying down, had chosen to blaze up anew—or, to use an image that may be more correct, was like a seed that, tossed out at random, with barely any soil, no water, just a little sun, inexplicably rises as a green stalk between two dry stones. Love had returned, and with it complete confidence, entailing the certain prospect of unhappiness, but one so circumscribed, so familiar, that it was nothing very frightening, nothing unforeseeable or not already experienced.

These were their halcyon days, these winter days in which, according to legend, Zeus calmed the tempest so that Halcyon, the kingfisher, could lay her eggs on the sea: a sort of miraculous springtime in the midst of winter, an island, an oasis.

Even the temperature outdoors rose: twice Pierre came to see Laure at three o'clock wearing a light jacket, his collar open. He brought flowers from a florist.

"You make me think of summer," Laure said. But it was better not to dwell on summer.

"It's true," Pierre said, "I long for the warm weather, open windows." Then, coming closer to Laure: "But with you I want to be shut up indoors." He drew the curtains and switched on the bedside lamp. And Laure, turning away from the weak sun that tried to force its way in through the blinds, had a brief pang of guilt for having violated a natural law by shutting herself in with Pierre; then she looked at Pierre's face, felt his hand rest on her, and stopped thinking about it.

Pierre returned every evening during those weeks, and Laure did not ask any questions. Nor did either of them mention the preceding weeks in which they had been apart, or the silent acts of cowardice each had committed against the other. Pierre simply said, one day, "I've neglected you, my darling."

She looked at him in silence. It had rained that day, and Pierre's damp hair was clinging to his forehead. Neglected her? "I called once or twice, but you weren't here. Or you didn't feel like speaking to me." His jacket was damp, too; he smelled of wool and hay. She remarked on this.

"More like a wet dog," Pierre said, and took off his jacket. Already standing close to him, now she slipped her arm around his waist and leaned her face against him: under his shirt she could smell his warm skin, his familiar smell. "Come quickly," he said. "I have wanted you so much, all these nights."

A little later they were lying side by side, face down; as always, the light cast by the little bedside lamp soothed them. Pierre's watch ticked close to Laure's ear. For once this reminder of time passing did not bother her: wasn't everything all right, since they were together again? For his part Pierre felt cleansed of all worry, all uncertainty, all suspicion: he had even forgotten the distress that had driven him to seek out Lautier, his useless confidences. He turned toward Laure and, resting his lips against her skin, breathed in deeply: "I love the way you smell," he said, "oh, I love your smell." He sat up and looked at her.

"Don't look at me that way," she said.

"I will," said Pierre. "Open your eyes. Look." He was kneeling at the foot of the bed, and forced her to open her legs. She resisted.

"No," said Pierre, "let me." With his eyes still fixed on her, Pierre leaned down slowly and finally buried his face between Laure's thighs. His hands, grasping her hips, seemed icy to her, and she put her own hands over them as if to warm them. But from that moment on, the lower part of her body, which they were both holding, seemed separate from the rest of her, foreign, subject to its own brutal law. She was relieved when he came back to her and she smelled her own smell on her lover's damp chin as they both drifted off to sleep.

CHAPTER 23

LAURE opened her eyes again in the room's artificial twilight and looked at her lover's muscular shoulder near her own, his trusting mouth half-open against the pillow. One of Pierre's legs was lying across hers, almost on her stomach. She caressed the top of his thigh softly, so as not to wake him. Pierre's right arm was pinning her down to the bed. Playfully she tried to lift it, then gave up. Six o'clock chimed. They could stay this way a little longer. She had just about fallen back asleep when something stopped her: a sort of chill, a pain, a regret. Did it come from being with Pierre again? From their having resumed the succession of days, the bondage of the constraints they had to endure? Maybe.

Thinking about it, however, she felt that it was something

else, something that had happened when Pierre, without lifting his eyes from her, had grasped her by the hips and leaned down toward her. At that moment she had seen Pierre change into a different person, someone rough, determined, and— yes, this was the word for it—violent. A stranger had appeared between the time when they lay side by side and the time, later, when Pierre, awake, dressed again, lingered near her for a moment as he always did, tenderly caressing her cheeks, gently saying goodbye to her: a stranger who was not only Pierre—his body, his gestures, his features—but her own body as well. Sometimes she had complained about that violence, had moaned, "You're hurting me," and Pierre, who probably saw the meaning hidden behind her words, had answered, "Yes, I'm doing it on purpose, I *want* to hurt you." But it seemed to her that today she had witnessed for the first time the merry, obscene, and brutal game their two bodies played in sly harmony before her own eyes and as though without her participation.

But wasn't it Pierre's fault? Every time, as soon as they went to bed together, Pierre began behaving in a way that was at once deliberate and ecstatic, as though in the grip of an immutable determination it seemed he must yield to, having no other choice. As though physical love were a duty, a sorrow, a curse, she thought, comparable to the struggles of a suffering body, the writhing of a snake as it sloughed off its old skin. Sometimes an involuntary motion of Laure's would annoy Pierre: he would push her away impatiently or else pull her toward him again without her knowing why, as though he were obeying laws unfamiliar to her, as though he were the more skilled, trained partner in a complicated game or dance whose moves no one quite understood.

At the same time Pierre, despite the confidence of his motions, seemed as subject as she was to an invisible law, from the moment when he found himself alone with her and saw her naked on the bed. From that moment whatever the two of them might want no longer counted: in them, through them, something else was speaking, something alien even to them. Weren't they simply responding to nature's imperious law— by which a woman had to be taken and impregnated at all costs? But even if they had been driven solely by a need to reproduce, such activity, such virtuosity, such fatigue would hardly have been necessary.

Having sex—an expression she never used, even to herself— suddenly seemed to her to be something overwhelming and terrible, like being born or dying, a difficult and dangerous passage, the sooner done with the better. During this exchange, which resembled a struggle, a duel, more than anything else, they always remained separate; deceived by the welcoming warmth of the room where they had thought it possible to come together, they were in fact thrust back into the cruel and solitary mechanics of a pleasure as crude as a sports event. Each had set to work, sweating, excited, with a rather grim mixture of technique and animal hunger. Especially Pierre, who was now fast asleep, exhausted. She turned to him and gently rested her lips against his shoulder with admiration and pity and the desire to tell him that they would certainly have succeeded just the same, without his muscles straining, his expression tense, his forehead sweating, his chest heaving, his heart pounding. With that thought, she drifted back to sleep.

And when he woke up a few minutes later, Laure was looking at him with a renewed tenderness, the way one looks at a sick person who has peacefully fallen asleep after suffering a dangerous attack. She stroked his forehead. Nothing bad could happen to him as long as she was there; wasn't she there to lighten the burden he carried—not only his family and the parceling out of his time but also the hard law of the species, of the body? She hugged him to her, her eyes against his.

He woke up slowly, looked back at her. "You're making me cross-eyed," he said. "What time is it? I think I fell asleep." But he did not get up. He closed his eyes again. "It's so nice to sleep with you," he added. She stroked his hand. What else could happen to them, what sorrows could afflict them beyond those they had already experienced? Other people might be afraid of disorder, a loss of confidence, the assault of a jealous rage, arguments, the burden of worry. But not them; their future was clearly indicated, patterned on their past. "Like the dead," she thought—she had read this somewhere—"who are at least relieved of their fear of dying."

Because the reading room was being reorganized, Laure had much more work to do than usual, but she went to the library every morning with a sort of joyful briskness that had something to do with the fact that she and Pierre were together again. Sometimes they even met as they used to, on the Place du Vieux Théâtre; it was hardly possible for them to sit together, and they did not, but they would exchange a few words and could not help smiling and looking into each other's eyes constantly. Pierre, seeing Laure so happy, breathed more freely and became more cheerful himself. His family benefitted, too, because he was more open to proposals to play charades and take walks, and one rainy Sunday he even agreed to a game of cards, something he hated.

These signs might have aroused Annie's suspicion if anything could; but Pierre had been right when he told Lautier that "for Annie these things simply don't exist." Not that it couldn't happen to other people, like one of her coworkers at the office, a certain Fromanger, of whom she always spoke with an amusement quite free of any disapproval. For twenty years he had maintained "two households": now that he was a widower, he had broken completely with his mistress. Annie had smiled sympathetically as she told Pierre the story.

February was going by, the cold had not returned, and Pierre suggested an excursion out of town. They could even have lunch at an inn somewhere—why not? Laure found someone to take her place at work (though she did not like to do it), and on a Tuesday, since Pierre taught only every other

Tuesday, they found themselves alone together, surprised, in a landscape that was bare but softened by a premature spring. A few green shoots had appeared, birds were singing. If they turned and looked back, they could see the town in the distance like a Turner drawing, a bristling mass of church towers and roofs, though dominated now by factory chimneys to the east and farther off by a row of low-income apartment high-rises.

Pierre kept Laure close to him; he had caught hold of her hand and did not let go of it but squeezed it tenderly against his chest. Deep in the park was an inn, and that was where they had lunch. Neither of them dared count the days that had gone by since they had last eaten out together, and it was better not to. Laure was calm, and she was surprised to think she had so recently been worried and discouraged. She looked at her lover's beautiful, square hand resting decisively on the table, his massive shoulders in his blue tweed jacket. He was even wearing one of the scarves Laure had given him, which he always "forgot" to put on, perhaps to avoid embarrassing questions. He seemed to have caught cold: his eyes were red, and his voice was gravelly, though it cleared after a few swallows of wine. Laure could not stop smiling at him.

"Don't look at me like that," he said, "I can't eat anything. I want to touch you, right here in the restaurant, under the table." He had leaned forward, slid his hand under the tablecloth, and laid it on Laure's knee, stroking it tenderly. "Your legs are so smooth," he said.

"It's my stockings," Laure said simply.

They finished the bottle of wine with their cake, and Pierre ordered another glass while waiting for coffee. His eyes were shining. Behind them a few tables were occupied. A rather plump man was speaking emotionally to a middle-aged blond woman, who seemed to be listening to him without pleasure.

"I really have to get back to work," said Pierre. "No kidding this time. Last summer I was only fooling around, there was no sense in what I was doing."

Laure nodded.

"You agree," he said.

"Yes," said Laure. "Yes, I agree."

"I need you. I need you to encourage me." He stretched his hand across the table. "What I need is to give myself a subject and a time limit. It doesn't matter—three years, five. And the plan of writing a short book, not a dissertation. Of course, it could be a dissertation, too. Shall we walk around a little?"

They were the last ones there, and the maître d', who had been keeping a discreet eye on them for the last few minutes, brought the check, already made out, as soon as Pierre signaled.

Outside he took Laure's hand again and squeezed it against his chest. "Give me your hand, give me your hand," he said. But she had already given it to him. "You will help me, we will do research together."

At the other end of the park a small museum had been set up in the former stables of the château, which itself had been partially destroyed during the Revolution.

"Let's go in," said Pierre. "Would you like to? It's not that warm out."

"I'm not cold," said Laure.

At a table that stood perpendicular to the entrance a red-faced woman seemed to be dozing. She woke up and grumpily held out two tickets to them. "Start over there," she said, pointing vaguely into the room. "The upper floor's closed."

"What's upstairs?" asked Pierre.

"Temporary exhibits."

The small entryway had been decorated with posters showing pastel drawings, butterflies, giant crystals, and Maori masks. They walked into the room, and in the silence their footsteps echoed on the flagstones. Faded tapestries hung from the two largest walls. The closer one showed a woman with loose hair kissing the ground before a throne on which a king sat, surrounded by blue trees and warriors with faces framed in dark beards. The woman's breast spread generously from the embroidered bodice of a dress with a train.

"Esther," said Pierre. "That's Esther revealing to King Ahasuerus that she is Jewish and asking for mercy for her people. I've explained that story so often!" He seemed pleased.

"Where do these tapestries come from?" asked Laure.

"I don't know, probably from the château."

The caretaker had overheard them. "No, Monsieur," she said. "Goodness no, everything there was ransacked."

"During the Revolution?"

"Yes, but the château wasn't torn down until 1820. This was a legacy from the last owner, who had a mansion in town. When he died, they opened a museum here, in the old stables. And His Honor the Mayor had other things brought here."

An ornate clock on a spiral-legged table chimed three.

"I'm suffocating," said Pierre. "A moment ago I was cold, now I'm too hot. I feel as if I don't have any room to breathe." He unbuttoned his coat and put his arm around Laure's shoulders.

"How the colors have faded," he said. "Imagine when these beautiful pale pinks were reds and these trees were a brilliant green."

"I like them better this way," said Laure.

Pierre continued, without looking at the pictures, "You see, I should have gone away, traveled, taken a job in a foreign country. In Italy, for instance. There I really could have worked."

Between two pictures the park came into view again with its beautiful trees, trunks glistening with dampness, and a very bright lawn.

"Yes, for instance I might have studied painting. I realize I love it. Not the painting you see in museums but the painting in little churches, the frescoes."

Laure had walked up to another wall. She pointed to a picture that seemed very dark because the daylight was coming in behind it. "Look," she said. "That's us."

CHAPTER 24

AGAINST a background of very dark forest, darkened even more by layers of varnish, stood two naked figures: a man was leaning toward a woman, holding out to her a branch loaded with fruit. Their bodies were very white, cold. Tiers of mountains behind them rose to the horizon in lofty, deep-blue profiles. An animal was lying at the man's feet, teeth shining in its red muzzle.

"What is it a picture of?" asked Laure.

"I don't know," said Pierre. "You can't see anything."

He maneuvered the window's inner shutter, and as soon as the shadow vanished, the tiny picture burst out in bright light.

"Is it Adam and Eve?" asked Laure.

"Where do you see Adam and Eve?" asked Pierre.

"I don't know, isn't she holding an apple?"

Pierre read aloud: " 'Allegory of Love, School of Patinir.' Aha!" he added.

Then he turned to Laure. "Really, listen to me. I swear I have to get back to work."

"Of course you do," said Laure quietly.

"Have you read *Lily in the Valley?*"

"I don't remember."

"It has nothing to do with this picture, even though . . . But I think of it often, it has a magnificent subject. It's the story of Mme. de Mortsauf, a middle-aged woman—or rather, she couldn't be more than thirty, but for that time . . . A young man, Félix de Vandenesse, is in love with her, and she loves him, too. But she doesn't dare admit it to herself, because she's married and has children."

Laure began to feel upset. But he went on, apparently without noticing, ". . . toward the end of the book she is ill and dying. During her death throes she hears women returning from harvesting grapes and singing as they go by. At that point she is seized by a sort of fury, a regret, at dying without having known what life was, without having been able to take hold of it."

Again Laure thought of them: loving each other, had they been able to "take hold of life," free themselves of constraints, conventions?

"You're not listening to me," said Pierre in the tone of an irritated child.

"Of course I am," said Laure. From the entrance they heard, faintly, some piece of popular music. The caretaker was playing the little radio she had turned off when they came in.

"I need you to listen to me," Pierre said. "I need you to approve of me. You're the only one I can tell this to."

They had stopped in front of a beautiful fireplace, which obviously had been added to the room. A painted figurine stood on the mantelpiece.

"She yielded," Pierre continued, "to an imagined duty, she never experienced the physical side of life, and now she is dying. Perhaps she even suspects that there is no life after death. And so she has lost everything."

Laure's attention was drifting again. How does he see himself? she wondered. How does he see us? Pierre's voice, as he continued, seemed distant to her, rang false: "Whereas those simple, primitive harvesters know, as in a dionysiac allegory, a bacchanal, the certainties of the joys of the flesh." He had drawn close to Laure.

An imagined duty? she wondered. An *imagined* duty? What did that mean? But if he really thought that . . . She became muddled, confused, she backed off from what she was thinking. All she said was "Yes."

"But good, pure love is not within her reach," Pierre continued. "The kind of love that brings salvation. Her despair is a blasphemy, the absence of love is a blasphemy."

A picture hanging near the fireplace showed a woman stretched out luxuriously on a bed, her head in profile, her body facing forward. She was turning away from an old, black-skinned, wrinkled servant woman with severe features who was pouring a stream of pale-blue water over her hand. Behind them a raised curtain revealed an open window and a forest.

"You're beautiful, like her," Pierre said. "Like hers, your face is severe, but your hips are broad and fecund." He was silent, then said, "I like talking to you. I know you understand me, encourage me. With you my plans have some substance. Do you believe in them just a little? You don't seem to, and that upsets me. I used to go to the library every day, I would pretend to be working, and from time to time I would slyly lift my eyes from the page, like some depraved schoolboy, and stare at your legs."

"Depraved," said Laure. "Thanks."

He put his arm around her waist, pulled her close to him,

and kissed her neck. "Are you too hot?" he asked. "I love your neck when it's damp with sweat. Oh yes, yes, here, right now." He pushed her away. They laughed.

"Did you see the little dog?" Laure asked. On the fur covering the bed a flat-muzzled pug was baring its teeth at the black woman.

"That's a dog?" said Pierre. "What a monstrosity."

"If I were writing a dissertation," Laure said, "I would write about animals in pictures. Dogs, cats, lions."

Pierre continued to gaze sadly at the beautiful naked woman with her straight nose and her headband woven into her golden hair.

"We won't make love anymore. We won't have time anymore, and besides, all the great scholars are chaste. And they smoke pipes, their clothes have an unbearable stink that repels women." Then he went on, more seriously, "I'll be forty soon."

"In three years," Laure said.

"Yes. That's not long. When I look back, what do I see? Nothing. I thought about it this summer: there's nothing to show for what I do, it all disappears. I'm not like Lautier, I don't believe in my vocation."

"Lautier? Do you still see him from time to time?"

"No, or rather, yes, I saw him the other day at the market."

It's the same for me, Laure thought. What do I have to show for what I do every day at the library? Does it really have any importance? Not really. For Pierre yes, not for me.

Some time passed, they looked at one or two pictures without seeing them, and some plates and dishes from the time of Napoleon III in a glass case.

"What a hodgepodge," Pierre said. "It's all rather ordinary stuff."

"Yes, but the room is pretty."

"Sometimes I wonder. I wonder what I'm really worth. I'm very afraid of being someone who 'has plans,' or rather, someone who once 'had plans.' "

Laure had stopped in front of a small, very bright canvas. Standing near a broken Greek column, a slender young boy was playing the flute. Behind him were ruins, a temple, and mountains that glowed with light; the boy's eyes were strangely dreamy, in contradiction to the lascivious position of his body, which was already mature, and his lips, which seemed to smile around the pipe.

Now the woman at the small table had taken some crocheted work out of her purse. What was her life like? Laure wondered. "Look at her," said Pierre, who had followed Laure's glance. "Spending all day surrounded by these pictures. Do you think she's ever looked at them? Never."

"Maybe not, but still, it matters that she's surrounded by them. Like me, surrounded by books all day."

"Yes, but you read books."

"Not many. I don't know what's the matter with me, but I seem to be reading more and more slowly. Six pages takes an eternity."

She looked more attentively at the woman. This was a living woman, she thought, the only living, flesh-and-blood woman among all these women in the pictures on the walls, or in the books Pierre was talking about. By doing this work, she had no doubt avoided more demeaning jobs—as a factory worker, a packer. Here she had found work that was restful, rather monotonous, but in a well-heated and clean room. Laure did not agree with Pierre at all. Yes, no doubt this woman was quite unfamiliar with all the things around her, she did not care, she came into contact rather haphazardly, involuntarily, with these vestiges of a time which she knew nothing about, in the same way she would have watched over an ill person. The emphatic gestures of the woman being bathed, the beautiful Esther baring her bosom, the tender couple nude in the forest, the radiant adolescent—all were as alien to her as the country and the period in which these pictures had been painted. And what of it? she wondered. Did she, Laure, really need that mythical landscape of mountains, that dreamy mist, that melancholy light, that blue which Pierre seemed to find so beautiful? These things did not speak to her, either.

Laure suddenly felt a great sympathy for the woman with the gloomy, torpid face. These gestures, these colors, these characters turning their eyes and their beautiful white arms toward the sky were celebrating something from which both of them had been excluded from time immemorial.

" 'Jakob van Hayden,' " she read below a picture. "Do you know him?"

"No," said Pierre. "The name means nothing to me."

A groom was tying some horses to a boundary-post while a young man in doublet and feathered cap crept up on a group of bathing women. " 'The nymph Aristaeus,' " Laure continued, " 'surprised while bathing by Apollo.' Apollo with a plumed hat?" she asked.

"Aristaeus," said Pierre, "from what I remember, was a shepherd from whom Apollo had stolen his bees, but I could be wrong."

"There's a bee in the corner," said Laure.

"Keep it for your dissertation," said Pierre.

Close to each other again, they were filled with a sudden warmth, and Pierre leaned over to kiss Laure. The woman had started her music going again, and as they passed in front of her again, she turned it down as far as possible without turning it off completely.

"She seems like a good woman," said Pierre. "But how bored she must be." The stealthy music surrounding her seemed like a demand, stubborn and strong, like a voice that insisted on recalling the existence of a world in which there was neither art nor beauty nor books nor pictures but—this was evident in the furious glance the caretaker hurled at the door—a constant desire to be protected from drafts.

I'm just like her, thought Laure. Yet as they left, she took one more look at the enigmatic couple in the picture, so fragile, so naked against the cold background of the blue mountains.

After nodding to them, the caretaker had gone back to her

crocheting, following the directions for a complicated design out of a folded newspaper. The young singer's voice had fallen silent, succeeded by a banal tune that Laure did not recognize. In the car Pierre hugged her. "We could even work together. I would leave my notes in your place. It would be one more secret we shared." Once again she resented his use of the word.

Now Pierre set to work with a true assiduity that surprised him even more than it did her. He rediscovered the pleasure of having a precise daily routine, of working with notecards, of underlining passages in his reading. He had left notes, notebooks, rough drafts at Laure's place; he went back to them with a childlike joy at accepting a constraint that did not cost him anything. He arrived every afternoon around four, sometimes before Laure, who would find him sitting at the round table, his tie loosened, an anxious expression on his face amid clouds of cigarette smoke. "Get thee behind me, Satan," he would say. "Don't tempt me." But he would stop anyway, for a cup of tea, and then it would be too late to go back to work. "It all seems less and less clear to me. But that's a good sign, it's a sign that I'm making progress."

Toward the middle of March, not long before Easter vacation, there was a rather unfortunate incident at the school, an argument between the headmaster and a young philosophy professor during which—or just after returning to his office: stories differed—the headmaster had a mild heart attack. He recovered very quickly, but the school split into two factions: According to certain people (though not all of them were witnesses), the young man's attitude had been arrogant, "intolerable." He was also a rather untidy person, they added; "his nails are always dirty," said Mme. Feider, the English professor. The others had taken his side because they did not like the headmaster, an unbearable man, a busybody, standing guard on the front steps every morning at eight sharp, watching to see who came in late. "Monsieur Timonnier!" he would say, "stop in to see me later when you have a moment." Timonnier was a good man. He rode to school on his motorbike and did not always remember to take the clips off his pant legs before entering the classroom. "Late again, Monsieur Timonnier?" the headmaster would say. "My bike broke down, sir," Timonnier would answer. "I had to stop and clean the spark plugs on the way here."

Though he sided with the second group, Pierre sent a get-well card to the hospital, expressing his hopes for the headmaster's "quick recovery." He also tried to invite the young professor to dinner as a public sign of his support. But twice his colleague answered with evasive excuses, rushing to take the train back to Paris, so he gave up.

Nevertheless, the incident affected the philosopher's career at R.: when one or two pupils were "unmanageable" in the class that followed his, no one was very surprised, any more than when several of his pupils failed the first round of exams. One of the two gym teachers, Mme. Groulty, who had a son in that class, "didn't want to say anything." The young professor asked to be transferred, but his request was not granted. The teachers' lounge and the trimester student conferences were also in an uproar. Laurencin, according to Mme. Rougier, had been wonderful and had shut him up; no one knew why, but she had stopped speaking to Pierre.

Pierre was tired, anyway. It was the end of the trimester, he was overwhelmed with papers to correct, conferences; and he could not shake his cold. He sneezed in the street in front of the school—he remembered Babeth's red eyes and husky voice the first time he had driven her home—and during his classes (he gave two hours of detention to one pupil he caught counting his sneezes: that had never happened to him before).

And the atmosphere in the school, he told Laure, was thick enough to cut with a knife, he was "up to here with it." He looked nostalgically at his pile of notes, which he no longer touched. "After Easter," he said. Laure poured him another cup of tea and gave him an aspirin. He sneezed again. "I feel so good with you, but I can imagine what I must look like! I

have to take off. Laumonnier"—that was the headmaster—
"has slapped us with a meeting at five-thirty to discuss the
senior theses."

"The senior theses?" asked Laure. "I thought you weren't
reading any this year!"

"Unfortunately, I am. You know I had to take over a part
of Gabert's work."

He took a few files home so that he could go on working
after dinner or on Sundays, at least. But when the table was
cleared and calm returned, he was tired, drowsy, the television
was on, and its gentle purring invited him to be lazy.

He stood up anyway and closed the door of his study, where
he had set himself up, but felt like a child being forced to
work while he hears his brothers and sisters playing at a distance. He would go back into the living room, and Annie
would prepare him a hot toddy—something Laure always refused to do: "When you have a fever," she would say, "alcohol
is very bad for you. They tell you specifically to avoid it."
Then he would sit down for a moment and watch the movie.
The theme he was looking for would slip between his fingers,
he would review titles—but the idea itself had lost its substance. Yes, everything he wanted to say had already been
said in a certain book, what else could he do but repeat it in
an inferior version? In the end this idea discouraged him. He
tried to talk about it with Annie, but clearly it did not interest
her. "Ah, I'm going to sneeze again," he would say. And he
would leave the room, because his attacks of sneezing irritated
her. "It must be an allergy," she would say, "take care of
yourself!"

In the first place, what did he have to say about impossible
love, whether his own or Mme. de Mortsauf's? What was he
championing—prisoner of a family he loved and of the sweet
images he came home to every evening, a child's bicycle aban-
doned on the grass, his little girl's tender kisses covering first
her dog's muzzle and then her father's face? His defeat was
even worse than the defeat killing his heroine. He shook him-

self. "Anyway, I'm not some romantic bourgeois—what a comparison! She was just an hysterical woman, that's all."

Nor was he a beaming, authoritarian "head of the family," a procreator proud of his line, he was simply trying to live his life. As for his love for Laure, it was not in the least a savage, violently disturbing impulse or an admirable revolt. It was something sweet, comforting—well, most of the time, anyway—and agreeable. And it was possible to preserve all that, together, as long as one agreed to be oneself: weak, sensual, submissive.

For her part, Laure saw clearly that Pierre "wasn't sticking to his work," as her father said of his painting. He would no doubt keep his notebooks and notes beside him all the rest of his life, just like her father with his canvases and brushes. Like her grandfather, who used to make napkin rings with a wood lathe. And she was almost relieved when she noticed that Pierre had permanently cleared all his notes out of her place and did not talk about them anymore. What he did "there," after all, was none of her business.

CHAPTER 25

PIERRE'S cold turned into bronchitis. He stayed in bed for several days at the end of March, and the first few times he went out he felt light-headed, fatigued, his legs like rubber. "You worry me, you look awful!" said Annie.

One evening, home from the bank, she remarked, "I spoke to Fournier, he suggested we go and stay in his house at Calvados, on the coast."

"You're getting to be pretty chummy with Fournier," Pierre said.

"Oh, if you met him you wouldn't talk that way. But never mind that. They don't use it in the winter, it's all ours if we want it. You could go off ahead of me by train, and I might be able to join you for Easter Sunday. Could you manage all by yourself for a week?"

"You bet! I'm an old hand with a boiled egg."

"Don't joke. You'd have to eat sensibly. You've been sick."

Pierre coughed.

"See? You've hardly begun to get well."

"I warn you," Fournier had said, "it isn't very big or very new."

Pierre left the twenty-sixth, without saying anything to Laure, without resorting to his usual excuses: "I wasn't very eager to do it," "it will be hard for me to call you," "vacations are always a bit of a chore for me." He arrived late in the afternoon, opened the kitchen, which smelled of mildew, and went upstairs to leave his suitcase in the bedroom with its sloping ceilings.

The next few hours were blissful. He went back out to eat fried fish at the port, walked under the arcades, and came back rather late, tired, to the little house with its tiny courtyard behind a scalloped gate and its low second story littered with summer clothes, a chaise longue, driftwood, and children's beach toys, amid a melancholy smell of old wallpaper, dampness, wood, and the sea.

The next morning he called Laure from a public phone booth. "You'll never guess where I am," he said.

She was in her office, a group of children had invaded the reading room. "I can't hear you very well," she said.

"What are you doing this week?"

"Well, I'm not sure I can take off. The woman I work with needs a few days with her children."

"Never mind her. Let's think of ourselves for once. I'm in Normandy."

She felt a twinge of pain, discouragement.

"A coworker of"—he hesitated—"a friend has lent us, has lent me his house. Do you want to come join me?"

"Yes," she said. "Explain it to me a little more clearly."

* * *

"I didn't want to tell you about it before," said Pierre, when she arrived. "I wasn't sure of anything, I was really sick, you know, I had a fever for two weeks."

But Laure was not listening. She was eager to explore the house. In the tiny kitchen, behind a cretonne curtain hanging from a string, she came upon some boxes of pebbles, pretty shells, and two dried starfish. "Look what I found," she said.

Despite Pierre's fatigue—the first few days he had trouble covering the distance from the house to the port and went to bed at nine o'clock—they took some long walks. Not having brought anything warm, they outfitted themselves at the seaside co-op with oilskins, scarves, woolen socks, and sailors' caps.

Two days went by, then a third. Early on the fourth day Laure began thinking about how they would soon be separating, though they had not talked about it; she had not dared ask Pierre if he would be going back with her or staying to wait for his family. In the midst of her happiness at waking up next to Pierre, walking out into the streets with him, strolling to the port arm in arm with him, lunching on crêpes with him, she felt stabs of pain, apprehension, worry. This Tuesday, this Wednesday together were so conspicuously more special than the days that would follow, which would adhere to the usual pattern instead of being made out of this precious substance. Every moment of the day thus prefigured a similar moment when they would no longer be together. And just as the idea of death looms up behind the delightful spectacle of a beautiful day—the sun shining straight down on the sea, a lane of trees filled with birdsong—Laure sometimes made calculations, reckonings, that drained her strength and more than once came close to spoiling their time together for her, as she counted up how many hours she had left with Pierre, how many dinners together, how many nights. Then she would forget it all.

They found a wounded gull on the beach and wanted to feed it. The wary bird tried to fly away when it saw them, took a few steps, turning its head sharply this way and that to see where the danger was coming from. "But we don't want to hurt you," said Laure. She broke open some shellfish with a stone and left them close to the bird. The next day she found it huddled in a crevice, but the shells were empty.

One night Pierre was sick. He tried to get up quietly so as not to wake her, but she heard him anyway. He walked in and out, shut himself up in the bathroom, and vomited for a long time. When he came back to bed, after spraying himself with eau de cologne, he was trembling violently. "I'm cold, I'm so cold," he said. She covered him up, snuggled against him to warm him, made him drink two glasses of hot lemonade. "It was the shellfish," he said. "I'm not a seagull— they're not good for me."

This episode redoubled their affection for each other. She had to go to the drugstore for him. He was really pale. But by evening he was feeling better, and in one of the few restaurants open in town they had a light dinner, face to face behind the narrow window, which was covered by rather ugly red-and-white-checked curtains. "Do you think a little wine would hurt?" he asked. And they walked back slowly through the main street. The shutters on the houses were closed, and on their walls were traces of brown rust like dried blood.

That night Pierre slept for hours. When he woke up, he felt completely well again. "Come on," he said, "let's have breakfast at the port."

They dressed and went out. The wind was still brisk, the sky clear, clean, cloudless, the seagulls crying loud.

They sat down at a table in the front. With the sun coming through the glass, it was almost hot. They gazed at each other tenderly. As they were preparing to pay the check, Pierre realized he had left his wallet back at the house.

"Oh dear," said Laure, "I don't have any money on me at all." This was one of the pleasant habits they had fallen into these days, as they were constantly together: only Pierre carried any money on him. "Shall I go back with you?" she asked. "No, stay here, have a cup of coffee. I'll run all the way, I'll be back in five minutes."

Outside he was struck once again by the beauty of the light. The boats were bobbing in the rising tide. The birds were shrieking. The sun shone on the rooftops. He had already gone up the main street and was turning into the Avenue des Bains when he saw his own car parked on the left side of the street. He stopped. Was it really his car? But there could be no doubt about it: strangely, he could not tear his eyes from the spot where he had scratched it recently against the garden gate, leaving a little green paint on it.

He moved toward the house. Annie was standing in the little garden. The gate was never locked. She had a large bag at her feet and looked excited. "It's so pretty!" she said. "What a pretty little house! Honey, I couldn't let you know in advance, but I finally did arrange to get away."

"But you told me you wouldn't be free until Sunday," Pierre said absurdly, as though he could still change the situation.

"Well," she said calmly, "as you see, it worked out otherwise."

Pierre was not listening. He felt all his energy directed toward a single end: first to stop Annie from going in, then to warn Laure. Obviously, he had to act quickly, or else Laure would begin to worry and come looking for him. One thought soothed him, though he felt ashamed of it: they did not know each other. His head ached, he felt like throwing up, he wished he were dead, he wished he could disappear, then and there, leaving a little spot on the sand and forgetting everything. His hands were trembling. The sun felt cold to him.

Annie was looking at him. "I'd like to go in. It's not exactly warm out here."

"Uh oh. You know what? I left my keys on the table in the café!" Later he wondered how he had managed to think up something so quickly.

"You were eating out?" asked Annie.

"Yes, it was easier. I'll go get them. I'll only be a moment." This was exactly what he had said when he left Laure.

"Is it far?" asked Annie.

"Pretty far," Pierre said, to dissuade her from coming, but she answered, "I'll drive you," and then, before Pierre had time to protest, changed her mind. "No, you take the car, I'll wait for you at the corner." ("At the corner" meant a rather untidy café that sold cigarettes and newspapers and smelled of pernod and stale tobacco.) "I'll have a cup of coffee to warm myself up."

Mechanically, Pierre groped in his pocket again: at the very bottom of it he felt a bill, and he breathed a sigh of relief. At least that was all right. He was about to leave Annie when another thought troubled him: there was Laure's car, right in front of the door! But how stupid of him, he realized—Annie had never seen it before. Of course, the license plate showed that the owner also lived in their district, but Annie never noticed things like that. "Here!" she said. "Take the keys!"

He went over to the car, recognizing the mess left by the children in the back seat, but his hands were trembling so hard that he tried twice before starting it up.

Laure was waiting for him outside, sitting on the stone edge of the jetty. "Back already!" she said. He had left the car a short distance away. "But what's that?" she added. "Did you drive?"

Pierre went inside to pay, came back out, took a deep breath, and grasped Laure by the arm. There was no time to break it to her gently. "Yes. My wife has arrived. I found her standing in front of the house."

"But you told me . . ." Laure said weakly.

"Yes, I know, but now we have to hurry."

Laure felt she was turning into a solid mass of indifference. She could not take her eyes off a large seagull that was clambering awkwardly onto a rock. It had a rust-spotted breast.

Is that our seagull? she wondered. The bird flew up, suddenly powerful, weightless.

"We have to hurry," Pierre said again.

"I never should have come," said Laure.

. . . Easy to say now that the damage is done, Pierre thought, but said only, "Listen. Here are the keys to the house. I'll go back and tell Annie that I've lost them and take her along with me to look for them. I'll make sure it takes some time, I'll distract her. Meanwhile you go in and tidy everything up, take everything out, and when you're finished . . ." He hesitated to say "go." Instead he said, "Throw the keys in the garden. I'll pretend to find them there when I come back."

When she did not move, he squeezed her arm. "Let's be quick. You can come along after me in five minutes. I'll be gone." His tone was so brusque and tense—as though he were afraid, Laure thought—that she burst into tears. "Don't cry, oh please don't cry, not now!" said Pierre, and there was more exasperation in his voice, even a kind of panic, than tenderness.

When he found Annie in the café, Pierre thought he saw the owner giving him a strange look, but the man was an alcoholic, always holding a drink—what could he have seen? He immediately led her off on a long, roundabout walk, from the little station, where he claimed he had bought cigarettes that morning, to the barber, and even to the port café, where of course no one had found his keys.

"Obviously not," the owner said.

"Why 'obviously'?" Annie asked.

"I don't know," said Pierre.

At noon he found the keys in the garden.

"They're in plain sight," said Annie. "Funny we didn't notice them before."

Pierre felt torn up inside. They had left each other without saying goodbye. They had left each other angry. Even worse, separate—in a way they had never been before. And he nearly cried when he saw the rectangle of light-colored, dry pavement in front of the house where Laure's car had been. He tried to call her that evening. He let the phone ring a long time. No one answered.

They talked about it once, much later. Pierre simply asked, "Did you ever forgive me for that?"

"Did I have a choice?" was Laure's answer.

Laure drove back feeling empty and despondent, her head cloudy, unable to think. Once home, she was at first just extremely tired. She went to bed early and fell asleep immediately. She woke up after a few hours. The night was very dark, and she found it hard to breathe. Something had happened, something monstrous and better forgotten. Suddenly she remembered everything, and she felt defeated, humiliated, ridiculed. Her eyes were dry, wide open in the darkness, as she grew more and more ashamed and angry. She turned on her bedside lamp and did not move again for some time. Then she began to cry.

She went back over everything in her mind. She blamed herself for everything. It was all clear to her. The true nature of their "understanding" revealed itself to her all at once: it was abominable—or rather, pathetic. She had seen Pierre's face, and she wouldn't forget it. He had been tense, annoyed with her, and several expressions had flown across his face in quick succession: she had seen shame, fear, and—worst of all, worst of all!—submissiveness; an air of gravity and importance rather than any staunch resolution. She had had to leave, and in Pierre's attitude there had been no trace of pity for her, none of the sentiment expressed by the endearments he so often used on her ("my sweet," "my beautiful mistress," "the best thing I have"). Or rather, even if Pierre had suffered for her, felt pity for her, that suffering, that pity could not change, could not affect *that*. That? What was this "that" to which Pierre yielded without a murmur?

Something completely incomprehensible, a mystery, was involved here. And Laure saw clearly that it resolved nothing to ascribe it to Pierre's sense of duty, or to the nature of that duty, the gravity of the commitments he had made and his awareness of them, for at the same time he had not appeared to her as some intransigent embodiment of the law. Nor had he seemed tortured: it was clear which direction he was going in. He had acted like someone under a spell, prey to an influence he could not control, some hypnotic power of suggestion. His actions had confirmed, in Laure's eyes, not the strength of his attachment to his family but his weakness of character. She felt he was backing down before something—taking Laure and the whole precious substance of their "understanding" with him in the process—that he respected even if he no longer believed in it, the same way people continue going to Mass long after they have lost the faith.

Well, maybe that was the very nature of the conjugal "faith" whose empty forms men like Pierre continued to honor. But wasn't it precisely when—and because—it had become an empty form that honoring it could no longer be avoided? What would have been left of it without that? Nothing? Laure, too, wanted to die, she felt so miserable, frail, exposed. Or rather, she wished she were dead, or had never lived, never gotten mixed up in all this horror.

This was what she had had to acknowledge: the existence of a paradoxical loyalty no longer based on a love that would have justified it but adapted to all sorts of betrayals—for in Laure's eyes Pierre, by loving her, was undeniably betraying his wife, his children, his family. And the elusive nature of a bond that outlasted the death of all feeling, or the appearance of another feeling—theirs! which was so strong!—if indeed all "feeling" was dead between Pierre and Annie.

She was glimpsing a world that astonished her: a world in which men were dependent on women, in which women acquired a singular power over them, compared to which Ghislaine's sensual power over men was only a joke; a world in which women made men incapable of taking care of their own daily needs—feeding themselves, clothing themselves, living.

Or did men do this to themselves? She no longer knew. In return for this, men appeared to gain a certain freedom, though it was illusory: the male freedom to run around all day long, like dogs, sniffing alluring odors left on walls. At night, though, they all returned home.

Her head was full of chaotic images. She was worn out. She wept. She dried her tears. She kept dozing and waking again. She thought about the division of tasks, of roles, of which so many couples gave an admirable and sometimes stifling picture: weren't even the most unified of marriages—especially those—only a deception that consisted in separating for good those whom they were supposed to bring together, making of them not complementary beings, as was mistakenly supposed, but incomplete beings, forever dependent on each other? And finally, the worst of it was that despite this, in Pierre's case, the necessary cement was lacking, a faith that would have explained and justified all the rest: fidelity. But what she could not forgive him for was that he wanted both—the law and also the violation of the law.

Then she realized that in condemning Pierre she was also condemning herself, since she joined in that betrayal and even benefitted from it. What right had she to reproach Pierre? Didn't people change sometimes? Were they always in control of what they desired? Like Lautier, and without knowing it, Laure eventually began to think that not only several souls but also several bodies were needed to continue to honor one's commitments and also their opposites. What should one do? What could one do? Close one's eyes to the world, lock oneself up? Or accept a compromise, as Pierre was doing? Or, every time a new love came along, abandon everything else, start over from zero, "remake one's life"? However she looked at it, Laure could see only disaster: monotonous constraints, voluntary servitudes, short-lived revolts, and above all the misfortune of the law, universally respected and universally mocked, since in the end anyone might get married yet disdain to respect the commitment undertaken.

And as Laure went back to sleep, she pictured a world of people attached two by two to the same tasks by the same obligations, sitting down together to an endless succession of meals, sleeping in the same bed, concealing from each other— or confessing, which was hardly any better—one escapade after another, escapades that brought them no joy but deprived them forever of any peace of mind.

"It's funny," Annie said a few days after they returned from Normandy. "I didn't say anything to you at the time, but in front of the house there was a car with a license plate from our district. Don't you think that's a strange coincidence?"

CHAPTER 26

A FEW days later Laure found a letter from Pierre in her mailbox, undated, containing these words: "I love you." Indeed, what else was there to say? Should he explain, ask her forgiveness, beg for her understanding, her indulgence? Overcome, she abruptly remembered that morning: the little beach, the cries of the birds, and her pounding heart as she took her clothes out of the closet, put away the dishes, the spoons, the plates upturned on the drainboard, removed her towel, checked for any underwear, hairpins, perfume she might have left.

She had invited Ghislaine to spend a few days with her. They had not seen each other for almost two years. The visit was good for her: the second evening she described the scene to her, altering it somewhat; the first evening she had resisted. Ghislaine had not changed. Her "idea of men"—she would not admit any difference among them, only a few nuances—was more pessimistic than ever.

"I'm not surprised," she said. Where men were concerned, nothing could surprise her. No anecdote was ever anything more than the predictable illustration of a general rule. And after a silence, having stretched out comfortably on the couch, she threw off her shoes, put another match to her cigarette—now she was smoking long brown ones—and said, "Listen, I want to tell you about something that happened to me two or three months ago."

She had met this guy, as she said—Laure had never liked the way she used the word *guy*—and, well, "to make a long story short" (but Ghislaine never made a long story short), they had fallen passionately in love. "But as you know," she immediately added, parenthetically, "these things don't last. They're like a disease, but they pass. The root of the word *passion* is *to pass*."

"Not at all," Laure said. "It comes from *to suffer*."

"Even better," said Ghislaine, who did not try to be logical. "That makes even more sense."

To make a long story short, then, "he loved her so much" that he contemplated giving up everything for her. One evening he had left home on some kind of errand and on the way suddenly decided to head for her place. She had come to the door and opened it right away, rather surprised. He was pale, he seemed distraught, he sat down without saying anything, then he said it was all over, he was going to move in with her. "Do you really want me?" he asked. The evening went by. He didn't say a word. He hugged her without kissing her, refused to eat. He only wanted endless glasses of water: he was dying of thirst. At ten o'clock he stood up. "I can't sleep here," he said. "I'm going to phone home and go sleep at a hotel." Yet as he was leaving, he was so undecided that Ghislaine "practically had to push him out the door."

Late that night he called her: "I couldn't do it. Not that way. It wouldn't have been worthy of you or me."

"I'll never forget those words," said Ghislaine. "They're engraved here," and she delicately tapped her forehead with two red fingernails.

She had understood. Afterwards there had not been the slightest sign of life from him.

"Not even a letter?" asked Laure. "And did you write?"

"You must be kidding . . . Though he wasn't as bad as the one who sent me a wedding announcement two months later."

Laure was thunderstruck.

"I'll tell you about that one some other time. Between the two of us, you and I have enough to fill a book. But as I told you, it will pass. Passion is a passing thing: it's a disease."

"No other recourse but to run away, they have no other recourse," Ghislaine said. But Laure did not believe her. From time to time she studied Pierre's note: "I love you." There was a confidence in those letters, so firmly placed in the middle of the page. But what was that confidence? She hesitated. Only then did she notice that he had not signed the note.

A month went by. Still no word from Pierre: he was angry, ashamed, a coward. But whatever the case, he was still Pierre, and she no longer had any news of him. Anything could have happened to him—maybe a simple case of bronchitis, or a more serious problem, one of his children ill, or his mother— and she would know nothing about it. When he was even one hour late, he always telephoned home; he had telephoned every evening at six during that dreadful stay in Normandy: "They would worry about me," he said. Yet he felt no need to let Laure know what he was doing. And didn't she worry? True, perhaps they had separated for good now—though in her heart she did not quite believe it. But during the summer it was the same, they behaved as though nothing could have happened to either of them. It was as though they lived outside of time, outside of any time in which things happened.

Once Laure could not help bringing it up with Pierre. "You're certainly very cheerful," he said. "Thank you very much."

Laure insisted. "But if you were really sick, you—" Pierre interrupted. "What an idea! Do you want me to promise in writing?"

"Yes," she said.

"Really," he answered curtly, "if you don't mind, let's talk about something else."

Between us, she thought now, there is no place for . . . She hesitated. For death. No place for Pierre's death in her life and no place for hers in Pierre's. Talking about it with anyone else would only make them the object of a hypocritical sympathy that would soon be betrayed, their confidences whispered behind their backs: "the other widow," people would call her, or "the young librarian, you know?"

Yes, I certainly am cheerful, thought Laure. But the idea kept haunting her. She did not really envy the arrogant legitimacy of widows, their mask of pride, their certainty of having carried love as far as it could go. She had an intimation that death alone could give solemn consecration to one person's devotion to another: those who could be separated only by death were the only ones truly united. What death gave to marriage was not just its end but its dignity, even as it conferred dignity on the daily routine, which, without it, would be nothing more than a succession of unimportant shared tasks. Being excluded from death, Pierre and Laure were also excluded from life, from time. Their love seemed cold and artificial, a phantom life.

The reasons for Pierre's silence, however, were not what Laure had imagined them to be. One night shortly after their return from Normandy, Pierre and Annie received a call from the B. hospital: Annie's father had just been admitted into the intensive-care unit—they were afraid of an intestinal obstruction. Pierre spent two days there with Annie, went home and then returned to keep her company while his father-in-law was dying, and left her with her mother after the funeral.

Once back in R., he felt like calling Laure but decided to write to her instead:

"My darling, I wasn't able to call you, though I wanted to. I want to see you, I need you. I have just returned from B. My father-in-law is dead. As you know, I was very fond of him, and I think he was attached to me, too. I asked to sit up with him at the hospital the night he died. I stayed alone with him all night. They had disconnected the tubes, put away the instruments that weren't needed, and pulled up the sheet under his chin, but out in the corridor life went on—people were calling out, bells ringing, nurses and carts going back and forth. There was a bit of a lull about three o'clock, but at five-thirty someone died in the room opposite, and it was a much more difficult death than his."

He paused for a moment. He was alone in the room. The children were asleep. He lit a cigarette, turned off the radio. A great peace filled him. He went on:

"At six o'clock the nurse brought me some coffee. Then I left. It's late, my darling, I haven't slept much the past two or three nights, but I don't feel very tired. However, tomorrow I have to get up, my classes start at eight o'clock. I feel close to you. I wish . . ." He hesitated. "I wish you were here"? Instead he wrote, "I wish I could see you," a lesser commitment. "If you want, we can see each other again. I love you."

He called her on Monday and went to see her the next day. He was pale, thinner. Laure forgot her complaints. They lay down together on the bed for a while, fully dressed, without holding each other, but their eyes were closed, they were silent. They felt good that way. Explanations, questions were postponed to an indefinite future. At one point Pierre took Laure's hand, raised it to his lips, and kissed it at length with unmistakable fervor. Yet when it came time to leave, he said, "Let's let a little time go by. We both need it." And Laure agreed.

* * *

After a few weeks summer came, deciding everything for them. On July 3 Pierre took Bruno to the station. The boy was going off alone for the first time—to England, with his class. His sister was dispatched to her grandmother in Guérande, to "distract her a little." Pierre and Annie found themselves alone for the entire month of July.

By the fourteenth, as Annie's vacation drew near, Pierre felt completely well, strengthened, rested. He had lost more weight, and, gazing in the mirror as he shaved in the morning, he thought he might grow a mustache. He ran his hand over his cheeks twice and caught Annie looking at him. "You know what?" she said. "I'd like to go away somewhere with you for two or three days. I don't know—maybe we could go to Rome."

Pierre thought for a moment. What harm would there be in that? What difference did it make whether he stayed with her in Guérande the whole summer or went off for a short visit to Italy in the middle of the vacation? He smiled. "I'll find out about it this afternoon."

They left at the end of the week, catching the Palatino at Lyon and arriving in Rome by eleven in the morning. Pierre took Annie's arm and held it against him as they emerged from the station. She hugged him tenderly.

It was July 20, and the heat was oppressive. On the Corso the asphalt had softened. For the entire five days Pierre thought ceaselessly about Laure, but with no trace of sadness, regret, or remorse: yes, he could have been there with her, but it would have been different. Anyway, being there with Annie deprived Laure of nothing.

Their hotel fronted a narrow street, and they slept badly the first night because of the noise. Then they were given a room that faced the back courtyard, as did the rose window of a church—this detail struck them. The following evening they had dinner on the Piazza Navona (and often, later, recalled their voluble waiter, who spoke to the tourists in a completely idiosyncratic English). Then they walked through small streets permeated with the smells of frying oil, overheated engines, overripe vegetables, stones warmed by the sun all day long. They went back to the hotel. In the darkness Pierre slid over against Annie, who was asleep. One evening he felt himself come gently against her thigh. She said nothing, and he did not move away. He breathed in the smell of his wife's warm face close to his own, the light film of sweat at her hairline; the linen pillowcase smelled cool.

The next morning, while shaving in front of the bathroom mirror, he heard Annie's voice. She was saying, "How thin you are. You know, you should grow a mustache. I'm sure it would look very good on you."

"I can't hear you. The water's running."

"A mustache—you should grow a mustache." She looked at him in the mirror, his face covered with foam—she liked the strange asymmetry his face always had in reverse. "You think so?" he asked. He decided to begin growing it that very day.

They returned from Rome with mixed feelings. "You know," said Annie, "I don't like Italy that much, it's too hot. Of course, it's amazingly beautiful, but one would have to have more time, or go in the spring." Then, moving closer to him, she added, "But it was nice. It was nice being there together." Pierre agreed. Yes, it really was. He smiled at her.

That summer was unusually hot: even by the time they returned from Guérande, at the end of August, the temperature had not dropped. Pierre had set up a pool in the garden for the children, and in the evenings all four of them would get into it. Then they would have a simple dinner outdoors—it was getting dark a little earlier these days.

By now Pierre had a short blond mustache, and the children complimented him on it. He turned to Annie. "And what about my hair?"

"You don't seem to be losing it as fast," she answered.

"Anyway, it suits you, it shows your temples. But look! There's a gray hair. What about that!" The little girl climbed onto her father's knees to try and pull it out.

"Well?" he asked Annie every morning.

"Still nothing," she said, "but I'm not worried. It's the heat." In fact, it was the heat, and everything was all right a few days later.

Laure set off for the library again on September 3 without any great pleasure. As she was leaving that morning, she thought she heard the telephone and went back in, but whoever it was had already hung up. It was raining. She had not spoken with Pierre, though he was undoubtedly back.

Yet it had been Pierre on the line. He called her again in the afternoon, but he had forgotten which days she was off work, and she was not there.

On Sunday she decided to go to the movies. She hesitated between the theater close to her house and the Variety, then opted for the Variety. When she came out of the theater, though nightfall was not far off, the lowering sun was shining unexpectedly bright and a dark-red cloudbank lay on the horizon. A gentle wind swept over the promenade, creating an illusion of spring. She had gone only a few steps down the sidewalk when she saw Pierre waiting in line. She blushed hot, and at the same time her face broke into an irrepressible smile. She was happy to see the same reaction on her lover's face. So it was not all over between them—that seemed clear. But his mustache! He smiled again but turned his head slightly to the left. Then she understood that he was not alone, and looking down she saw, close to Pierre's side, the bright face, attentive and serious, of a dark-haired little girl. Pierre is so fair, she thought, it must be . . . The little girl held her father's hand very tight and, in silent surprise, kept her eyes fixed on Laure and her mouth open, showing rosy gums with a gap where two teeth were missing.

Pierre freed his hand and held it out to Laure. "How are you?" he asked.

"Very well," said Laure.

She heard a voice behind her: "It wasn't easy, but I finally found a spot."

Laure turned around. A dark-complexioned, short-haired young woman looking at her through sunglasses said, "Hello."

Laure had time to notice the beautiful pendant hanging from her tanned neck.

"It is thanks to her efficiency," he said, gesturing toward Laure with an exaggerated, amused solemnity, "that we have a library worthy of the name."

"Oh, you're the one," said Annie. "I feel so bad that I never stop by the library! I envy you—it's the sort of work I would have liked to do."

The two women smiled at each other. Laure felt her heart pounding, and her palms became damp. Cats are supposed to do that, aren't they? she thought. Their palms sweat when they're frightened. Does that mean I'm frightened?

The little girl was pulling on her father's arm. "What's the matter?" he asked. "What do you want?" He bent down and she whispered in his ear. "Wait a minute, wait a minute." Did she ask what my name was? Laure wondered.

Pierre's wife turned to Laure again solicitously. "What did you just see? *Star Wars?*"

"No," said Laure, "*The Lady from Shanghai.*"

"I confess I would rather see that," said Pierre, "but with these two . . . Where is Bruno, anyway?"

"He went to get an ice cream," said Annie.

Laure stepped back. "I've got to go," she said, and they shook hands again.

In the street she passed a boy running toward the movie theater, an ice-cream bar in his hand. His hair was sandy, thick, like his father's, though already a little darker. He looks like him, Laure thought, with a strange excitement. But when she looked back, it seemed to her the boy had joined another family.

"She's nice," said Annie. "She has pretty eyes."

It was the same with the nurse, Pierre thought. God! Does my wife have to think well of all my mistresses? He felt like smiling, but his heart was full.

This was what I was most afraid of, Laure thought as she returned home, and now—"You see? It's all over," as her mother used to say when they came out of the dentist's office.

When Pierre stood before Laure in the entryway of her small apartment, their emotion was so strong they had great difficulty speaking.

"I was so moved," Pierre said at last, "the other day in front of the theater, I wanted to take you in my arms. You were so pale, you looked so frightened. My God, what pain!" And he added—he would not have thought himself capable of such a liberty—"My little girl thought you were very pretty."

No, that came a little later. Before that she had smiled, he had moved close to her, and once in each other's arms, they calmed down, felt no more uneasiness, no more doubt, no more worry. Hugging each other tightly, they went into the bedroom, mouths pressed together, hands wandering aimlessly over each other's faces. Hardly had they touched the bed before he was inside her, his face buried in her neck, his teeth closing over her skin. She moaned, and soon she began to cry, and for the first time Pierre cried, too. They let the warm water flow over their faces, washing everything away.

Outside, Pierre hesitated a moment, but at the top of the bridge he suddenly turned off toward the road that led to the plateau. The countryside was deserted, the car purred softly, the low sun shone bright. It was not long after five o'clock: he had time. Once in the flat open country, he breathed deeply. A mass of clouds sped by, casting shadows across the fields that moved before the wind. As he gazed at them, the feeling of peace inside him grew and grew. He drove slowly, his face whipped by the wind. He rolled up the window a little. Suddenly the clouds overtook him, and the landscape was plunged in a menacing darkness. Only one spot of light remained in the distance, an inexplicable, dazzling yellow. He accelerated suddenly, he had to reach it.

He glimpsed his tense face in the rearview mirror, his animated expression, and thought, How curious—Laure said nothing about my mustache!

ABOUT THE AUTHOR

Danièle Sallenave is currently a professor of literature at the University of Nanterre. She is the recipient of France's Prix Fémina and the author of numerous novels, including *Les Portes de Gubbio*, winner of the Prix Renaudot, and *Adieu*, forthcoming from Pantheon. *Phantom Life* is the first of her work to appear in English.